DROWN THE WITCH

SUALI'S SURPRISINGLY COMPETENT DETECTIVE AGENCY: BOOK ONE

MICHAEL COOLWOOD

COOLWOOD BOOKS

Acknowledgements

I'm eternally grateful to Magdalena Knitter, murder consultant, for her assistance in crafting the murder at the heart of this story.

Persons of Interest

Victims

Lady Marie Callas – Recent corpse – Probably deserved it

    Susan Fletcher – Not dead. Yet – Give it five minutes and we'll see

    A.O.V. (Any other victims) – TBC – Taking all bets

Suspects

Charles Varma – Friend of the deceased - Posh twat

    Praxi Tollis – Friend of the deceased - Unconscious

    Betsan – Head of security - Don't cross her

    Teleri Parry – Caterer - Why hire *her* of all people?

    Mr Das – Housekeeper – Suspiciously quiet

Others of Note

Alison Dewan – Other initiate – <u>She mustn't find out what I am</u>

    Victoria Callas – The deceased's wife - Tempestuous relationship with Marie

    Lady Octavia Dewan – <u>DO NOT APPROACH UNDER ANY CIRCUMSTANCES</u>

    Paget Belacourt – Lives with Octavia – Betsan's scared of her

    Tova Oster – Died fiftyish years ago – Charles' protégé

Chapter One

Silver had only been bestowed on me twice in my life. The first gift, a pendant which glittered even under half-light, had been from my mother. I'd sold it during my sixteenth winter to cover the cost of biofuel for our geriatric stove. The second gift of silver, a second chance from Lady Marie Callas, lay on the kitchen table between me and dad, whilst papa, my other dad, paced in front of the windows, hands shoved into his pockets. Occasionally, he stopped to glare at the second chance.

Dad scratched at the stubble on his chin, staring at the sheet of notes I'd handed him. "Who are they?"

I tapped the back of my left hand, "Magissa. A secret society. Probably people in silly robes who sacrifice goats and play akvopilko together at the weekends."

Fog soaked the street outside. The gas lamps had been shut down for hours, so, for our purposes, the outside world didn't even exist yet.

"What mustn't you do?" asked dad.

I tapped my left thumb, "Take off my shoes, break cover in front of the other person in the coach, and forget why I'm there."

Papa stopped pacing and rolled his shoulders, "I've been thinking."

I groaned. "Please stop doing that."

He stared at me, his expression stern. Unforgiving. He could only hold the expression for a moment before he gave in and grinned. "I just thought that... if I went back to work then maybe you wouldn't have to take on this commission. You could retake your final exams next year. Secure a new scholarship. Show the University of the Silver Key what an awful mistake they made."

Dad's gaze met mine, amber eyes glittered over dark crescents. I shrugged. He sighed. "Honey, we've talked about this."

Papa held up his hands in mock surrender.

Dad circled a finger over my notes, then stabbed down and read the bullet point he'd picked. "Who are you?"

I tapped my left wrist. "I'm a Charites."

Papa frowned, an adorable V formed at the bridge of his nose. His gaze flicked from the second chance to the notes I'd handed dad, and finally to the missing finger on dad's left hand. "I don't like it."

Dad reached out and squeezed his hand. "None of us like it, honey."

I stared at the ceiling, counting to five, then checked out the window for what felt like the seventy-seventh time. "It's a commission."

Dad nodded. "It's a commission."

Papa sighed. "It's a commission. Look, I know... Commissions a re... I get why you'd be so taken by the idea. The fall of the house of LaCroix, the investigation into the origins of the Angel Plague... I'm getting distracted. My point is, we don't know how many callous aristocrats went around offering commissions to desperate people which never led to anything or got everyone involved killed. It's... what's it called? That thing where you only remember the successes and not the horrible danger your only daughter is being put in? What's that called?"

"Paranoia?" I suggested.

"Survivorship bias," said dad.

Papa clicked his fingers and pointed at dad. "That's it!"

I sniffed. "It's really not going to be that dangerous, Papa. Also, calling me desperate is a little harsh."

"Oh, no, sweetie, I didn't mean…" He deflated, and collapsed onto the only empty chair. His gaze returned, inevitably, to the silver gift. He picked it up. He turned it over and over in his hands. "It's lighter than I expected."

"What's your objective?" asked dad.

I didn't need a memory anchor for that question. "Observe, make whatever notes I feel necessary, prepare a report on my findings."

"Did she say why you?" Papa asked.

I held out my hand. He hesitated, before handing over the gift.

"She said she was in he business of offering people second chances," I said. The gift sat heavy in my palm. A simple, elegant bracelet. A fraction of my payment given up front, and a passkey rolled into one. Twenty silver mountings were spaced around the outer face which, on a normal bracelet, might have held jewels. On this bracelet, the mountings held human teeth.

In the distance, muffled by fog, a steam engine chuffed. All three of us leapt to our feet, our chair legs screeching against the kitchen floor.

"I love you, kiddo," said Papa. He hugged me. Dad hugged me from the other side, making a Susan sandwich.

"I love you too," I said, my voice muffled.

The chuffing drew closer. Wheels rattled against cobblestones. The dads drew back. A light glimmered in the fog. My heartbeat quickened. I exhaled and scrunched my toes in my shoes. Gently, casually, as if it were the sort of action I performed every morning, I snapped the second chance around my wrist. I checked my pockets – notebooks, pens, pencils, emergency whistle.

"Good luck," said Dad.

"You've got this," said Papa.

I turned and winked at the dads, then pointed at the notes Dad had been quizzing me with. "Burn that, please. I wasn't supposed to make any copies of Lady Callas' information."

I'd left my sword in its belt by the front door. I still wasn't sure if I wanted to bring the thing. It was shorter than your average xiphos, its double-edged blade flaring closer to the fearsome tip than many others my schoolmates had owned. A short xiphos compensated for my lack of strength, making it easier to wield. It didn't compensate for my lack of talent, but it would make Papa feel better if I took the thing. He'd been brought up in a house where being armed was assumed, merely one aspect of being properly dressed. I buckled the sword belt around my waist, waved to my dads, and slipped out into the fog.

The coach clattered to a halt in front of me, its engine venting excess steam. It looked either brand new or fastidiously maintained. A coat of arms featuring birds, laurel wreaths and half a dozen other miscellanea had been painted on the door.

A driver sat hunched over the controls, her overcoat buttoned up tight, her hat pulled low against the fog's chill. The boy who sat next to her wasn't so encumbered. He dropped down to the cobbles and opened the coach door for me.

I glanced back at my dads, who were staring at me through the window. Dad looked proud. Papa looked on the verge of tears. I could let the commission go... but Lady Marie Callas didn't seem the sort of person I could safely cross. I thanked the boy, stepped up, into the coach, and the door clicked shut behind me.

Soft lighting – a glow globe set into the roof. Grey silks, red silks. Decorations? Partly. They dampened the noise from the engine as the coach drew away from my home. Empty bench seats at the front and rear. After the notes had got me all worried about the person who'd be sharing the coach with me, it was anti-climactic to find it empty. I settled down on the bench furthest from the engine and tried, unsuccessfully, to relax.

I ran through my memory anchors as the coach swayed through Selen's suburbs. We crossed the soot-stained bridges over the city's canal network. Shimmers of light broke the fog here and there – the mills must be up and running, even at this hour. The fog thinned as we rattled through Nocturne district's warehouses, then Cavoletti's slums.

We rolled through Nine Dials without slowing down, before turning north. I groaned as I sat back in my seat. With this heading, our destination had to be somewhere in Elizabeth-Dane. A district filled with wealth and those who wielded it.

After a few minutes, the coach clattered to a halt outside a mansion which could easily have housed ten families. Ornate stonework framed each door and window, but... I frowned. There was definitely something wrong.

The coach rocked as the boy leapt down from the driver's box. He hesitated at the foot of the steps leading up to the front door, which remained resolutely closed. The fog swirled around him.

He'd approached the front door without passing through a gate. That was what had been needling at me. The house had no gates. No wrought iron railings to keep intruders away. The place also lacked coats of arms. I'd never met an aristocrat who neglected the opportunity to stick their coat of arms on anything which would stay still for long enough, or one who wasn't terrified of poor people stealing their hoard.

The boy gave up waiting, and climbed the steps to the front door. Only then did the door open. The boy scurried back down the steps to the coach door and stood by to open it.

A figure emerged from the house. Their form was enveloped by a long cloak, a hat covered their head, and a veil concealed their face. A pistol hung at one hip, and a sword at the other. Probably the person Lady Callas' notes had warned me about.

The boy opened the door for them and they stepped inside. They paused in the doorway, considering the available seats. After only a moment, they sat next to me. The door to the coach swung shut and, with a cough and splutter from the steam engine, we were moving once more.

"Good morning," I said, in my best 'talking to rich twats' voice.

"Well, isn't it just," said my companion. Her voice was soft, but confident. It carried easily over the engine's noise.

I held out a hand. "Susan Fletcher. Delighted to make your acquaintance."

The woman took my hand. "Alison Dewan. The pleasure is mine. If I'd known I was to have company such as this, I'd have... ah, but I'm forgetting myself. I'm about to remove my veil. Have you encountered Hydros before?"

Hydros was one of the code words I'd learned over the last few days. Other than that, the word meant little to me. I'd attempted to research the term but had only found references to a long dead water goddess. I shook my head.

"Please," said Alison, and I thought I caught the ghost of a smile beneath her veil, "don't scream."

I dearly wished to raise a sceptical eyebrow, but I kept my face carefully neutral. It was fortunate I adopted that strategy, because it meant that I was already concentrating on maintaining a placid face when Alison removed her veil.

Alison's face was daemonic. Her mouth was too wide. Ridges of bone jutted from her forehead and, as she slipped her top hat from her brow, she revealed small horns jutting from her hairline. I didn't cry out. I didn't breathe in sharply. I was composed, even upon finding myself trapped in a coach with a monster.

"Well done," said Alison, mildly. "Most people can't hide their shock nearly so well on first meeting me."

I needed to respond. How? What should I say? What was correct for this situation? I was lost – I was *completely* unprepared.

Alison smiled, her face cracking open, displaying far too many teeth. "Don't worry. With a face like mine, you become accustomed to seeing fear in others. A moment of shock, followed by the sudden realisation that you don't know how to react in the face of my magnificence. I'm used to it. It's tiresome, but I'm used to it."

"I apologise unreservedly for my rudeness," I said, unable to meet her gaze.

Alison raised an eyebrow. "Do you indeed? Well then, I think we shall be friends. There. The day's barely begun and we've both made a friend. With any luck, the rest of the day will be equally productive."

She hadn't immediately decided to eat me, which was a relief. I held my curiosity with both hands and throttled it. I wouldn't sneak glances at her face. I wouldn't trespass on her no-doubt formidable temper. No Susans were going to be eaten today.

"In case you're wondering," Alison said, "Hydros provided the basis for the classical representation of daemons. Not the other way around."

"Of course," I said, as if it was the most natural thing in the world to be having this conversation. She couldn't possibly be real... and yet, here she was.

The coach was supposed to be taking us to Lady Callas' mansion on the Obsidian Coast. I'd make damn sure to talk to Callas as soon as we arrived. She had some explaining to do.

Alison grinned at me. "So. Your name is Susan Fletcher. I might be so bold as to ask what you are."

What I was? Wait, I had a memory anchor for that. I tapped my left wrist. "I'm a Charites," I said.

Alison winced. I'd made some sort of mistake. Was I discovered? The monster leaned towards me. Her mouth opened. Her teeth glistened. Saliva linked two razor points. "My adorable little possum," the demon said. "Have you only discovered your magissa status recently?"

I swallowed. "Quite recently, yes."

"Quite recently, indeed. Well, rather than saying 'I'm *a* Charites' you should ideally say 'I'm Charites.'"

She hadn't reached for her weapons or denounced me as an infiltrator. I decided to push my luck. "Why's that?"

"Because," said Alison, "our osto names come from the names of ancient gods. You wouldn't say 'I'm an Apollo' for the same reasons you wouldn't say 'I'm a Susan.'"

I bowed my head, "My thanks." Sweat was sticking my shirt to my back.

"Don't give it a second thought. So, you're to be Lady Callas' new protégé? It's fortunate that we've decided to be friends, as we'll certainly be allies as well. You'll have to show me what you can do when we reach our destination, and I'll show you what *I* can do."

She clearly thought I'd be a great deal more impressed with her than she'd be with me. She didn't seem like a braggart. I didn't know what to make of her – or of her expectations. I smiled to cover my fear.

Our coach headed north with no other stops. We moved from the comfortable suburban housing belt to the fields which fed the city. Beyond the fields, the road ahead wound towards the obsidian coast.

Alison and I passed much of the journey in idle chit chat. My initial shock upon seeing her having faded, I was able to take a stab at doing my job and make some careful observations of the daemon.

Beneath her cloak, she wore a precisely tailored business suit, whilst her pockets bulged in a way which would probably have made her tailor cry. Silver shone from two places - her wrist – a bracelet lined with teeth, the mirror of mine. The second was an elegant ear cuff, surging wave engravings caught the light at every movement of her head.

I learned that Alison lived with her mother along with a family friend and a truly staggering number of dogs. The worst part, Alison said, was they couldn't even use incense to cover up the wet-dog smell, because that would undermine the point. What point she referred to remained unstated.

The sun was rising as the road ahead flattened out and curved, following the coastline. Black rocks flecked with silver kept the breaking waves at bay. The coach turned, and we clattered onto a bridge. I stuck my head out of the window and got my first proper look at our destination. The bridge led us over a jagged mess of dark rocks to a promontory which jutted out into the sea.

A driveway led up to a neat garden and a two-storey cottage, whilst a blood-red brick wall ran around the promontory keeping everything within its perimeter sheltered from the spray. I frowned at the cottage before returning to my seat. Lady Callas' notes had said she lived in a mansion, not a cottage. I'd expected an intimidating monstrosity with ivy climbing the walls.

The coach drew to a halt outside the cottage, and the boy jumped down to open the door for us. Alison stepped out and I followed, hoping my shaky steps wouldn't betray my fear.

The cottage was quiet and dark. The clocks hadn't struck six yet, so the stillness wasn't exactly shocking, but I'd expected to see lights in the windows. Servants should be preparing for breakfast and attending to the residents. It was unusual to do such things in total darkness.

"Something's wrong," growled Alison.

The boy took a step towards the front door, possibly assuming we wished for him to knock. Alison held out a forestalling hand. "I don't like this," she said. "Susan, do you know how to use that sword?"

"Yep," I replied, after only a moment's hesitation.

She nodded, playing with her bracelet of teeth. "Then you'd better get ready."

Unsure of what to expect, I rested my hand on the hilt of my sword so I could draw it at a moment's notice. Alison rapped twice on the cottage door, then folded her arms. The coach's steam engine rattled and clanked behind us.

Alison rolled her shoulders, then tried the door handle. No movement. She bent down and peered through the letter box. "Oh, that's not good." She knocked on the door again. "Betsan? Betsan? Wakey wakey! Betsan?"

Betsan was the name of Lady Callas' head of security. My briefing had described her as 'remarkably professional unless roused'.

"Is she okay?" I asked.

"No. She's passed out behind the front door. Hold on a tick." She knelt and scrabbled at the crack under the front door. "Got it!" She passed me a piece of paper, before resuming her attempts to rouse Betsan.

I unfolded the slip of paper. "*Key: Eurydice and Orpheus.* What does that mean?"

Alison thumped the door. "Key to the security system. Hey, Betsan! Treat your passwords with more care! Betsan? Betsan, if you're ignoring me I swear to the spirits I'm going to boil the blood in your veins!"

I rocked on my heels and glanced back at the coach. It wasn't too late. But... damn it all, not only was the commission too good an opportunity to pass up, I was also intrigued. Alison had been extremely restrained, having not eaten me even a little. So far. What sort of journalist would I be if I fled? Callas had answers. "We need to get inside," I said.

Alison shook her head. "The door's locked. Betsan's unconscious."

"Can we help her?" Concern. That was a good angle. Alison already thought I was hopelessly naïve. With a little luck, she'd sympathise and help me break in through a window or something.

Alison frowned. "What did you say was on Betsan's note?"

"*Key: Eurydice and Orpheus.*"

Alison nodded, then turned to the coach driver. "You'd better head to the village. We'll send word if we need anything."

The boy scrambled aboard without hesitation and the driver got to work turning the coach around without flattening us in the cramped driveway. I strode to the nearest window – curtains closed. I tried to lift it, but it wouldn't budge.

"I wouldn't do that if I were you!" called Alison. "This place has a security system. Can be tetchy about people breaking in. Come on, I think there's a side entrance."

I followed Alison down the side of the house. Gravel crunched under our feet, the sound merging with the waves crashing on the shore beyond the walls. The cottage windows at the side of the house were similarly dark.

"Alison," I said, "this security system. It would trip an alarm or something if we broke a window?"

Alison shot an odd look over her shoulder. "An alarm? Maybe? I suppose? It'd probably fry our brains first. That's what ours at home does."

"Right, right..." I hadn't heard of a security system that could do anything of that sort. I didn't think that was even possible. Alison might merely be eccentric, or maybe rich people had access to way more dubious tech than I'd suspected.

Alison turned a corner up ahead. I ran to catch up, turned the same corner and gasped at the sudden expanse of pristine lawn and artfully sculpted flowerbeds which confronted me.

The garden was fully four times the size of the house. It had two sheds, rather than one, because a rich twat could never do with having a single shed. Trees, each packed with nesting boxes, rustled in the distance.

"Wow," I said.

"Mm?" asked Alison, who was searching the ground by the back wall of the house.

"The garden, it's... who builds a garden on a rocky promontory all the way out here? They'd have had to lay down soil and... what are you doing?"

"Looking for a round hatch with a wheel in it," said Alison. "You know the sort? They have them in those amphibious vehicles that buzz up and down the canals sometimes."

"Oh, yes, those."

"Right. Those. The hatch is a secret entrance. And exit. An entrexit, if you will. Well, I suppose all doors work as both an entrance and... never mind."

My monster companion scanned the ground, then strode further along the wall and checked again. She wasn't being particularly thorough. Maybe I'd got the wrong impression of her in the coach.

I shook my head and joined in the search. I didn't think it particularly likely that Callas would leave an entrexit hatch out in the open. More likely it'd be concealed somewhere. I shoved a water butt aside, revealing only soil and worms beneath. A suspiciously large flower pot yielded similar disappointment. Someone had piled wood haphazardly up against one of the sheds...

I strode over and peered into the log pile. There was definitely something inside. Hopefully not a stag beetle burrow, those poor things had enough to deal with. I lifted three planks away from the shed wall, revealing a canvas sheet. I peered underneath.

"Alison!"

"Hello? Yes?"

"I've found it!"

"Oh hey, well done!"

Alison ran over to join me. She glared at the shed, as if outraged that it hadn't clued her into the hatch's position. I shoved the rest of the wood away and together we lifted the tarp, revealing the hitherto elusive hatch.

Alison bent down and spun the handle, until it gave a soft *thunk*. She grinned at me, and swung the hatch upwards. "Do you mind if I go first?"

I didn't know why she thought I'd mind.

She didn't give me a chance to answer because she snapped her fingers and exclaimed "No! No, I'm being selfish. I shouldn't be the one having all the excitement. You go first."

I stared at her. What was going on? She'd been quiet and reserved during the drive from Selen. Controlled, even. Now... well, that didn't matter. If using the entrexit was my only way to get to Lady Callas, I'd take it. I climbed through the hatch and down the ladder which lay beneath.

Chapter Two

The entrexit shaft was so dark I had to feel for the ladder's rungs. My shuddering breath filled the air around me, which wasn't too bad until one of my boots missed a rung. My stomach dropped and I felt as if I was falling, tumbling into the darkness below. I clung to the ladder for dear life whilst I waited for my heart to slow down.

Ten rungs later, my boot hit the floor, which was more shocking than painful. I dropped down and experimentally shifted my weight about a bit. The floor felt like poured concrete.

"Alison!" I called, my voice echoing back at me, mockingly.

"Yeah?" She was dreadfully quiet up there. I had to hope she wasn't going to close the hatch and jam it shut.

"I'm at the bottom! It's a long climb but safe!"

"Right. See you in a second!"

I backed away from the ladder so as to avoid being struck by descending Alisons. Other than the small disk of grey at the top of the ladder, my world was dark.

I don't like darkness. I've never liked darkness. I used to have nightmares about lurking horrors in dark rooms. This time, the person descending the ladder towards me was a far greater threat than whatever nameless horror lurked in the dark.

I reached into the darkness until my fingertips brushed something solid. It was... yes, it was concrete. I ran my hands across the wall experimentally, until I found a thick layer of insulation wrapped around something, probably a steam pipe. Below that was a cable the size of my thumb. I followed it to an enormous knife switch. I only hesitated for a moment before throwing it.

Somewhere in the distance, pipes clonged and clanged. A pump thumped. Liquid churned. One by one, glow globes set into the ceiling bloomed into life. The globes were filled with bio-luminescent fluid which reacted to the fuel being fed to them from an interconnected network of pipes, bathing the area in a brilliant white light.

I was in a tunnel, cramped and grey – so grey the walls, ceiling, and floor blended together and I had trouble making out what was at the far end. Alison cried in triumph and leapt from the ladder to fall the remaining distance.

"Good work," she grinned, brushing herself down. "So, all we need to do is walk down the tunnel to the end. Eurydice and Orpheus is the key to the security system. Once we're there, we'll need to find a way through the door. Simple enough?"

"Err..."

Alison sighed. "Which bit's the problem?"

I didn't really know where to begin.

"When Betsan said the key was Euridice and Orpheus... what did that... mean?" There was a classical poem called Euridice and Orpheus. Well, actually there were about twelve different versions from various centuries. There were also a couple of modern versions – an opera that Dad had hauled boxes for a while back, and a song that the anarcho-socialists were enjoying last winter. I doubted Alison would know about that last one, however.

Alison shrugged. "We have to recite Euridice and Orpheus. You know. The classic?"

I winced. "Recite it?"

"You didn't study the classics?"

Dad and Papa had both worked extremely hard to get me a shot at a bursary from Selen's least snooty private school. "Yes, I've studied the classics, but not to the point where I can recite the damned thing from memory!"

Alison tutted. "Ah, yes. Charites, with their enviable ability to leave the house without special clothing. Well, lucky for you, whilst you were leaving the house, I was at home, alone, reading. I'll recite for both of us. You've been through a security system before?"

Not wanting to seem like the most naïve person alive, and, if I'm honest, a little fed up with having to plead ignorance every thirty seconds, I nodded.

"Good. So you know what to expect. Good. That's good. Follow me, stick close and don't panic." She held out her hand. I stared at it. She flapped it at me.

"Come on," she said.

Did she... did she want me to hold her hand? I thought that was an activity undertaken by people who were doing a romance on each other. Or had I misunderstood all those stories my friends had told me?

I took her hand in the hope that she'd stop making me feel stupid. Alison took off at a brisk stride down the tunnel, yanking me forwards at such a rapid pace I had to scamper to keep up.

"She mustn't look back, mustn't look back," Alison spake, "Eurydice knew she mustn't look back, for to do so would doom her one true love."

The lights pulsed, then faded. Shadows reared up against the walls. They spread and merged until an endless tide of blackness swirled around me, leaving only a sliver of light around Alison. I shrank away from the edge.

An invisible force was dragging me forward. Someone called to me from the darkness. Was that Papa? Had he come to get me out of this mess?

I closed my eyes, trying to concentrate on what he was saying. It was no good. An unfamiliar chant was obliterating his words. I opened my eyes again and stared into the darkness.

My head felt as if it was stuffed with spider webs. I couldn't think straight. If I could get to Papa, he'd be able to save me from this madness. I needed to get out of the light. Papa was waiting for me. Had Dad come too? I needed to get to them, but I was still walking forwards. Why?

I tried to stop. That was step one. Step two was turning and walking back the way I came... but my hand was yanked forwards and I staggered onwards into the light.

A howl echoed in front of me. An indistinct shape towered, screeching and wailing. Enormous eyes swirled, fangs gnashed and snapped at me. The towering monstrosity dug its claws into my hand.

I recoiled, gritting my teeth at the agony in my hand, in my head, burning me alive. I needed to run. I needed to get *away*. The creature was too powerful. Again, it hauled me forwards, step by quivering step. Everything would be fine if only I could get away, if I could leave this horrible tunnel. I closed my eyes and screamed. The creature hauled me forwards once more—

I stood in front of a gate at the end of the tunnel. Alison held my hand.

"And he was cast, cast, cast back into the underworld," she said, glowering at me. "Eurydice's tears flowed like blood for she had doomed her love for folly."

Had someone stuffed my skull with packing foam and then split it open with a sledge hammer? Because if so, they'd done a lousy job putting me back together.

Alison sighed. "I think we're out the other side."

"Good." I shook my head, then winced and clutched at my skull as dazzling pain scorched into me.

"Was the system a bit rough on you?"

I looked up at her. What had she just said? I'd understood all the words, but I couldn't make sense of the sentence. Was that right? I wobbled and had to lean against the wall for support.

"Whoa, easy," said Alison, easing me to the floor. "Don't worry, security often has this effect on people."

I'd no idea what she was talking about, but I nodded anyway. She turned to the gate and wiggled the handle. She sighed, and rammed her shoulder into the gate. Metal snapped, and Alison careened through the gate and into the room beyond.

Not wanting to be left in the nightmare tunnel, I staggered to my feet and followed. I'd been doing something. I'd been trying to get to Lady Callas. Yes, that was it. Because all of this was impossible. She'd invited me here. Lured me here. I needed answers.

The chamber beyond the gate was small and clogged with dust. At the far end were some steps leading up, hopefully, towards the cottage. Alison ascended. I followed.

The stairs were cramped, and would be an absolute nightmare for anyone with mobility issues to navigate. At the top of the stairs was an empty landing. Concrete walls to the left and right, whilst the wall directly ahead of us was lined with wood panelling. Alison strode up to the wood wall and gave it a shove. Easily, silently, the panel rotated on its central axis. Alison cackled before stepping through.

Beyond the panel was a cavernous hall, lit only by glow globes. There were no windows. We were probably still underground. Other than a tang of damp in the air, the place seemed perfectly pleasant. Wood panelling, soft carpets, occasional tables, that sort of thing. I turned to look back through the panel and found it had noiselessly shut behind me.

"Have you been here before?" hissed Alison.

I shook my head.

"I have," she said. "Follow me."

She strode towards a doorway at the north end of the hall where a set of stairs led down. This, after everything that happened was infuriating.

"Alison, why are we heading down again? Won't Lady Callas and Betsan and everyone be up in the cottage?"

"Goodness no. The bedrooms, library and... all the residential bits of the mansion are below us. Our patrons both live down there. I suggest you seek yours out whilst I check on mine. It would be ideal if they were both absolutely fine, but maybe something ghastly will be happening to one of them. Or possibly both! You never know your luck."

"A prudent course of action," I said, trying not to sound too relieved at the idea of getting away from her.

We descended the stairs, and found a richly decorated hallway. Lamps illuminated tastefully abstract wallpaper, a few doors, and a discarded napkin. A little further along, a wine glass lay in our path. Alison stepped over it without a second thought.

We reached a T-junction. Alison spun on the spot, "Praxi is that way." She pointed to the left. "Lady Callas' room is down there." She pointed with her other hand, then twirled, and swept her hair out of her eyes with a dramatic flourish. "Let us potentially save our patrons from the no-doubt horrible fate which awaits them, possibly!"

I nodded and, with a wink and a daemonic smile, Alison strode away. I followed the corridor she'd indicated at a calm, collected walk. When I judged I was out of earshot, I broke into a jog, and then a run.

The rich indigo carpet lost its colour as I followed the hallway. At first, I thought it might be fading due to age, but I soon realised that the change was deliberate. By the time I turned left, the carpet was no longer a rich blue, but had instead become a brilliant white. The walls seemed to close in on me as I ran. Spots clouded my vision.

I slowed as I approached the door to Callas' room, and tried to get my breathing back under control. I was free of Alison's company and about to see the one person who could answer any and all of my questions. I knocked on the door. No reply. I shook my head, and opened the door.

A bedroom, huge and richly furnished. An enormous four-poster bed and a brace of reclining chairs were arranged artfully about the place. A bookshelf stood against one wall, full to bursting with leather bound tomes. There were two other doors – one in the west wall and one in the east. The door in the east wall was open, revealing a bathroom on the other side.

I took in these details as my eye tried to focus on something other than the one feature of the room that was grasping for – no, demanding my attention.

Across every centimetre of the south wall, across all six metres of its length, hung bones. Bones of all shapes and sizes, shockingly familiar. I recognised them from my anatomy classes. These were bones from hundreds of people.

I felt sick. My head swam. I focussed. The room was devoid of aristocrats, but the bedclothes had been thrown back. A trail of dark spots on the carpet led through to the bathroom. "Lady Callas?" I said, hating the way my voice shook. "It's Susan Fletcher."

No reply. I hesitated, before stepping into the bathroom. An elegantly crafted toilet greeted me, blessedly unoccupied. A portrait of a terrified teenager... no. A mirror, hung on the wall over a sink. A bathtub—

I gasped and staggered back. Someone was in the enormous brass bathtub – their knees broke above the waterline, but their torso and head were underwater. I took a tentative step forward, then another. Soaked silk shirt and trousers. Eyes wide and bloodshot. Staring up at me.

"Lady Callas?" My voice quivered.

Still. Completely still. No bubbles from her mouth or nose.

I wanted to cry or vomit or scream or perform all three actions simultaneously – but what if she was still alive in there? I reached into the water with one hand, then the other, and slipped my arms under Callas' armpits.

I hauled her up until her head broke the surface. Freezing cold. She was freezing cold. Water cascaded from sodden hair. I focussed. I breathed. I let her down gently, back into the water with barely a splash, before tugging the plug out of the bath.

I tapped her cheek with my free hand, as the water lowered. She didn't respond. I held my hand in front of her mouth and nose. She wasn't breathing. I felt her wrist, and then her chest, around where her heart might have been.

I closed my eyes. I opened them. I needed to collect myself. I glanced down, and saw Callas' bare feet. They didn't end in toes. They ended in vicious looking talons.

It was the talons that did it. I've no idea if I'd have been able to hold myself together without that final shock, but her unexpected mutation was too much for me. Noises ripped out of my throat, and I couldn't tell if they were screams or cries of despair. Callas was dead. The one person who might possibly have kept me safe in this storm was gone. My breathing felt shallow and lifeless. I just wanted to be back home. I wanted so badly to go back to a world where the worst thing to have happened to me was a disappointing set of exam results leading to prestigious universities withdrawing invitations of study. But I couldn't. I was here, and Lady Callas was dead, and all I could do was scream and cry and beat the floor impotently with my fists and clutch at my head and curl up into a ball and just desperately wish I was anywhere other than where I was.

Chapter Three

A claw gripped my shoulder. I threw it off, and scrambled into a corner of the room, a hollow wailing noise ripping out of my throat. Alison. It was only Alison – standing in the bathroom doorway, eyes wide, hands held up, empty. Fingers. Not claws.

"I'm so sorry, Susan," she said. She approached, and patted my shoulder a few times before withdrawing.

I needed to get out. I stood, keeping my eyes on the floor, and stumbled back into the bedroom. I leant against a bookcase, closed my eyes and tried to shut everything out.

"Were you very close?" asked Alison. I opened one eye. She was hovering, shifting from foot to foot. It was comforting to see the daemon's edge blunted, either by Callas' body, or my reaction to it.

I couldn't answer Alison's question truthfully. I'd met Lady Callas precisely once before. She'd set me a test, along with maybe twenty other school leavers who'd hit a wall when it came to formally studying journalism. We'd needed to meet her for breakfast at Selen's most exclusive hotel without an invitation, or the sort of bank account which would allow access to such a place. I was the only one to get to her without being thrown out by the hotel staff, and that had been by the skin of my teeth. She'd offered me the commission, given me a set of briefing documents, along with the bracelet of teeth and... that had been it. Twenty minutes from hello to goodbye.

My brain was too full to construct an elegant lie. Or any lies, really. The truth would have to do. "We hadn't known each other long, but she was like a mother to me."

"Oh Susan... I'm so sorry."

I closed my eyes again, and felt some of my shock and terror drain away. Anger rose in their place – partly at the thought of runaway mothers, generally, and mine specifically. Mostly, my teeth ground together at how unfair my situation was. It was supposed to be my second chance.

I had to make a choice. I could just run. I could get out of this underground death trap, head back to Selen, and forget any of this ever happened. The only snag was... how? Would the security system that had nearly melted my brain on my way in feel the same if I tried to break out? And could I find out without risking my life?

The other option... the extremely tempting option, was to stay. Do the job I'd been hired to do – learn all I could about the magissa, write up a report and... I'd worry what to do next if I got out alive.

I groaned, and sank to the floor, running my hands through my hair. Back in Selen, I had a pretty good sense for danger. Don't go to Nocturne after dark, don't talk back to people if they're obviously connected, running away from a fight is safer than winning one. Nice, neat, simple rules.

In the Callas labyrinth, I had no idea which was the least dangerous of my two options. I didn't have enough information. And if I was gathering information anyway...

Lady Callas was dead. I hadn't seen any injuries. She *could* have drowned in the bath by accident, but that felt wrong. We'd arrived to find the place locked down. Betsan, the head of security, incapacitated, and Lady Callas dead. She'd been murdered – it wasn't certain, but it was a good starting point.

Alison didn't seem to be an immediate threat. She was sympathetic, albeit awkwardly so, at my meltdown on seeing the Callas body. What's more, she'd been with me every moment inside the house until she'd gone to check on her mentor, after which I'd come straight to Callas' bedroom. If Callas had been murdered, Alison was the one person who couldn't be responsible. Alison was very possibly the safest person I could be around, currently.

To flee, or to stay... To flee, or to stay...

I was here. I was in the middle of something I didn't understand, and I *hated* not understanding things. Why did I want to become a journalist, anyway? It wasn't because the pay was great. I wanted to uncover dark, awful things such as the magissa, and shine a light on them. Lady Callas had wanted that too. If I really wanted to be a journalist, I should stay. I should stick with this.

Having made that decision, there was one obvious starting point. I was generally in danger from the magissa, but if there was a murderer in the house, they were a direct threat. I opened my eyes and clapped, cementing my decision. I rose, and turned to the daemon who might be able to help. "Alison?"

She was still hovering a little way away, unsure of what to do. "Hello? Yes?"

"Lady Callas has been murdered?"

"I think so, yes."

I frowned. "Why do you think so?"

Alison pointed at the wall of bones, "People who can amass that many bones don't just happen to wind up drowned in a bathtub."

"Right?" Alison's logic made sense, but I was also clearly missing context. "Will you help me find out who did this?"

Alison's eyes widened. A hazel storm danced in her gaze, and her grin grew even wider. "I was hoping you'd ask that."

Questions clouded my mind – I dearly wanted to ask 'why?', but working out exactly what Alison's deal was would have to wait. "Great. First, I really need your help."

"Yes, of course, anything."

"Lady Callas had promised to explain the magissa to me when I met her here. Now she's gone, but I still need to know. What are we?"

Alison nodded to herself. "I was wondering why you didn't have a familiar. All right. All right, I'll explain, but we should go. We need to check if everyone else is okay."

"Thank you," I said, following her out of the bedroom. "Is your patron alive?"

"Unconscious. Her heartbeat's strong, her breathing's regular. I just can't wake her up." Alison stopped mid-stride. "Did you hear something just then?"

I frowned. "Something scraping against a wall?"

"Let's move," whispered Alison, "we might not be alone down here."

I nodded, and we picked up the pace.

"Okay," said Alison, "to explain the magissa, I need you to give me two of the teeth from your bracelet."

I hesitated. This seemed like something a member of this secret society would be extremely reluctant to do.

Sensing my discomfort, Alison laughed. "You're cautious! You're right to be cautious. Very well. We'll use one tooth each. I've plenty to spare, and now that Lady Callas has passed on, your next patron will no doubt replace them."

"Thank you. Shall I give you any particular tooth?"

Alison waited for me at the top of the stairs to the great hall, and took my wrist in a confident grip, rotating my arm until she saw a tooth she thought suitable. She gripped it with her fingers before locking her gaze with mine. Was she asking for permission? I nodded and, smoothly, she twisted the tooth free of my bracelet, leaving the rest of the bracelet intact.

"I'm Hydros," she explained, taking a tooth from her own bracelet. "My osto is rapid evaporation. One second..." She pulled out a flask from her jacket pocket and offered it to me. "Try some."

"What is it?

"Just water. I don't want you to think I've got explosives or anything else in here."

I took a swig – just water. I shrugged and handed the flask back. Alison poured a few drops from the flask onto the carpet at our feet.

She handed me the flask, then held up our teeth, one in each hand. "With tiny bones like this, my osto will only work over a short distance and in limited ways. Crucially, the osto remains the same. It's the bone chosen to activate the osto that affects the outcome."

Alison lowered the hand containing my tooth and focused her attention on the one from her bracelet. "This tooth's a molar. Looks like it came from an elderly female. It's damaged – there's a large chip taken out of the distal side, see?"

It just looked like a tooth to me. I nodded anyway.

She grinned at me. "With a tooth like this, I'll be able to evaporate only a fraction of the water. Observe." With that, she popped the tooth into her mouth, and swallowed.

I bit my tongue. Thankfully, Alison was too busy pointing at the drops of water soaking into the carpet to notice my flash of agony. After a moment, the damp spots on the carpet began to fade, and a thin trail of steam twirled into the air.

"Evaporating the water? That's an osto," said Alison. "And, based on that example, you'd be forgiven for thinking it's not particularly powerful. You're Charites? With a tooth like the one I just used, you'd be able to communicate with simpler animals, or you might be able to compel a certain type of creature to perform simple tasks, that sort of thing."

I nodded. Alison thought I could communicate with animals. That seemed the sort of thing I should remember, no matter how disconnected from reality it sounded. I began the process of seating a memory anchor into the motion of scratching the back of my head.

Evaporating water and talking to animals. Was Alison deluded? She thought I was a member of her secret society. She had no reason to lie to me, so she might be deluded. But... her face was unique. It couldn't be an accident of birth, and her features were perfect – far beyond the skills of any cosmetic surgeon. Callas' feet had boasted claws rather than toes, and the security system had caused me to hallucinate. No tech I knew of could do that.

Alison held up the other tooth. "This tooth is an incisor. It came from a young person, most likely a male. It's in fine condition. All these factors, the size of the tooth, the type of tooth, the person it came from, what type of person they were, their general health – all these factors affect how the osto manifests. With a tooth like this, my osto should be a little more impressive."

She popped the tooth into her mouth, and retrieved her flask. She flicked a stream of water from the flask, pointed at the sparkling shower and—

BOOM

A cloud of steam burst from where the water had been. A shock-wave struck me in the face a moment before the furiously expanding steam enveloped me. I backed up, and stared at Alison, who'd pre-emptively sidestepped the mist.

Alison hadn't been trying to fool me. She thought I was already part of her order. She wasn't trying to con me out of money or power, no simple trick to fool me and win my loyalty. She had simply been attempting to demonstrate the intricacies of her art.

Alison gazed smugly at the look of awe and shock on my face. "Exactly."

Everything I thought I'd known about the world was wrong. Magic was real. Alison strode towards a ramp at the far end of the hall, but turned when I didn't join her. "Come on, let's go! We should check on Betsan and the others."

I shrank back.

She smiled. "I know it's a little shocking, but you have nothing to fear from me. I said in the coach we'd be friends, and I'd like that very much. You can trust me, Susan."

She strode up the ramp. I followed in a daze. Magic was real? *Magic.* The mystical force from children's books was here and real. There had always been rumours – stupid, credulous rumours but they always came from a conveniently distant country beyond the wall of chains.

"Are you okay?" Alison asked. "Because you look like you're having a heart attack. You're not, are you?"

"Oh no," I said, trying to get my breathing under control. "I'm fine. I'm fine. Fine."

"You're fine?"

"Yes. I'm fine."

In the silence that fell after my lie, I heard something stir behind us. I turned just in time to see a shadow dart out of sight at the far end of the hall, and a strangled yelp escaped my lips before I could stop it.

Alison whirled round, her hand on the butt of her pistol. "What is it?" she hissed.

"Someone watching us. Other end of the hall. Ran down the stairs as soon as I saw them."

Alison strode back down the ramp and dropped into a squat, peering into the gloom. "Interesting. They must have been drawn by the sound of my osto demonstration. It's possible I should have been more discrete. Well, it might not be *too* much of a problem. This house has several people living in it, other than our patrons. It might have just been one of them. Or..." She scrunched up her nose. "Let's watch for a bit. See if they come back."

She drifted to the side of the ramp to lurk in the shadows. I moved to stand behind her. Silence reigned for a few moments before I mustered the courage to speak.

Something had been gnawing at me since... Something had been gnawing at me since learning that m... Something had been gnawing at me since learning that magic was real. Those last three words shrieked through my head and I nearly whimpered out loud. I got myself back under control.

"The bones in Lady Callas' room," I said. "Where did they come from?"

"Humans," said Alison.

I must have gasped, because she glanced over her shoulder at me. "You've lived with humans up to now?"

I nodded.

"Well," she said, turning back to observe the great hall, "we get them from a variety of places."

"Graveyards?" I asked, hopefully. Grave robbing wasn't unheard of in Selen. It's traditional to bury loved ones with a valuable item or two, and the city's growing problem with homelessness and destitute citizenry complicated the tradition. Grave robbing has its upsides, of course. Medical students need bodies to practice on, after all.

"No. Our osto won't activate if the bones we use are taken from deceased humans. Those teeth will have been each extracted from a living donor. Sometimes they're acquired voluntarily. Sometimes they aren't."

A creeping horror skittered through me. I'd wondered about the teeth biting into my wrist many times since I'd first seen them, yet hearing them discussed so matter-of-factly felt unreal. I stared at my bracelet. Some of the teeth were old, some were new. Some were small, some were large. Some were stained and damaged, some were nearly perfect.

"Why are the teeth so varied? Wouldn't it make more sense to take all the teeth from one mouth? Say, a prisoner? Why take individual teeth from individual mouths?"

I managed to get the question out without stammering, to my relief. These people, these magissa, *ate* these teeth. The thought of feeling a tooth judder down my throat made my stomach turn.

"That's one of the limitations on a magissa's power," said Alison. "We can't use multiple bones from a single human. As a result, collections of bones are a mark of considerable status. They show you have power, and plenty to spare. These bracelets we wear mark us out as initiates of a very powerful house."

"The bigger the collection of bones, the more powerful the magissa?"

"Exactly. You saw the wall of bones your patron had acquired. Lady Callas was very powerful indeed."

Two years ago... two winters ago, my dads and I had been struggling. Biofuel prices had skyrocketed because the three large suppliers had bought out the smaller companies, and started price fixing. Dad was working every shift he could. Papa was still too ill to work and I could only work a few hours after school.

One day, dad mentioned a rumour he'd heard. Someone – a friend of a friend, was offering serious money for bones. We still had my baby teeth, so dad asked me if I'd mind him giving them to a mysterious tooth pervert. The chance at being able to pay for the fuel to get us through winter was enough. We'd all been shocked when the tooth pervert had paid dad a month's wages for the delivery.

Of course I tried to work out what the tooth pervert actually did with the things – I was deputy editor of my school paper, I was hoping to study journalism at the University of the Silver Key. I was born to investigate that sort of shit.

Unfortunately, the tooth pervert wouldn't talk, and every trail I chased went cold. After two months, I had to give up. And, the next winter, when dad had come home missing a finger and papa had begged me just to drop it... I dropped it.

So, the real question was, had the magissa mutilated my parents? The anger I'd felt in the wake of discovering Callas' body had started to fade. This thought brought it back with a vengeance. I welcomed it. Anger would keep me alive until I could get used to this nightmare.

"We should check on the rest of the household," I said, running a finger from my forehead to the bridge of my nose, focussing on that particular memory anchor. "I know about Betsan, the head of security. There's a housekeeper as well – Mr Das I think his name was. There was another servant named Teleri. Finally... Charles? A friend of the family, I think."

"Exactly."

"Right. Let's check on them all, then we can get to work on finding out who murdered my patron."

Chapter Four

The ramp levelled out and stopped abruptly at an unimposing door which wouldn't have looked out of place as the door of a linen closet. Alison swung the door open. A small brass plate with the words 'linen closet' had been affixed to the other side.

Beyond the door was a narrow corridor which ended at a curtained window, a sliver of light cutting through a gap at the top. The walls were decorated with a cream paint that had probably been the height of fashion fifty years ago. Rugs covered the stone floors. Exposed beams gave the place a traditional feeling. Doilies perched smugly on top of occasional tables.

"Hey." I said.

Alison drew her pistol. "What?"

"Why is the door to the lower levels marked 'linen closet?'"

Alison huffed, and holstered her pistol. "It's a disguise, dummy. Curious intruders are loathe to investigate areas reserved for the domestic staff. It's a well-known fact. Now shush, we might not be alone up here."

That... was a point I'd not considered. Alison nodded to me and stalked down the corridor. I followed, resting a hand gently on the hilt of my xiphos. The grip felt like home. Practice with papa in the nearby park.

We crept past a set of stairs, then turned a corner and nearly tripped over Betsan's scraggly form. She lay curled up on the floor, shoulders jammed against the house's front door, knees squeezed by the opposite wall. She looked as if she'd been stuffed into a packing crate. Sweat plastered chestnut hair across her face.

"Betsan?" I asked. I rocked her shoulder, gently.

Her eyelids fluttered. "You made it. Good. Have you checked on the others?"

"Some of them, yes," I said. "Betsan, what happened?"

She groaned. Her fingers twitched and her legs shifted. Finally, her eyes opened. "We were all fine until about half way through dinner, but then Mr Das collapsed. Teleri followed. Lady Callas sent word that the three residents were in a similar state."

"Could it be food poisoning?" I asked.

"Not a chance," said Betsan. "This was deliberate. Designed to incapacitate."

Alison frowned. "Not kill?"

Betsan groaned. "I think so. Hard to be sure. Think I'm past the worst now, it just hurts." A tendril of drool leaked out of the corner of her mouth. "A lot."

"Is there anything in the house that might help?" I asked.

"Medicine kit. In my room. Painkillers. Common antidotes. Fetch it."

"Which is your room?" Alison asked.

"Up the stairs, turn left, follow the corridor, last door on the right," Betsan said, closing her eyes. "Leather bag on the back of the door."

Alison turned to me and shrugged. I nodded "Be right back."

I ran back to the stairs I'd passed earlier. It felt strange to be away from Alison – safer in one way, less safe in a host of others. Up the stairs of the cottage, the corridors were tighter, and the ceilings lower.

Whitewashed walls and functional furnishings. A place only intended for servants.

Betsan's directions led me to a room that looked as if it belonged to some sort of warlord. Bladed weapons of every shape and size hung from racks on the walls, meticulously organized and maintained. Commendation ribbons hung in a display case set against one wall.

Betsan's bag was where she'd said it would be. I grabbed it and staggered a little under its weight. I composed my face, which had been set in an expression of naked horror since I'd left Alison's company, and scampered back downstairs.

Betsan moaned in pain as I reached the bottom of the stairs. I picked up my pace. "What's wrong?" I asked, when I reached the patient and my daemonic companion.

"I told Betsan about Lady Callas," said Alison. "She asked. Seemed rude to remain stonily silent."

I scurried over to Betsan. "Here's the bag."

She blinked up at me, possibly in thanks, and then unclipped the bag's fastenings. She hauled out a small derringer pistol, a set of wrist cuffs, a bundle of candles, and finally a small leather case. She flipped the case open - glass vials glinted in the light.

Betsan glowered at each vial in turn. "Not you, I'm not nearly dead enough to be suffering from Antediluvian Fever. Not you, because my fingers haven't turned green. Not you..." she continued like this for a while before she reached the final vial in her case. "And not you, because my eyes are still very much inside my skull rather than in little pools on the floor."

She rolled back her head and swore, loudly. Alison covered her ears.

"Will none of these antidotes work?" I asked, not really convinced Betsan knew what she was talking about.

"No! None of my symptoms fit any of the common poisons these are supposed to counteract. I've been hit with something exotic and really quite nasty. We've just got to hope not everyone in the house is as incapacitated as I am. However, *this* will help."

She grabbed a twist of paper from the bottom of the case and emptied the grey powder contained therein into her mouth.

"Someone's definitely doing better than you are, Betsan," Alison said. "Someone was watching us from the great hall as we made our way up here."

Betsan growled. "Find them. They might know who did this. They might be the one who did this. Check on everyone else. Find out if anyone is unaffected. Find who... who killed Lady Callas."

Yes, The Callas murder. Where to start... We'd got in through the entrexit. Could anyone else have done the same? I squatted down by Betsan. "Who else knows the passphrase for the secret entrance? Could the murderer have got out the way we came in?"

Betsan shook her head. "I changed the code when I locked the site down a few hours ago. No-one else knows what it is, other than the three of us."

"Got it," I said. "Thanks. Let's go, Alison."

I led the way to the stairs I'd recently become familiar with, affecting my best confident saunter. I needed to focus on the Callas murder. If Alison saw me as someone she could rely upon, she might question my ignorance a little less.

My confidence shook a little as I climbed the stairs. The noise of my feet on the carpet sounded just a little too loud, and I was sure Alison would be able to hear my heart hammering. I tried to breathe normally.

Where to start? Doors. Check each of the rooms on the first floor. Gather evidence. Hope inspiration strikes. Get out alive.

The first room I checked turned out to be a dining room. A table might have once been set for four, but was now a chaotic mess. Glasses had been knocked over, serving dishes overturned, plates scattered across the table and floor. Bile green sauce soaked into the carpet.

The next room had a brass plaque on the door marked 'visiting staff'. I raised an eyebrow at Alison, who blinked at me. I wasn't sure what that meant, so I peeked inside. I shrugged. I threw the door open so Alison could see. The place was bare – nothing but a bed frame, a mattress and stale air.

The next room over was also marked 'visiting staff'. Its bed was occupied by a woman who looked as if she made her living hauling bio-fuel tankers into port. Her breathing was ragged, like a saw grinding against a nail.

"Hello?" I said. No response. I approached, and shook her shoulder. Still nothing.

"She's unconscious?" asked Alison. She seemed on edge.

"Looks like it." I shrugged. "Your mentor was like this?"

"Yes. Can you sense anything?"

It was a good thing that I was facing towards the unconscious hulk rather than Alison, because I couldn't keep a momentary flash of panic from my face. "Yes," I lied, "there's definitely... something..."

Alison grunted. "Exactly," she stalked from one side of the room to the other, her gaze darting disjointedly. "There's something, I just can't tell what. It's at the edge of my senses. What is that? What is it? It's sort of – no, not that. It's like a splinter I can't get at. Do you—"

"Let's check the other rooms," I said, not wanting her to ask any more questions about whatever it was that I was supposed to be able to sense.

"What?" Alison blinked, then focussed on me. She shook her head. "Oh. Maybe? Yes. Yes, good idea."

The next doors we tried led to a lavatory, linen storage and then Betsan's room, where Alison eyed the bladed weapons with ill-concealed envy. The last door had a brass plate marked "Mr Das."

Mr Das was Callas' housekeeper, according to her notes. The mansion wasn't large enough to warrant a butler, or sizable full-time staff, but a housekeeper was essential. Apparently.

There were other servants employed by the Callas family, but they commuted from the nearby village of Irinna. Maybe the servants didn't know about the underground sections of the house.

I opened the door to Mr Das' room gently and, as with the visitor's room, I found a figure curled up on the bed. Mr Das made a strangled gasp as the door opened, and appeared to be trying to turn over to see who I was.

"Mr Das? It's Susan Fletcher – Lady Callas' protégé. I've got Alison Dewan with me." The figure twitched a little. "Mr Das?"

The figure twitched again. This time, I realised that he was trying to nod his head. I entered the room, cautiously. Alison followed.

As my eyes adjusted to the dark, the shape in the bed became clearer. A slight man with loose, curly hair. He wore a black formal tunic – a housekeeper's uniform. It was battered and creased, far more than I'd have expected, but then he'd probably slept in it whilst being racked with the effects of the mysterious poison.

I approached the bed. "Is there anything we can do to help, Mr Das?"

"Nnnnnn." Mr Das said, his teeth grinding together.

"Has your condition grown worse?" Alison asked from my side. "Should we summon a physician?"

"No!" The word slammed out of his mouth. We both took a step back. Alison and I exchanged worried looks.

"Can you tell us anything about what happened last night?" I asked.

Mr Das screwed his eyes shut. "No,"

He was clearly in pain, and while that might explain his behaviour, there must be something else going on...

"Mr Das," Alison said, "what are you?"

The man breathed deeply. It seemed to be taking everything he had to force even this one word between his teeth. "Erebus." Something red bloomed at the corner of his mouth. Wet. Glistening.

Alison drew in a shocked breath. "My apologies. In that case, we'll continue with our investigations."

My companion backed out of the room. I glared at her, and waved for her to come back. She caught my flailing arm and hauled me outside.

"What was that about?" I asked, as Alison strode back down the landing, away from Mr Das' room.

"He's Erebus," said Alison. "We won't be able to get anything useful out of him. It's not his fault."

"What is Erebus?"

Alison covered her face with her hands, groaned and then spun to face me. "I'm sorry. I wonder if it would be worth me just telling you everything that Lady Callas should have told you."

I wanted nothing more than to fall to my knees and beg for her to do exactly that. Instead, I tried my best to appear insulted.

She shook her head, and strode to the head of the stairs, "We don't have time. Erebus are mistresses of stealth. Mr Das will have some sort of camouflage ability. Their curse is they find communication difficult. Some can only speak in riddles, some can never make a noise above a whisper."

"A curse..." I was finally putting some pieces together. "Like..."

Alison rolled her eyes. "Like my face, yes. And your claws."

Callas' feet had ended in claws. Was that why she'd instructed me to never take my shoes off? It'd reveal me as someone only pretending to be Charites?

Betsan looked a little more lively when we returned to her. She was still drenched with sweat, and a lot greyer than was healthy, but she no longer looked like she might actually be dying.

"Mr Das is in a pretty bad way," Alison said, without preamble. "Oh, and there's someone in one of the visitor's rooms, but she's unconscious."

"Big woman?" asked Betsan. "Looks like she could bend a poker in half?"

I nodded, "Thats the one."

"That'd be Teleri," said Betsan. "She's a caterer that Lady Callas got in to cover the event tomorrow."

"Don't you have a cook?" Alison asked. "We've got a cook. His name's Eric."

"Yes, we do have a cook," growled Betsan, "and she suits our needs perfectly. Victoria thought we should get someone who catered to the wider magissa society's needs a little more closely."

"So, she was the only stranger in the house when you were all poisoned?" Alison asked.

"I checked her out myself," said Betsan. "There were a few things that raised my concerns, but nothing that suggested she'd do anything like this. She's not political, and has no reason to have a grudge against any of us."

Politics. I hadn't a hope of getting to grips with a secret society's politics in the time I had. I'd have to take Betsan's word for that, at least for now. "Thank you Betsan. We need to check on Charles next."

Chapter Five

Alison led the way to Charles' room, which turned out to be next door to the room occupied by Praxi Tolis, Alison's patron. I took a moment to centre myself before I knocked.

"Come in," called a plummy voice from inside. I raised an eyebrow at Alison before turning the handle and walking in.

Charles' room was elegant and tidy. Three portraits hung on the walls. One was unmistakably Callas. Tall. Elegant. Deceitful. I didn't recognise the other two. A desk sat against the west wall, fastidiously stacked papers at one end and a silver-framed picture at the other. The frame contained a photograph of a young woman in practical, everyday clothing.

No, that wasn't right. I looked closer. Her clothes were, indeed, practical, but were of a distinct style which had last been popular fifty years ago. Wide collars and reinforced cuffs had been in fashion back then. She was either into retro clothing, or this picture was ancient.

Charles sat on the edge of his bed. He looked to be in better shape than Betsan, but that wasn't saying much. Sweat beaded on his forehead, and he appeared short of breath, but seemed otherwise unharmed. That was, until he attempted to stand, causing him to wince in pain and drop back onto his bed.

"Charles?" I asked.

He nodded. "Charles Varma. Are you the initiates?"

"That's right. How do you feel, Mr Varma?" I asked.

Charles wiped sweat from his brow. "Terrible. I can barely move. I'm of a mind to complain to the chef. I say, don't touch that!"

Alison paused with her hand outstretched. She'd spotted something on the bookcase. A document folder bound in crimson. "Why not?" she asked.

Charles looked at my companion as if she'd just asked for some of his used underwear. "Because it's mine," he said, eventually. "Look here, could you two please leave? I've barely slept and am still not feeling tip top. I'm sure we'll get to know each other a little better during the ceremony."

We were going to have to break the news of Callas' untimely demise, but perhaps not yet. His ignorance was useful. We could question him in a relatively unguarded state. I fought to keep my expression neutral, but the aristo's brow furrowed.

"What?" he said. "What's the problem?"

I clasped my hands behind my back. "The ceremony's likely cancelled. or at least delayed."

"What? Why?"

"Lady Callas has been murdered," said Alison from behind me.

Shock, surprise and fear fought for dominance on his face. "What? But – but that's terrible!"

"I'm sorry for your loss." I said. "I wonder if you would be so kind as to tell us what happened last night?"

Outrage glistened in his eyes. But then, his accent, his surroun dings... I'd met this man hundreds of times before, even if this was my first time encountering Charles Varma. I could practically hear his thoughts: *Who was this girl to ask such a question? I'd just been told some truly devastating news! But then again... she was a child.*

She'd surely need some distracting from the horrific sights she must have witnessed.

"Of course," he said, his expression softening. "Well, we had dinner at around seven in the evening. I started feeling a little queasy afterward, so I retired to my room. I slept fitfully until a few hours ago when I woke to find myself unable to rise from my bed. I've been slowly recovering since then."

Alison stirred – she was fidgeting about near the bookcase. Charles' head turned in her direction.

"I see," I said, a little too loudly. Charles' gaze snapped back to me. "And what did you do just before dinner?"

"Well, I did a little reading," said Charles. His manner had subtly changed – the pained expression from moments ago had all but vanished. "Then I had a chat with Lady Callas about my visit to Irinna, our nearby village."

"And you went straight to dinner with her ladyship?" I asked.

"Well, I might have slipped upstairs to have a quick word with Mr Das about the evening meal. I have allergies, you see."

"I see." I nodded, gravely. "Well, thank you for your candour. Do you have any questions, Alison?"

"None whatsoever," replied Alison, a little too quickly.

"Very well," I said, not wanting to give Charles an opportunity to ask what was going on. "We shall leave you to your thoughts."

Alison slipped out of the door ahead of me. I followed her down the corridor, but paused in front of Praxi's door. "Alison!"

Alison was already halfway to the staircase. "Hello, yes?"

"Can I speak to Praxi?"

"Oh, yes, good idea. See if she's awake."

I knocked on the door – no answer. I opened the door and saw the familiar sight of a figure tangled up in her own bedclothes. Her face was similarly demonic to Alison's, although there were some significant differences. Her horns were a little longer, and the ridges of bone at her forehead lacked the elegance I'd grown used to when regarding Alison. Her skin might also have been lighter, but it was hard to tell in the sliver of light from the doorway. "Ms Tolis?" I called. No response. I approached her bedside, and shook her shoulder. Nothing. Out cold, like Teleri.

I retreated back to the corridor, and reported Praxi's state to Alison, who nodded. "Same as when I checked on her. Anyway, feast your eyes on this!" She pulled Charles' crimson document case from under her jacket.

"You're stealing from the residents now?"

"He didn't want us to have it, there must be something interesting inside."

I pinched the bridge of my nose. "Do you do this often?"

Alison shrugged, "I get bored easily. Anyway, we're trying to find out who murdered Lady Callas! We need clues. I found clues!"

She opened the document case and spread the contents out on the floor of the corridor. The documents turned out to be a police report, concerning a murder which had taken place in the year 690 – forty-nine years ago. The victim had been a young woman named Tova Oster. On the last page was a photograph – unmistakably the same girl I'd seen in the framed photo on Charles' desk.

Charles hadn't looked over fifty. Mid forties at the absolute oldest. Could Tova have been a parent? Or maybe...

"Alison?"

"Yes?"

"How long do we live?"

"Say again?"

"The magissa. How long do we live on average, compared to humans?"

Alison sighed.

"I'm sorry," I said.

Alison sat on the floor, next to where I'd been examining the papers. She leant against the wall, the back of her head thumping against the plaster. "Look, I'm Hydros. I'm used to only talking about this stuff to Hydros. Do you know why?"

"I'm honestly amazed you felt the need to ask that question."

"Magissa, for the most part, aren't born. We emerge. You were discovered recently, yes? At a guess, you noticed your toes were morphing into claws and you went to see a physician. The physician referred you to one of our people. Our people paid the physician a vast amount of money to keep their mouth shut, and here we are."

"Right."

"That didn't happen to me. magissa gifts and curses aren't passed down in the usual way because most magissa can't breed. They're sterile. There is one exception to this rule, and you're staring at her."

"You're the only magissa who can breed?" I asked.

"No, you dope. Hydros. Hydros can breed, but magissa from other clans can't. You can imagine that this had caused a certain amount of resentment towards us, which I know isn't *your* fault. You've never shunned me like the other Charites I've met. I like you, Susan, though I dislike others of your kind, and I find your ignorance infuriating."

She paused, sighed, and hauled herself to her feet. "So, to answer your question, we don't actually know how long magissa can live naturally. I've never heard of one of us dying of old age."

"Huh." Another impossible thing to add to the pile, although this one seemed more sad than shocking. "So, how old would you say Charles is?"

"I've no idea, we'd have to check the records."

"Could he be over, say, a hundred years old?"

"Oh yes, easily. My mum is about five hundred."

"How..." I began, before realising my mouth was dry. I swallowed and started again. "How old are you, Alison?"

"What? I'm eighteen. I'm sure I told you that."

"But..."

"Oh, I see where you're getting confused. Initiations into the magissa happen at the age of eighteen. We could technically wait for longer than that, but you know how tradition is."

I was getting lost in the weeds, but this felt important. "So... how come the humans outnumber us and not the other way around? Humans die after only about eighty years in the best case scenario."

"Because new magissa are extremely rare. I don't know the actual statistics, but it's something like one in every thousand human children are born with the gift, and only a fraction of those children mature into magissa. The odds improve if they're found in time. The odds diminish if their curse is discovered by superstitious humans. The claws on your feet would still be a death sentence for you in the wrong circumstances. You could claim they were a birth defect, but enough of us have been found over the years that we've made our way into folklore. You'd have probably been accused of being a daemon. Imagine that! You! A daemon!" Alison cackled.

"Mm."

"Come on, grab the papers, I want to check the rest of the house. See if our mysterious stalking figure is anywhere obvious."

She strode away without waiting for me to get to my feet. I found her at the staircase - it turned out there were stairs leading down as well as back up to the great hall.

I followed Alison down, trying to work through the papers I'd hastily gathered. There were a few letters from Tova Oster to Charles, which I found utterly bewildering. Still, one thing quickly became clear: Tova had been Charles' protégé. Next in the stack was a hand-written report concerning Tova's death. The name Teleri Parry was mentioned several times.

"Oh, wow," I said.

"What?" Alison asked, over her shoulder.

"Charles had a pupil, a woman named Tova. She was murdered. It looks like Charles had someone investigate the killing. The investigator returned Teleri Parry as a person of interest."

"Teleri Parry?" Alison asked. "Do we know if that's the same Teleri as the one sleeping in the cottage upstairs?"

"We'll have to check."

"Does it say what Tova's clan is?" Alison asked.

I scanned back through a few sheets of paper. I'd seen one of those blasted code words somewhere... there, at the bottom of one of the letters Tova had written to Charles. "Deimos."

Alison whistled.

"Are Deimos powerful?"

"Very," said Alison, before making a noise that I first thought was a groan but morphed into something akin to delight. "This is so amazing! I've been waiting all my life for something like this! This place has everything. Dead mentors, dark figures stalking us, mysterious pasts of shadowy individuals!" She shivered. "It's a dream come true."

She turned to look at me. Her grin faded when she saw my expression. "And I've *just* remembered that Lady Callas was *your* mentor. Sorry, Susan. I get carried away sometimes."

"It's fine," I said, weakly. We turned a corner in the hallway. Had this been the floor above, we would have been heading to Callas' room.

Silence was thick in the air. It felt as if Alison wanted to say something, but was holding back. "Have you done much work of this sort before?" I asked.

"Not so much," said Alison. "I've had lessons, of course. Stealth, espionage, combative use of tie pins..."

"You made that last one up."

"Oh, you poor, sweet, delight. My point is that Hydros tend to gravitate towards investigative work. We excel when operating in the shadows. Influencing matters whilst out of sight."

"Oh, why?" I asked.

Alison gave me a look which she had evidently spent some time perfecting. She twirled her fingers in a half circle around her face. Her horns seemed to grow slightly as she glared. Her grin was too wide. 'did you really need to ask that question?' her expression asked.

"Right." I said, my cheeks burning. "Sorry."

"My point is that I've been examined on my investigative techniques. I'm excited to be finally using them."

"Did you do well in your exams?" I asked, jealousy gnawing at the back of my brain.

"Damn right I did, but it's not like the real thing. I'm just pleased to be able to get some practice in, and to have someone else helping."

We reached a door marked 'library'. Alison strode in without breaking her stride, and flicked the light switch, causing glow globes in the ceiling to ignite. The library was immaculate. Bookshelves lined the walls, whilst the centre of the room was occupied by reading desks and armchairs. It was the size of Callas' room, which was to say, massive.

I paced a circuit of the room whilst Alison examined a bookshelf.

Had my head been a little clearer, I believe I'd have noticed an object or two that seemed out of place. Maybe a bookshelf wasn't standing quite with its back to the wall. Maybe there was a conspicuous hole in a shelf where a single book had been suspiciously removed. But, with my head reeling from the 101 impossible things I'd learned so far that day, all I saw was a library.

"Nothing jumps out at me here," I said. "Do we have time to search thoroughly?"

Alison shrugged... and I heard something move. I waved to get Alison's attention and tugged at my ear, trying to communicate what I meant silently.

There it was again – a scraping sound. Maybe cloth moving against stone? I glanced at Alison, who nodded. It had been coming from the south wall, behind a book case. There were no doors in the south wall, nor were there any other rooms past this one.

Was someone in the wall? Was that a sensible thing to think? Or was this place warping my sense of reality? It was hard to tell.-I moved to Alison's side as silently as possible. "Could there be someone behind that wall?" I whispered.

Alison nodded. "There must be. They're probably in the steam tunnels. Let's move."

We left the library, and crept back the way we'd come, occasionally pausing to listen for more mysterious noises behind the walls.

We returned to the stairs, and then past them, to the next room – a guest bathroom. Thankfully, the bath was empty. The next room was a dining room. The place was a shambles, an opulent mirror of the dining room upstairs. I fished a notebook out of a pocket, and sketched a quick plan of the room, along with curious features – spilled food, overturned chairs, and mysterious stains on the carpet.

The next door led to a room with padding on the walls and floor, which Alison explained was designed to help the magissa hone their powers. To my relief, it was also entirely empty.

No more noises from the walls, and we'd checked every room on the floor. I led us back upstairs, and felt as if I could breathe properly again once we were back in the great hall.

"How are you doing, Susan?" Alison asked, patting my shoulder.

I laughed at that, although I felt more relief than anything else. "Hanging in there, but I've had a thought. We should establish how the poisoning of the household occurred."

Alison nodded. "You think the poisoner and the killer are one and the same?"

"Exactly. They might be an outsider who has infiltrated the house and found themselves unable to leave, or they might be someone we've already met. We should work on the assumption that they aren't an outsider."

"Why's that?"

"The murderer has been in the house, alone, and unchallenged for hours. They could have murdered Betsan, Praxi, or anyone else whilst they were unconscious and feeling the effects of the poison. They didn't. They killed one person, and only one person, which indicates that this was a precisely motivated act. Come on, I want to ask Betsan something."

Alison nodded, slowly. "I get you. The killer targeted Lady Callas, but they could still be an intruder, just someone who came in with the plan of murdering her. Or maybe stealing from her before they were caught, and they murdered her to get away."

"Sure, that makes sense," I said. "Either way, we should ask Betsan about the steam tunnels. I want to know where the entrances and exits are, so we don't get ambushed."

"Ooh, good idea," said Alison. "And we could maybe go into the tunnels to try to flush our spy out."

"I wish you wouldn't keep having ideas like that."

Chapter Six

"Okay," I said, striding across the great hall. "The household fell ill during dinner. All six began to feel sick simultaneously, so it's likely the meal was the cause. One of the six must be faking their poisoning, unless they poisoned themselves deliberately to allay suspicion. If we find a single setting at the dinner table where some or all of the foodstuffs are untouched, that would suggest that person is the poisoner."

"Right," said Alison. "If you say so. So why did we leave the dining room? We should have checked the meals."

"I did. I sketched the room, and noted the status of each meal. They were all mostly eaten. I hadn't considered this factor when I was last in the servant's dining room, so let's head there next."

"Tell you what," said Alison, as we strode up the ramp and into the cottage, "why don't you check the plates and I'll ask Betsan about the entrances to the steam tunnels? Divide and conquer!"

I didn't want to be left alone in this death trap. The anxiety that I'd been fighting down for a long time now bubbled back up fiercely, its fingers encircling my throat for a brief moment before I could smother it again. I should be safe if we were only separated for a short time. I should be safe.

I returned to the servant's dining room without being murdered, which was a relief. I sketched the room, as I'd done for the rooms downstairs, then checked on the meals. They were mostly consumed, except... when I checked under the table, I found a stray plate. It was lying pretty much under the centre of the table. Not a natural place for the plate to have been dropped accidentally. Further inspection revealed that the cut of pork once forming the centrepiece of that meal had been left completely untouched.

I grabbed a napkin, wrapped the pork up in it and returned downstairs, where the sounds of Alison and Betsan talking made me feel safer. I explored until I found the kitchen, and then resorted to opening doors more or less at random until I found the pantry. The air inside was chilled, thanks to a steam powered heat exchanger. I stashed the pork somewhere no-one was likely to stumble across it, and nodded to myself. I was making progress.

I had a moment. I sank to my knees. I wanted to scream. What was I doing? I wasn't a detective. I should run. I should run. So, I should run. Good, I'd made that decision. Then what?

If Alison didn't pursue me, I might be able to get back to Selen before nightfall. I could try to get my life back on track some other way. But what would happen when the magissa tried to find me? Because they *would* be able to find me. I'd not hidden my name. I'd not thought I'd need to. What of the killer? What if they followed me back home?

Over the course of the next ten minutes, I pulled myself together. Solving this murder was a much more sensible thing to do than making plans for the future, seeing as I first needed to ensure that I had a future at all. Once that was certain, I could then worry about making it a *long* one.

I dried my eyes, straightened my clothing, and clapped my face between my hands a few times. I rooted about in the pantry a bit until I found the remains of a steak and ale pie, which I grabbed, before slipping back into the kitchen. Breakfast had been long time ago. I helped myself. The food, far more than slapping my face, made me feel better.

I went to re-join Alison and Betsan, but then remembered that they would likely be in the same state I was. I cut the remains of the pie into two sections, grabbed what plates and utensils had been left out and presented it to the two magissa.

Betsan didn't so much eat her pie as savage it. Alison ate with her hands rather than use the spatula and escargot tongs I'd presented her with. Every time she took a bite, she looked down at the pie in her hands and giggled.

"I should take some food to my patron," said Alison, brushing crumbs from her hands..

Betsan stretched, "That can probably wait. The effects of the poison are fading. You might not have long left to explore the house as it was at the time of the murder."

Alison and I glanced at each other.

"Did you ask where the entrances to the steam tunnels were?" I asked.

"I did!" said Alison.

"Then shall we proceed?" I asked, bowing to the inevitable.

"After you!"

I was about to leave when I remembered what I'd been meaning to ask Betsan. I snapped my fingers and whirled around. "Betsan? What's Teleri the caterer's surname?"

"Parry."

"Thanks!" I nodded to the head of security, then followed Alison.

"Why did you ask about Teleri's surname?" asked Alison.

"You remember the red folder you stole from Charles?"

"Ah, yes, Teleri Parry was a suspect in the murder of Charles' protégé."

"So, we have a poisoned aristocrat, a bereaved magissa, and the person responsible for said bereavement just happens to be invited to cater at their home," I said.

"It could just be an awfully big co-incidence," said Alison. I gave her one of my looks.

She shrugged. "What? I didn't say I thought it *was*."

I grinned. "So, tell me about the entrances to the steam tunnels."

"They're all either in the great hall or on the mansion's lowest level. Betsan told me how to find most of them; they're well hidden. Shall we go and have a look?"

"I want to have a better look at the crime scene first. You're sure there aren't any entrances on the level below the great hall?" A nasty, dangerous little plan was growing inside me.

"The tunnels run through that level but there aren't any ways in or out."

"Okay," I said. "Okay. I propose that I poke around the crime scene whilst you lurk in the great hall. If our spy hears me in Callas' room and emerges from the tunnels to come and get me, you can surprise them."

Unsurprisingly, Alison agreed enthusiastically to my plan. She didn't try to talk me out of it. Not even for a second. Blast her.

I made it to the opulent white bedroom without getting attacked, and added a check to a mental tally I was keeping under the 'success' column. This small victory failed to balance out the thirty or so checks I'd already placed under the 'fail' column, but it was a start.

I closed the bedroom door behind me and then spent a few minutes hauling a writing desk until it was propped against the door. Then, I wondered what would happen if there was a steam tunnel entrance leading to Callas' room which Betsan didn't know about. In that case I'd created a Susan trap for the murderer to take advantage of. I shoved the writing desk back out of the way, and propped a chair under the door handle instead, that'd have to do.

I looked about the bedroom. Where to start? The bed was probably a smart place. Something about it was bothering me, but I couldn't work out what.

I pulled out my notebook and sketched the scene before me. I captured the odd way the bedclothes lay – they were crumpled up at the foot of the bed. They didn't look as if they'd been flung aside so Callas could make a quick trip to the bathroom. I also drew out the shape of the huge sweat stains on the mattress and pillow.

I then sketched a plan of the room, complete with the water trail leading to the closed bathroom door. This activity was surprisingly relaxing. For the first time in hours, I felt some of my muscles start to unclench. My chest stopped clamping around my lungs. In Callas' room, in that moment, I felt able to concentrate.

I tapped my pencil against my teeth for a few moments whilst I pondered where to explore next. I'd seen the bathroom on my last visit, but there was another door in the Callas bedroom I hadn't checked. Maybe it was a wardrobe, but you never knew.

I opened the door to find a decently decked out study. It wasn't as charmingly tacky as Papa's, but it was significantly larger. I'd guess it was shared by Callas and her wife; there were two desks at opposite ends of the room. One of the desks was beautiful and ornate, sculpted from oak with brass handles adorning the drawers. A silver-framed picture of the couple had been placed at a carefully calculated angle at the desk's left edge, while the rest of the surface remained clear except for a blank page of writing paper, and a pen.

The other desk was a disaster area. Papers lay strewn across it, and on the floor around it. A drawer was half-open, and a drift of paper wrappings lay inside, the names of various expensive chocolate manufacturers embossed on the papers.

When I'd met Callas at the hotel, she'd been wearing a simple business suit. A pocket square had been her only snippet of flare. I sat at the neater of the two desks and started opening drawers.

The first drawer mostly contained spare writing paper, which I ignored, and expensive looking pens, which I stole. Other than that, I found a thick book with a blank cover, which I hauled out and dropped on the desk with a thud. In the lower drawers, I found a small, unlabelled bottle of liquid and a battered leather pouch. I raised an eyebrow at these before placing them next to the book.

Bag. Book. Bottle.

I opened the bottle first and sniffed gingerly. I winced. Strong alcohol, although exactly what type was a mystery. The dads had let me have the occasional glass of beer. Cider had been my drink of choice when out with school friends.

The contents of the pouch clicked and clacked as I weighed it in my hand, as if it contained pebbles. Given how my day had been going, I didn't have to wonder too hard at what was inside.

I teased open the thong constricting the bag's neck and peered inside. The day's magnificent detective award went to Susan Fletcher. Inside were thirty or forty teeth. I found myself still staring at them after my moment of smugness had passed. Having a pouch like this was probably the magissa equivalent of having a roll of used bank notes in the bottom of your desk. There might be legitimate reasons to have such a stash, but why weren't they on display in the main bedroom like the rest of the bones?

I shrugged, and slipped the bag into my pocket to get Alison's opinion on later. For all I knew the pouch was a completely normal thing to have in a desk drawer. Finally, I opened the book, which turned out to be a diary.

I recognised Callas' handwriting from the letter she'd sent me. Flowing and precise. *12th of Mist 737. Victoria and I visited Selen for the first lecture in the series on assassination by Ariana Aetós...* etcetera, etcetera. Nothing mind-blowing on the early pages. I flicked to the last entry.

20th of Frost 739, it began. The day after we'd met at the Hotel. The entry was about some book she was reading, and little else.

The previous entry was marked the 19th of Frost, the day of our meeting. It was three paragraphs long, and was solely focused on preparations for the upcoming initiation ceremony. There was no mention of a trip to Selen to meet me.

Maybe there wouldn't be anything useful in this diary after all. Callas had either considered our meeting not worth mentioning, or she was worried that someone would do what I was currently doing.

I glanced across at Victoria Callas' desk. Was there a lack of trust between these two? Possibly. Where was Victoria, anyway? I made a mental note to ask Betsan about that when I next saw her.

I started flicking to pages in Marie's diary at random, keeping an eye out for anything that grabbed my eye.

Victoria is the sun on my face, read one entry. *Without her, I'd truly be lost. I wonder if she knows what she really means to me?*

She's going to leave me, read another, and *Victoria was distant today*, read yet another. It was hard to tell if these darker entries were well founded suspicions, or merely evidence of paranoia.

I was about to close the book and recommence my search when one last entry caught my eye. *Confronted Betsan about her fighting, She practically snarled at me when I told her to stop. Not for the first time, I cursed the day when I allowed Victoria to bring a wild animal into our home. I can only hope Victoria's words restrain the beast as firmly as she says they do.*

I raised an eyebrow. The other eyebrow followed its sister. What was it they always talked about in detective novels? Means, motive, and opportunity.

Could it be possible that Callas had sacked Betsan, and Betsan had murdered the aristo to keep her job? It had holes I could drive a coach through. Victoria wouldn't have been happy if her wife had been murdered, and probably wouldn't keep a head of security who'd let it happen.

Betsan had also been the one to let Alison and me into the mansion, and whilst she could have been faking effects of the poison, she'd have to be a prodigious actress to replicate them so effectively. Callas painted Betsan as a vicious beast. Vicious beasts are not often known for their phenomenal acting. Still, motive was motive, even if it was shaky.

A better motive would have been murdering Callas because the murderer learned she'd planned to reveal the magissa to humanity. If that turned out to be her motive, I had to really, really hope the murderer didn't know about me.

I stood, leaving the murdered aristo's diary on her desk, stretched, and braced myself before investigating Victoria's desk. The drifts of paper that lay on the desk itself turned out to be blank. As did the paper on the floor. And the paper in her drawers. There were plenty of pens – much more mundane pens than the ones I'd stolen from the aristo – along with inkwells, ink stains... There was a notable lack of books, letters or anything at all in Victoria's hand.

That was interesting, but possibly not entirely relevant to my current investigation. I went through the desk once more to check that I hadn't missed anything, but nothing jumped out at me, other than a few stray chocolates Victoria seemed to have overlooked. Those, I ate.

I returned to the bedroom and cast my gaze slowly from one side to the other. I didn't notice anything obviously out of place, so I made a quick circuit.

I paused as I passed a dressing table – a decorated box lay discarded nearby. Everything else was squared away neatly, yet this box had clearly been tossed aside. What had been inside it? It looked like a jewellery box. I pursed my lips and made a quick sketch of the dressing table, complete with empty box.

Robbery was another possible motive for murder. If someone had sneaked into the house to rob the place, only to find Lady Callas in the bathroom, they could have... No. There were too many holes in that theory. If the killer was only stealing the contents of this one box, it would be much easier to flee the scene rather than commit murder. Besides, would a burglar have poisoned the entire household?

I resumed my circuit of the room. I passed the wall of bones, shuddering as I did so. Each bone was secured to the wall by two twists of wire. Any one of them could be snatched from the wall at a moment's notice. It also meant the numerous unoccupied twists of wire were obvious, now I knew what to look for. Had several bones been removed from the wall? Or had Callas not yet replaced bones which she, herself, had used?

I completed my circuit of the bedroom without noticing anything else obviously out of line, and smiled to myself before moving to the bathroom door. I turned the handle.

My guts twisted. I felt as if I'd been climbing a set of stairs in the dark. I'd lifted my foot, and brought it down on a step which wasn't there. Alison and I should have been the only two people to enter

Callas's room since the murder. Neither of us had closed the bathroom door.

The door swung open. I couldn't move. A figure stood in the dark - tall, cloaked in deep purple and black, and adorned with a mask and a hat. One hand held a knife.

A strangled gulp died in my throat. I took one stumbling step backwards before my legs give out from under me. The monster strode towards me, and something inside me broke. I scrambled to my feet. I sprinted for the door and kicked aside the chair I'd used to block the handle. I lost my balance and nearly fell again, but I grabbed at the door handle, tore at it.

Footsteps behind me. I hauled the door open and bolted down the corridor. I skidded on that beautiful carpet as I rounded a corner. I thudded into the wall, rebounded, and suddenly all that separated me from the stairs and from Alison was a straight length of corridor.

Sprinting footsteps behind me. Adrenaline surged. Propelled me forward. I reached the stairs. So many stairs. I threw myself at them. My lungs were burning. My legs were screaming. I was climbing, I was climbing. Had there always been this many stairs? What sort of house needed this many stairs? Why were there so many? I was going to die. I was going to die here, and it was all my own fault.

CHAPTER SEVEN

I exploded up into the great hall. Alison was leaning against a wall, picking at her fingernails. I skidded to a stop next to her and drew my xiphos. That got her attention. In one fluid movement, she slipped a tooth from her bracelet, and flicked it into her mouth, while simultaneously drawing her pistol with her other hand and levelling it at the stairs.

"Intruder," I gasped, "in Lady Callas' bathroom. I only just got away."

I'd barely finished speaking when the figure that had been chasing me emerged from the stairwell. They had either been slowed by the stairs, or suspected some kind of trap. Alison, to her credit, didn't hesitate. She fired her pistol. The almighty crack of igniting gunpowder tore through my head. I stumbled, clutching at my ears.

The intruder ducked back into the stairwell. Alison grinned at me, dozens of perfect teeth glistening. "Come on!"

She holstered her pistol and bolted after the intruder. Fervently wishing I could just let her get on with it, I followed. The murderer was no-where to be seen when I reached the bottom of the stairs, but Alison was haring towards an entrance to the steam tunnels. She threw herself at the concealed door in the wall, which had been in the process of closing. She hauled the door open and slipped through, leaving space for me to follow.

The tunnel on the other side was a smooth corridor cut through concrete. It would have been quite roomy, were it not for the pipes that jutted from the walls and ran across the floor at regular intervals, threatening to trip up a careless interloper. The space was dimly lit by glow globes. Their bio-luminescence was only just kicking in – the intruder must have tripped their proximity sensors.

The cloaked intruder shimmied up a ladder at the far end of the tunnel. Alison was already in pursuit. I followed, slowing down briefly to sheathe my sword. The lost seconds seemed a fair price to pay to avoid knocking into a stray pipe and cutting my own knees off.

Alison was already at the top of the ladder when I reached it. She climbed the last rung up, yelped, and let go of the rungs. She dropped a full meter before grabbing the nearest rung, just as an enormous *CLANG* rang from above. Hanging precariously from one hand, Alison grinned down at me, before finding the rungs with her feet.

"Well, they have a sword," she said, redrawing her pistol. She scuttled back up the ladder and made sure to shove the pistol into view before she followed. She poked her head into view before withdrawing quickly in anticipation of another attack. The intruder must have resumed their flight, because she clambered up through the hole.

I scrambled up the ladder and was just in time to see Alison disappearing around a corner. I followed as fast as I could, but was hampered by the tunnel's constant trip hazards. Rounding a corner, I found myself alone. Alison and the killer had outpaced me. I set off after them, my breath ragged, my legs aching.

I dodged past pipes which blocked off the entire right side of the tunnel. I scrambled over a pipe jutting across my path at knee height, then I turned another corner, and screamed. I didn't have time to turn and run, or even skid to a halt. The murderer stepped out of a shadow in which it had been lurking, its sword swinging.

I flung myself sideways. The rough concrete wall clawed at my shoulder, and I felt blood seep into my shirt, but the sword missed me by a breath. I stumbled and rebounded off the wall. The tunnel ahead was a thicket of pipes, I'd never escape the murderer.

I drew my xiphos and held it in a classical Hoplite style. I'd been taught how to stand, and how to wield my weapon well enough, but I'd never dreamed of using it for combat outside of lessons. The intruder advanced on me. I steadied my grip.

The shadow lashed out with their blade. I blocked, but the clash of steel on steel ripped my sword from my hand – it clanged to the ground and I had to dodge back to avoid another swing. I had two choices. I could turn and run, or I could stand here and die. Or, perhaps, I could try and get my sword back and die. Three choices. I had three choices.

I spun and ran – at least my brief flirtation with close quarters combat had given my legs a rest. Thundering footsteps followed close behind me. Tears streamed from my eyes. I could picture the gleam of light on the intruder's sword rising behind me.

I didn't slow enough to turn the next corner – I rammed into another wall. My left shoulder bore the impact again, but I ignored the pain. I'd not yet felt a sword in my back. Nothing else mattered right at that moment.

I scrambled over a pipe, and was delighted to see Alison approaching at a dead sprint from the other end of the tunnel.

"Susan!" she yelled. "Duck!"

My eyes widened and I skidded into a crouch. Alison flung something over my head which burst into scalding steam, right in the figure's face. The intruder stumbled back. Their hand hovered around their wrist before they turned, and fled.

Alison drew her pistol, and fired. The shot went wide. She took off in pursuit, but I was done. I needed to get out of the tunnels. The light around me seemed to be fading. I was sure the walls were creeping closer towards me, sensing my fear.

A figure rounded the corner and I yelped, hauling myself to my feet. It was only Alison.

"I lost them," she said. "Well. Wasn't that exciting?"

I glowered at her, although I was pretty sure she wouldn't be able to see in the dim light.

"Come on," she said, as I dusted myself down. "Let's get out of here. We need to report this to Betsan."

Frustration, anger, and fear fought for control of my face. I kept quiet and followed Alison as she poked about, looking for one of the doors that would allow us to escape the tunnels.

"Did you detect an osto?" Alison asked over her shoulder, after a few minutes of searching.

"Er," I stalled, trying to remember what a osto was. My hand moved by itself, scratching the back of my head. Of course! Magissa powers. Now, what had been the question?

"An osto?" Alison prompted, with a commendable amount of patience. "Did the intruder use one? You should have been able to tell if one was used. It feels like a wave of sound washing over you, only without the sound. You remember how you felt when I showed you my osto?"

"Yes," I lied.

"Well, it's like that."

"I didn't feel the intruder use their osto," I replied, honestly.

"Mmm," said Alison. "Nor did I. It's interesting, isn't it?"

I shook my head, thankful that I was behind Alison and that she didn't have eyes in the back of her head. At least, I presumed she didn't. I slapped my cheeks in an effort to wake myself up.

"Are you okay?" Alison asked, turning to look at me.

I smiled at her. "Yes, sorry. I'd say there are two possibilities."

Alison raised an eyebrow before resuming her search for an exit. "Two?"

"Right. The first is that the intruder was someone we've already seen. Charles or, I don't know, anyone from the house. They didn't use their osto because they didn't want their powers to identify them."

"That was the conclusion I'd come to. What's the second possibility?"

"Well.." I said, not sure if I should voice this particular thought. "the intruder could be a human. Someone without an osto."

Alison stopped so suddenly I walked into her. She spun to face me. "You don't really think so, do you?" she asked. For the first time since I'd met her, I saw genuine fear in her eyes.

"Maybe?" I said. "I mean, it's just a possibility."

"Oh, that's *all* we need," said Alison. She thumped the wall, winced, and went back to searching for an exit with renewed urgency. "I'm too young, and far too clever to die at the hands of one of those bloodthirsty monsters."

"Would it really be that bad?"

"If a human has made it this far, that means they know how to get past the security system. The chances are they know about *us*. They know about the magissa. And if just *one* of those creatures finds out about the magissa and we don't know about them, we'll all be in very serious trouble."

Alison found a section of wall which I could only barely distinguish from the rest of the tunnel and pushed. The wall gave way, and we stepped out into the peaceful menace of the great hall.

"Can one human be that much trouble?" I asked, scampering to keep up as Alison strode towards the stairs.

"Oh, believe me, when you have a face like mine, you know just how bad things would be if the magissa's secrets got out. You might survive for a year or two, Susan. I mean, as long as no-one takes off your boots to reveal the claws on your feet, you can pass. But they'd find you eventually."

"But..." I said.

Alison rounded on me. "I know," she snapped. "I *know* that you were raised by humans. And I know that can be very confusing. I'm open to the entirely theoretical possibility that some humans are not bloodthirsty monsters, but seriously, Susan, you can't trust them.

"When you start manifesting your powers around them... When they see the curse of your clan... even if they don't try to drown you themselves, they won't stand in the way when the mob comes for you. I wasn't raised by humans. My vision isn't clouded like yours. I see them for what they are."

"We could try explaining to them—"

Alison laughed. "Explaining? We feed on their *bones*, Susan. There's no nice way to explain that. Have you ever read one of their newspapers? They spend their entire time talking about other humans as if they're monsters determined to ruin their own society. Immigrants, socialists, people of strange and sinister faiths, they're all the enemy to humans. Imagine how they'd react if they found out about a secret society of people who *ate their bones*."

"But we could... I don't know... go to war with them? We could fight them and win."

Alison laughed again, bitterness souring the air around us. "No. No, we couldn't. Maybe if this was two hundred years ago, but this is the year 739, Susan. Humans have zeppelins that can rain explosives from the sky. They have incurable poisons, firearms, and long-range communications. There are millions more of them than there are of us. Our only real weapon is our secrecy."

I blinked. A woman who could evaporate water fast enough to cause an explosion was saying her only weapon was secrecy.

"Look," said Alison as we reached the door to the cottage, "you're young, you haven't seen much of the world. I understand. I wish I was in your position, but this face forced me to do a lot of growing up very quickly. If the intruder is a human, and if you find them before I do, you need to kill them. Please. It seems ruthless, and maybe it is, but we *can't* let word of the magissa slip out. If we do, my family and I are as good as dead. I'm serious."

"Okay," I said. The lie caught in my throat but Alison nodded.

"Thank you. Now, let's hope we weren't chasing Betsan just now, or I'm going to feel like a right ninny when I tell her about what we've been up to."

I followed her. In the time I'd spent with this woman, I'd grown used to her company. She was brave and she was cunning. It was a bit of a shock to remember that, no matter what experiences we shared, Alison was not my friend. Alison couldn't be my friend. If she found out who I was, or why I was really in the Callas mansion, she'd kill me herself. She wouldn't even hesitate.

CHAPTER EIGHT

"Hi, Betsan," said Alison.

"What news?"

"There might be a human in the mansion."

Betsan actually managed to leap to her feet for a moment, before collapsing back to her knees. Her recovery seemed nearly complete. "A human?"

"It's possible," I said. "That, or someone we've already interviewed is faking their own poisoning so they can run around and try to kill us."

"They tried to kill you?"

"Unsuccessfully," said Alison, studying her fingernails. Betsan glared at her.

I'd managed to collect my thoughts a little which had, in turn, enabled me to get my heart rate down to a level that felt closer to normal. At least, my chest no longer felt like it was about to explode.

Perversely, I was starting to enjoy myself a little. Yes, I was living a nightmare, fearing both the phantom killer and, more immediately, the possibility that I might say or do anything that would reveal my true nature to Alison. Would she execute me on the spot, or enact some form of slow, torturous revenge for the fear she'd lived with her entire life? Who knew? Nevertheless, there was a tiny, tiny part of my brain that was thrilling at the mysteries this mansion concealed.

"Are you closer to knowing who killed Lady Callas?" Betsan asked.

The tiny part of my brain coughed, and presented the list of questions I'd been preparing in Lady Callas' room before I'd been ambushed. "Yes, Betsan, I actually had some questions about your relationship with Lady Callas."

Betsan's eyes widened. "Oh?"

"Why did Lady Callas consider you a dangerous animal?"

I didn't even have time to blink. Betsan leapt to her feet, howling in pain as she did so, and launched herself at me. She grabbed my throat, and slammed me against the wall. Stars danced in my vision. I couldn't breathe, I scrabbled at Betsan's hand, but couldn't loosen her grip.

Betsan growled. I was just realising that I'd finally made a fatal mistake when she loosened her grip. She slowly released me, and I collapsed into a heap on the floor. Alison helped me to my feet, whilst Betsan swayed and had to lean against a wall for support.

"Susan asked you a question, Betsan," said Alison, once she was sure I was no-longer at risk of passing out.

Betsan growled, a low rumbling which rattled the windows. "How do you know what her ladyship thought of me?"

"She wrote as much in her diary," I said.

Alison turned to me. "You read her diary?"

I glanced at my companion. "Yes. We're investigating her murder. Of course I read her diary. Anyway, you did you know what with a certain person's red folder."

Alison raised an objecting finger, then squinted. We stood frozen for a moment before she slumped and waved at me to continue. I turned back to Betsan and raised a quizzical eyebrow.

"Her ladyship found out about one of my hobbies," rumbled Betsan. "She didn't approve."

"What was this hobby?" I asked.

Betsan tossed her head from side to side, clearly unhappy about this line of questioning.

"What was this hobby, Betsan?" I repeated. I may not be one for fighting in the dark, and I may not be as academically gifted as I'd once thought, but I was a journalist. I could bloody well get information out of people if I needed to.

"I go to this bar," said Betsan, "and sometimes, only occasionally, some of us participate in boxing matches. Sometimes we meet up with other organisations and have tournaments. It's nothing sinister."

"You're not part of the Pitt Club?" said Alison.

Betsan turned her steely gaze on my companion. "How do you know of the Pitt Club?"

"One of my mother's house-guests is a member," Alison said. "Paget Belacourt."

Betsan slumped. "Oh, Paget. Well, yes, I'm a member of the Pitt Club."

"Paget says it's a network of bloodthirsty maniacs, many of them Silenus or Hephaestus, who enjoy nothing more than beating seven shades of snot out of each other whenever they can get away with it."

Betsan grumbled to herself before speaking up. "That isn't quite how I'd describe it myself."

"And Lady Callas found out that you're a member of this club?" I asked.

"She did," Betsan said. "She wanted me gone, but Victoria stood up for me. My mistress is kind to those loyal to her."

"I thought Lady Callas was your mistress?"

Betsan growled again. "Victoria Callas is my mistress. Her ladyship merely had the good fortune and sound judgment to marry her."

"You sound as if you don't approve of the match."

"It's not my place to approve or disapprove. I'm bound to Victoria Callas, thanks to a service she performed for me many years ago. I merely do as she asks."

Coming from another mouth, Betsan's words might have revealed her as one of those tragic figures who had fallen in love with their employer. Instead, she sounded like a lioness who was choosing not to eat her gamekeeper.

I flipped open my notebook. "Could you tell me a little about Victoria Callas? You said she was kind."

"I said she was kind to those loyal to her. There have been times when people have betrayed her or caused her harm. Those people were not dealt with kindly."

"That seems perfectly reasonable." said Alison.

"You might be surprised," said Betsan.

I twirled my pen, "Had Lady Callas—"

"No, Lady Callas had done nothing to cause Victoria to deal unkindly with her. Victoria loved her wife. They occasionally fought, but they made sure to work together to address the problems that had caused the fight. Issues such as my employment status."

"You're very keen for us to locate Lady Callas' murderer," Alison said, "which seems strange, given you have good reason to dislike her."

Betsan huffed. "My mistress will be most distressed by her wife's death. She will be inclined to look unkindly on those who hinder the investigation. She will be less distressed if the killer is apprehended."

Betsan looked from me to Alison, and then back to me again. "Do you have any more questions? Or are you going to stop wasting time?"

I pulled the small leather bag I'd found in Lady Callas' desk drawer out of my pocket. "Do you know anything about this?"

Betsan squinted at the bag, but shook her head. I pulled one or two teeth out of the bag and rolled them between my fingers. I felt Alison tense next to me but Betsan was unmoved. I shrugged, and dropped the teeth back into the bag. "One more thing - I found a bottle of alcoholic stimulants in Lady Callas' desk drawer. Did you know anything about that?"

Betsan coughed, uncomfortably. "Her ladyship had a complex relationship with alcohol. She often indulged a little too enthusiastically when she felt Victoria's absence."

I nodded. "Where is Victoria Callas? Should she not be here with the initiation scheduled for tomorrow?"

"She's on a diplomatic mission to one of the other city states. She's due back tomorrow, which is why time is of the essence. I hope for all our sakes that you're making progress."

"Thank you for your candour, Betsan," I said. "Do you have anything else you wish to add to your account at this time?"

Betsan didn't immediately say no, and a pause hung between us which I found most enticing. She clearly wished to say something. Were I capable of physically intimidating someone of her stature, I'd possibly have pressed her on the subject. As it was, I let the silence grow. I didn't break eye contact. I didn't allow my expression to change. I tried to convey, as subtly as possible, that I already knew most of the facts, and that I was giving her the opportunity to put the record straight.

Guilt is a wonderful thing. It only took fifteen seconds for Betsan to crack. "It's probably nothing. Probably. But... well, I performed a background check into Teleri, the caterer."

I nodded. "You mentioned that you had some concerns."

"Yes. Yes, that's right. Well, one of those concerns was that Teleri is also a member of the Pitt Club. I've fought her previously."

"And knowing this, you still let her into the house?" Alison asked. I shot her a look. This interrogation was mine.

Betsan held up her hands. "Lady Callas requested her, specifically. She had her heart set on Teleri. No-one else would do."

"Did you tell her she was a member of the Pitt Club?" I asked.

"Yes!" Betsan said. "She said it didn't matter!"

"And this all took place after she found out you were a member?"

Betsan's hackles were rising. "Yes! She said it didn't matter! She tried to have me banished from the house only two days earlier for that same crime, but for *Teleri* it didn't matter!"

"Did that make you angry, Betsan?" I asked, feeling like I was finally getting somewhere.

"Damn right!" Betsan snarled.

"Angry enough to do something about it?"

Betsan opened her mouth to reply, but no sound came out. I frowned. She'd been visibly agitated mere moments ago, but now, all her energy appeared to have dissipated.

Betsan sighed. "No. Not angry enough to do something about it."

I was floored, left scrambling for a follow-up question. I couldn't think of one, so I left a silence for Betsan to fill. To my surprise, she obliged.

"I don't appreciate being questioned like this," Betsan said, fatigue showing in her voice. "I think it's disrespectful of you. But... I understand, and I'm glad. You're right to ask these questions. If you're questioning everyone like you just questioned me, you might just find the killer."

I glanced over at Alison, who gave me a thumbs-up.

"Thank you," I said, "Well, I think we should see if Teleri is awake, given this new information. We are yet to interrogate her, Mr Das and Praxi."

Betsan grimaced. I nodded, and made for the stairs, Alison falling in behind me.

"That was smartly done," said Alison as we climbed the stairs to the servant's quarters.

"Thank you."

"Right, so.... Betsan's condition is much improved. The poison's wearing off rapidly. If we want to be able to interrogate people whilst they are still incapacitated, we need to act fast."

"What are you saying?"

"I'm saying we should split up." Alison said.

"No," I said, a sudden jolt of panic drenching me.

"I just—"

"No." I didn't trust myself to be able to say more than that one word.

"Can I—"

"No?"

"Can I finish my mother-effing sentence?" Alison snapped.

My mouth was too dry to reply.

"I know last time we split up led to a spot of bother but... think about it. Teleri is up in the second floor of the cottage. There are no steam tunnels up there. There's no-where for anyone to hide, and Betsan is on the ground floor, nearly recovered. She'll raise the alarm if the murderer starts sneaking up after you. Susan. Look at me. Look at me."

I tore my eyes away from the patch of carpet they'd been locked on and met Alison's gaze. I saw warmth there. For a fleeting moment, losing myself in those eyes, I knew that everything was going to be all right. I nodded. "Okay. Thank you."

Alison waved this away. "Don't worry about it. See you in a bit! Do you have anything you want me to ask Praxi?"

"What her experiences were of the poison, and if she could think of anyone who would want to harm Lady Callas, I suppose. Try to find out if she'd have a reason to harm her herself. Not that I think she'd have hurt Lady Callas. I'm sure your patron is beyond reproach."

Alison grinned at me. "Very diplomatic," she said, before stomping cheerily back down the stairs.

I smiled after her in spite of myself, before returning to the visitor's room where I'd last seen Teleri. I steeled myself. I knocked. There was no answer. I considered retreating back down the stairs but no. I was here to do a job. I needed to demonstrate a little spine. I eased the door open to take a peek.

Teleri was still lying on her bed. She may have rolled over since I'd last checked on her, but was otherwise unmoving.

"Teleri?" I said. "Teleri Parry?"

Teleri stirred. I approached the boxer. Her breathing was slow, but strong and even. I peered over to see what condition she was in. Her face was hard edged and muscular, but also grey and drenched in sweat.

Poking her would be the polite thing to do. Still, if she was still asleep, taking advantage of that would make sense. The room was for visitors, so few things present would have belonged to Teleri. A washbasin had been jammed in a corner, and a table had been squeezed in between the foot of the bed and a wall. A mirror lay on the table, but disassembling it revealed no hidden papers concealed in the frame.

The only item that looked like it belonged to Teleri was a pack stuffed under the bed. Its flap lay unstrapped, and a work shirt spilled from within.

I hesitated. It was one thing to rummage through an aristocrat's personal effects. Teleri didn't necessarily deserve the same treatment. Still, I needed to get out of this house alive. With this goal in mind, it was ridiculous to hesitate at the idea of going through someone's pack. Good manners could be suspended under such circumstances – a phrase, presumably, uttered by awful bastards the world over.

I drew the pack out from under the bed as quietly as possible, slipped from the room and rummaged through it outside. Spare clothing – mostly battered but clearly well cared for. A bag of yellowing, chipped teeth. Boxing hand wraps, a shaving kit and a small appointment book - only sporadically filled in. Flicking through it revealed nothing of note.

I laid the items on the carpet, frowned at them, and then rummaged about in the bag to see if I'd missed anything. Something clinked at the bottom of the bag. No, two somethings - small glass vials.

The vials were stoppered with study rubber corks. Fragments of wax clung to the rims – maybe they'd been sealed? Resting at the bottom of both vials were dregs of a milky white liquid. I held one vial to the light and shook it. The liquid was viscous and sickly, and it had left a residue against the vial walls.

There was also something etched into the glass. I turned the vial, trying to catch the edges of the writing in the light. 'Flower of Tartarus'. Ominous. Also... etching the words onto the vials seemed overkill. Why not use a paper label? Maybe if you wanted to identify the vials in the dark? I jotted the name down in my notebook and pocketed both vials. Did detectives get into the business because it gave them an excuse to steal stuff?

Mysterious, ominous vials kept in a visitor's pack. The Flower of Tartarus might have been the poison the household consumed. There'd been a meal discarded under the servant's dining table. Had it been Teleri's?

Teleri groaned as I returned her pack to its spot under her bed. I shot to my feet, expecting to see her glaring at me and reaching for a knife. No. She was still. I retreated to the door, and got ready to run.

"Teleri?" I said. She stirred. I tried again. Her eyelids flickered, and then eased open. She stared past me, unfocused.

"Teleri?"

A strange tension rose in the air, as if the world was holding its breath, and then suddenly let go. Memories rose inside me like a flash tide. Times I'd lied to my dads, or cheated at school. Times I'd called my school-friends names, or stolen from shops. Every bad thing I'd ever done flooded my mind in an overwhelming rush of guilt, despair, and self-loathing. Alison, and the staggering number of lies I'd told her, featured heavily.

I staggered, clipped the doorframe and collapsed to the ground, shaking. A swirl of ruby red under Teleri's bed pulsed, then faded. My guilt-ridden memories faded with it. My vision cleared, and my hands stopped shaking. I stood, supporting myself on the doorframe... and then I saw Teleri.

She was awake. Her eyes wide and staring. Her gaze locked on me.

"Teleri?" I stepped towards her.

Her enormous hand shot out and grabbed me by the collar. "I didn't mean to! You have to believe me! I didn't mean to!"

I pulled back but she held me tight – I wasn't going anywhere. "What didn't you mean to do? Are you talking about Lady Callas? Did you not mean to kill her?"

Tears streamed down Teleri's cheeks. "No, no, no, no, no, no, no! Not her, I never killed her. I meant *her*, the girl!"

Someone else. Not Lady Callas. "Who?"

A trickle of snot ran from Teleri's nose. It mingled with the tears at the corner of her mouth. "I was wasted! I didn't mean to keep hitting her, but then she wasn't moving, and I just had to run… but her face…"

"Who? Do you mean Tova Oster?"

Teleri grabbed my collar with he other hand and drew me closer. "I don't know! Don't you see? That's the worst part! I never even knew her name. But she knows my name. She's here with me now. She knows what I did."

Teleri let go of my collar and scrambled into the corner where the head of her bed met the wall. She drew herself into a ball, her gaze darting from point to point. Tears streamed, sobs wracked her throat.

"I need some help in here!" I called. No help came. I hovered, wondering if there was anything I could do. Nothing. Nothing. I was so fucking useless. I bolted from the room, and clattered downstairs, nearly cannoning into Betsan, who was finally up and about, albeit supporting herself on a wall.

"What's going on?" Betsan asked.

"Teleri's in trouble. She's raving about someone. Tova Oster, I think. Teleri is just… she's terrified."

"Wait, Tova Oster? Charles' old pupil?"

"Charles thinks Teleri killed her."

Betsan clutched at her hair. "Why don't people tell me these things?" She caught my flash of guilt and waved a hand. "Not you, you're doing great. Come on, let's get up to Teleri. I'll see if there's anything I can do."

I helped her up the stairs and had only just reached the top when Teleri moaned, piteously. Betsan bolted forward and I, fool that I was, followed.

Teleri's door was open, much as I'd left it after fleeing. Teleri's body slumped in the corner where I'd left her. Blood soaked her neck, her shirt, her legs, and the bed beneath. Her throat had been cut.

Chapter Nine

I sat on the landing outside Teleri's room. Alison had returned a few minutes ago. She was in Teleri's room with Betsan, seeing if there was anything that could be done.

I stared at the carpet, worn but cared for, cyan swirls decorated a field of indigo. I stared at the carpet, but all I saw was Teleri. Her right arm shone. It had been flesh and blood when she'd grabbed me. Her flesh had since turned to steel. Her fingers ended in blood-soaked blades.

Boots grinding into the carpet. A towering figure blocking out the light. The shadowy intruder had returned to finish me. Good.

A hand rested on my shoulder. I flinched. Frowned. Alison. Not the intruder.

"How are you doing?" she asked.

I wanted to say something bitter and sarcastic, but I couldn't think of anything. Besides, Alison had been in the room with Teleri's body. I hadn't made it past the doorway. She should be in a much worse state than I was.

Even so, she wasn't. She looked fine. Her hands weren't shaking, she wasn't sweating. Her features weren't... She looked calm. I stared up at her, a stable figure in the ever-shifting world of horrors which Marie Callas had trapped me in. "How are you so calm?"

"Mm? Oh, that's not my first dead body." She sat on the floor next to me. "Six years ago, my tutor was attacked in the street. She was Hermes, so she had all these scars... Anyway. She was walking home after teaching me something about, I don't know, pumping engines or expansion gambits or something.

"I just wanted to go to bed because my brain was full, but I had to train because of course I did. Study and train, study and train. Life, right? So, I was doing my warm up exercises when a maid burst into the training room. Good job I was working at the other end of the room or I'd have taken his head off. 'Mistress Alison,' he said, 'your tutor's in trouble.'

"Some humans had taken offense to my tutor's scars, or maybe they'd thought she was a prize fighter or something. Anyway, they wanted a scrap, and so they attacked her.

"I didn't think, right? I was twelve. You'd think I'd have learned. But I didn't think. I just ran out of the house. I didn't even grab a sword on the way out. So, I ran to where my tutor was, and then realised my mistake.

"Four humans had my tutor on the ground. I couldn't go back for my veil. I couldn't go back for a sword. I had to act right that second or my tutor would be murdered in front of me.

"I grabbed the flask of water I'd been training with and downed every bone I had on me. I ran into the middle of the group and threw myself over my tutor. I hurled the water up into the air and – *PSSSSSSSSSSHHHHHHHHHHHHHHH!*" Alison mimicked an explosion with her hands.

"So, my tutor is lying there, barely alive, and we're in this huge cloud of expanding steam. Three of the humans had fled, but one got it worse than the others – half their face got caught by the explosion and they died from the shock. They fell on top of me. Their hand splayed across my face. Still slick from the steam.

"Thankfully, our maid saw me leave without my veil and told our butler. *She* went and told mum, and came to help. She brought my veil, and not a moment too soon, because one of the neighbours came out and saw me as I was putting it on.

"There was a moment where I wondered if I was going to have to kill her, too, but she waved and said she hadn't known it was me. She'd asked if I was okay. I told her my tutor and I had been jumped by some thugs and I'd summoned an ambulance.

"The neighbour told me I was a good girl, and wandered off. I got my tutor back inside, and half the household worked through the night to make sure she didn't die. Mum sent Paget to take care of the humans who'd seen my face. They didn't cause any trouble."

I glared at Alison. I was absolutely furious. When *I'd* been twelve, some kids in my class had decided they didn't like me because I didn't know about some game or other they were playing. They called me names for a few months and I'd been utterly miserable the entire time. On the other side of the city, Alison had been hiding her face because her mere existence could mean a death sentence at the hands of my people.

"So," said Alison, slapping her knees and getting to her feet, "did you hear what Betsan and I were talking about just now?"

I had to mentally replay her question before it filtered through the wall of horrible thoughts that had been demanding my attention. "Sorry, no," I replied.

"Don't worry," said Alison. "Look, we think someone made Teleri do that to herself. This whole mess has developed into something we can't handle on our own, and we need to send someone to ask for help. You're the lucky messenger."

My hands were shaking again. "Are you sure? I can help…"

Alison bumped my shoulder with hers. "This *is* helping. We can resume the investigation once you're back but, for now, we need reinforcements. Someone in this house has killed two people. We can't risk them claiming a third."

"Does the house have a telephone we can use?"

Alison shook her head. "There's a telegraph office in the village, but that isn't secure. You're going to need to go and talk to my mum. She'll summon the astynomia – our police."

"How will I get there?"

"Betsan's going to open the front gate for you. You need to go to Irinna. That's where the coach that brought us here will have gone. Find someone there, and tell them you need to get back to Selen immediately. Don't tell them what's happened. Dropping Lady Callas' name should get people to listen to you well enough. Come on."

Alison held out her hand. I'd never seen a more wonderful sight in my life. "I'm going now?" I asked.

"The sooner the better. We need the backup."

I took her hand and she pulled me to my feet. "I'll come back as quickly as I can," I lied.

Alison's smile was warm and genuine. "You'd better. We have a murderer to find."

Betsan showed Alison how to work the emergency release on the cage barring the cottage's front door. After only a moment, a cold breeze struck my cheek.

Alison grinned at me. "My mum's name is Lady Octavia Dewan. If she's not in, Paget Belacourt will be able to help you. She works for the Senate."

"What's the Senate?" I asked.

"Work it out from context," said Alison, swinging the door closed.

I set off down the drive in a daze. I was out. I was free. I'd made it. It felt like a bit of an anti-climax.

I'd expected to go through some huge trial in order to get out of that house. I should have needed to work my way through a labyrinth. Maybe fight a dragon. If dragons were real. Dragons probably weren't real. But... I'd always assumed dragons weren't real, which probably meant they were real, given how today was going. I needed to leave immediately before a dragon disproved her own non-existence.

I crossed the bridge which led back to the mainland. The waves had calmed since this morning. They crashed on the obsidian coastline, throwing up diamond spray which tumbled around me, the scent of fresh salt transporting me back to childhood beach holidays.

The village of Irinna was further down the Obsidian Coast. All I needed to do was follow the road our coach had taken that morning. Walking away from the nightmare house wasn't enough. Energy rose within me, and I broke into a run. With every step, I became more free.

It only took around half an hour to get to Irina, and another five minutes to find the coach driver who'd transported Alison and me from Selen. She looked less imposing stripped of her high-necked coat. Her florid face spoke of cider and plenty of time enjoying the sun.

She glared at me suspiciously when I asked for a lift back to Selen, until I said there was trouble at the cottage. She nodded, disappeared into her bungalow, and emerged carrying a crank handle.

"Where exactly am I taking you?" she asked, cranking the coach's steam engine into life.

I gave the woman my address, and she nodded. "Hop in."

I climbed into the coach and shut the door behind me. In mere moments, we were driving back up the road I'd so recently run down. Soon, I'd be home. Soon, I could forget any of this had happened.

My right leg trembled. I glared at it until it stopped. I stared out of the window, but couldn't get comfortable. A question lurked at the back of my head. It wanted my attention. I ignored it. I ignored it until we rolled past the Callas mansion and the road began its long ascent back to Selen.

The question was this: was I really going to leave Alison and Betsan and the others locked in a house with a murderer, expecting backup when none was coming?

Alison wasn't my friend. If she'd discovered I was human, she'd have killed me. The problem I had was... I couldn't really blame her for that.

If I'd not been forced to spend time with Alison, I'd have been terrified of her daemonic face. Alison, meanwhile, was terrified of who I was because everyone like me represented a threat to her very existence.

Secret societies weren't supposed to actually exist outside the minds of schoolchildren and conspiracy theorists. There were rumours about some, like the Filiki Eteria, who supposedly controlled the banks, orchestrated Prince Abrams death, and all sorts of other nonsense. That particular conspiracy theory had deeply racist roots and was usually an excuse people used to justify persecuting Kipina.

The way secret societies were presumed to maintain their stranglehold on power was by maintaining absolute secrecy. No-one can oust you from power if no-one knows you exist. The magissa, by contrast, maintained their secrecy because to do otherwise would surely lead to the deaths of Alison and everyone like her. Plus, the secrecy must make it easier to harvest bones from the living.

So. Was I going to abandon a woman who had not harmed me in any way to a probably violent fate? She was counting on my help. Everyone in the house was, except for the murderer. The murderer was probably hoping I'd do something along the lines of what I was planning to do: run and never come back.

On the other hand... I'd been concerned about the magissa tracking me down if I fled the Callas mansion. What if I fled, and the murderer took care of everyone else? I'd be free.

But then, in that rather unlikely outcome, the murderer would probably come after me as well. If they could catch me. But if there was only one of them, I could probably evade them well enough. Evading one person had to be easier than trying to disappear from the sight of an entire shadow organisation.

But Alison... The real problem I was having was this: I really couldn't see any downside to going and warning Alison's mother. 'Hi, Lady Dewan, your daughter is in serious trouble. Send in the... what were they called? Yes. Send in the astynomia! Okay, I've got to go now, but good luck with all that. Thanks, bye!'

Alison wasn't my friend... but didn't I owe her that much? It would take five minutes. I could stick my head through the door, shout a warning and then run away. Okay, maybe it wouldn't be *that* quick, but...

I slid open the hatch in the coach wall which let me communicate with the driver, and hollered for her attention. She asked what was up without looking around. I asked if it would be okay to change destination, fervently hoping she'd refuse. She didn't. I slid the hatch shut again, settled back into my seat and got to work chewing my nails.

The journey into Selen was uneventful, but getting to the Elizabeth Dane district was a little trickier. The city had roused since we'd left, and many of the major roads were jammed by coaches, carts, and foot traffic.

We found our path blocked by two carriages which had collided, killing both drivers. The coaches were melded together and the street was being evacuated, lest the coaches' steam tanks rupture and explode. Chaos radiated away from the incident in tiresomely familiar patterns.

My driver did what she could to mitigate the delays, but it still took some considerable time to reach Alison's house. The delay did nothing to settle my nerves, but nothing caused such an inconvenience that I could justify abandoning Alison.

The driver pulled up as close to Alison's house as was safe. I jumped down, thanked her for her assistance and said I wouldn't be needing a ride back. I could find my own way through Selen easily enough, and with the roads jammed I could slip away with the magissa none the wiser.

Alison's house was less imposing than when I'd last seen it, wreathed in fog. It was still huge, and the lack of walls was still intimidating, but it was a house. Just a house. I sighed, walked up the steps and rang the doorbell.

A maid opened the door. I fished about in a pocket and handed him one of my cards. I made a mental note to try and get it back if the opportunity arose – I only had five left, and the blasted things had been very expensive to order.

I rolled my shoulders, trying to get back into professional journalist mode. "I need to speak to Lady Dewan or Ms Belacourt as soon as possible. I'm an associate of Lady Dewan's daughter." Without being too obvious, I moved my wrist to display the silver bracelet of teeth which still bound it.

The maid's eyes widened. He ushered me into an expansive reception room and asked me to take a seat. I selected a chair which appeared comfortable, but wasn't so richly upholstered it risked actually engulfing me, and settled in for a wait.

The Dewan residence was very different from the home I'd spent much of the day in. The reception room was well lit, and evidently furnished to prioritize comfort. It might have been any well-appointed home, had it not been for the decor. Whoever had decorated the place seemed to have a profound affinity for the colour red – the walls, floor, and ceiling all boasted various shades of the colour. The bone white curtains should have offset this saturation somewhat, but somehow, they only accentuated the colour choice. I'd only been in the room for a few moments before I found myself unable to shake off the feeling that I was drowning in a lake of blood.

I concentrated on keeping my breathing steady; it was possible that I was being observed. I couldn't let my nervousness show. I only had to complete this one task, and then I was free.

Muffled footsteps came from my left – apparently from behind a crimson wall. A section of the wall slid open, and a butler stepped through. She was all shiny buttons and stern correctness. I stood to acknowledge her presence, as it's best to have such people consider you well-mannered.

The butler took in my budget-conscious suit, my sword belt with no sword in it and my hastily straightened clothing. "Ms Fletcher?"

"I am she."

"Very good, ma'am. Follow me, please. Lady Dewan will receive you immediately."

The butler turned and walked back through the concealed door. I followed, mildly surprised. Usually, aristocrats like to keep unexpected guests waiting for hours. Lady Dewan appeared to be taking her daughter's safety seriously. That was good news. The door closed behind me as I stepped through.

Chapter Ten

Gas lamps illuminated a needle-straight corridor. Twisting silver vines climbed the walls. My footsteps were muffled by the thick carpet. The butler must have deliberately walked noisily in order to signal her approach to the spot I'd been waiting in. Had she wished to walk silently, I doubt I'd have ever heard her coming.

She stopped in front of an imposing oak door, unlocked it with a silver key, and swung the door open. "The mistress is waiting for you just down the corridor and to the right. Please don't delay." I nodded and stepped through, but the butler hadn't finished.

"Ms Fletcher," she said. I turned to look at her. "Please activate your osto as soon as I've closed the door. That's the key. The deeper into the house you go, the more the security system will be alerted, until it's used to you. Had we the time, I'd introduce you to it slowly, but I'm sure you'll manage."

She closed the door. The click of the latch jammed into my head, causing pain to dig in deep.

Evenly spaced lamps washed the corridor in bright, soft light. Two doors stood at the end of the corridor: one to the left, and one to the right. Intricate patterns of silver and gold criss-crossed the white wallpaper and cream carpet.

I cracked my neck. How long had it taken for the Callas security system to affect me? It had been a lifetime ago. I focussed on the right-hand door, gritted my teeth, and set off.

My shoes rustled through the carpet's tendrils, the sound scratching in the air long after it should have. My footsteps burred together in the air behind me.

I passed a lamp. Only six separated me from the door. I took another step and then another. The lamps darkened... no. I was wrong. The light was growing brighter, but the walls were darkening. The walls and the floor were changing colour. They had been green, hadn't they? No, they had been silver and gold with white patterns dancing across them. The white patterns were still there, but now the walls lurked a stone's throw away - dark grey slate, the colour of falling stone, shattering at your feet, shrapnel driving into your flesh.

My breathing, the rustle and thump of my footsteps, the gradual groaning which oozed from the walls echoed and morphed into each other, forming a constant roar. I felt as if I was listening to the sea, or rather, it was as if someone had taken the sound of the sea breaking on the Obsidian Coast, and then they'd taken just a fraction of a second of that sound, and made that fraction of a second fill the entire corridor for... how long would it last? How long had it lasted already?

I passed another lamp. There should have been four more in between me and the two doors, but I found myself standing with the doors on either side of me. The corridor stretched off in the direction I'd come. Which door should I enter through? The butler had said the...

The butler had said t...

Which door had the butler said to enter? My footsteps roared in the air, even though I was a stone cold statue, dust collecting on me from centuries of immobility. The patterns on the walls had wound around me, lashing themselves to my arms.

The butler had said I needed to enter the door to the right. The butler had told me to activate my osto. The fascinating white pattern leapt from the deep purple carpet and entwined my legs.

I slipped a tooth from my bracelet and popped it into my mouth. It sat on my tongue, a smooth pebble of a thing. It caught in my throat as I swallowed it. Had that been right? I got the feeling there was a reason I shouldn't have swallowed that tooth. But I'd been told to. It was the key to the security system. I had a right to be here, I *needed* to be here.

I lifted my right arm, my clothing cracking, showering the carpet with fragments of marble. Statuesque fingers wiped a bead of marble-sweat from my brow. I'd activated my osto. Help for Alison was a mere moment away.

The butler had told me to go through the door on the right, but that had been at the other end of the corridor. I was facing the way I'd come, so that meant I'd need to go through the door on my left.

I opened the door and stepped through.

"I'm sure you'll manage," said the butler. She closed the door behind me and I was left staring at a long, unbending corridor, bathed in purple and white. I set off, my gazed fixed on the right hand door.

I passed a lamp. There were seven in between me and the door. The roar of my feet in the carpet mingled with my breathing, and the gentle sighs emanating from the lamps as I passed them, into the constant drone of a zeppelin engine.

My feet felt light, as if I might float away at any moment. I took one more step, but my foot skidded away from me, and I fell to one knee. Light flared around me. I looked up to the ceiling, and found I was standing on it. I walked forward, only to find myself between two doors. I needed to enter the door on the right after I activated my osto.

I slipped a tooth from my bracelet into my mouth, and swallowed it, nearly choking as I did so. It was strange that an act I must have performed hundreds of times would feel so unfamiliar to me.

I needed to enter the door on my right. Which was my right? I was upside down; the floor was below me. That meant my right was my left. I stepped through the door on my left. Did Alison get this confused when she went through security?

"I'm sure you'll manage," said the butler. She closed the door behind me and I was left staring at a long, unbending corridor. A blood red carpet mingled with shimmering black walls. Howling voices cursed me as I walked.

Lamps hung from the ceiling, but I had no idea how many. Some turned to face me as I walked past them. I needed to activate my osto. I tore the bracelet from my wrist, and swallowed the teeth from it one by one by one by one.

At my next step, the floor sank beneath me, drawing my foot down, then my ankle, and then my knee. I swallowed another tooth and felt something in my throat rip. Two doors – one to either side. I couldn't remember which one I was supposed to go through. I couldn't think. I couldn't breathe. "Alison," I said, my teeth loose in my mouth, "I need your help. I always need your help."

I turned. The world swirled and curled around one single, focal point. A pearl, a round orb grinned at me, a mouth built wider than most, a mouth designed to smile. I reached for the smile, found a door handle, turned it, and stepped through.

"Oh, you poor thing. Come here and sit down."

Helpful hands guided me to a chair. Teeth juddered from my mouth as I sat. I stared down at my lap, my stomach twisting. I'd had nightmares of this exact moment. But... my tongue probed at my teeth

– no gaps. Marie Callas' bracelet of teeth was in my hand. I'd been using the teeth, or eating them or...

"Security was a little rough on you, was it?" It was the same voice which had sympathised earlier. A warm, kind voice. The sort of voice which might sit you down on a long winter evening and tell you horror stories alongside a mug of spiked hot chocolate.

I rolled my head – trying to raise it. My neck was too long, and it wouldn't bend the right way.

Grandma chuckled. "Don't worry, it'll pass in a few moments. You're through the worst of it, and the system has accepted you as an authorised visitor."

Security? Damn. I breathed, collected myself and looked up. In the chair opposite sat a middle-aged lady in the most understatedly elegant shirt and trousers I'd ever seen. She sat cross legged, a wry smile playing at the corners of her mouth. She superficially resembled Alison. Her eyes were the same – although laughter lines lay at the corners. Her smile seemed more guarded. There was only one person she could be. I gripped my chair's arm-rests. Tried to stand. My feet slipped from under me.

Alison's mum shook her head. "Please don't. You'll feel better in a moment, but you're clearly not in a position to stand on ceremony. You must be Susan Fletcher. I believe I have one of your business cards. Tell me, did you spent a vast amount of money hiring an artist to craft cheap looking, creased business cards as some sort of statement? Or did you simply buy cheap business cards?"

I'd been in this woman's presence... what had Alison said her name was? Octavia. I'd been in Octavia's presence two minutes and already she was asking loaded questions. I turned the question over in my head before giving up. "I bought cheap business cards. They were all I could afford at the time." My voice sounded rough. I fought back a cough.

Lady Dewan raised an eyebrow. "Are you sure?"

"I'm sure."

She tapped the armrest of her chair. "Hm. I'm not sure how I feel about that. Leaving that aside, I am Octavia Dewan. I'm delighted to meet you, possibly. I believe you know my daughter, Alison?"

"Alison? Yes," I shook my head, clearing some of the cotton wool.

"Is there a reason you came to ask for my help instead of my daughter?"

"A reason? Yes, she was needed at Lady Callas' residence."

The aristo frowned. "Why?"

"Lady Callas has been killed, as has a visiting magissa. We were investigating the murders, but Alison asked me to summon the astynomia."

"She decided she should stay in harm's way, because she can fend off almost any attacker, whilst you're less gifted in that area?"

"I... yes."

She smiled, her gaze drifting to a spot I couldn't see. "That's Alison."

"Yes..." I said, worrying that Alison's reputation was taking a bit of a hit, "Although I must stress that Alison has acted with courage, empathy, and wit during the investigation into Lady Callas' murder."

Lady Dewan studied me. "You must, must you? And who are you, Susan Fletcher? What are you?"

"I was to be Lady Callas' protégé." I frowned, stumbling over Lady Dewan's second question. Then, light dawned. I had a memory anchor for that question. I tapped my left wrist. "I'm Charites."

Her eyebrows rose. "Really? Well, then you must be introduced to Paget before you head back to the mansion. It may be that she is of a mind to take you on as her protégé in Lady Callas' stead. She is Charites as well."

No. No, no, no, no, no, no. I didn't want to be here any longer than I had to. I'd passed on the message. I should be leaving. The problem was... Lady Dewan's offer to introduce me to a member of her circle must be a huge honour. It would be inconceivable that a fellow magissa would refuse such a favour.

I dropped my gaze and tried to look humble. "That would be most generous, Lady Dewan. I'd be considerably in your debt."

She waved a hand. "You came here to assist my daughter. It's the least I can do to repay you." She tugged a bell rope which hung next to her chair. A servant slipped through a door behind her and circled the room until she could approach Lady Dewan from the side, rather than from behind. Lady Dewan smiled up at her. "Ah, Fida. Please take Ms Fletcher here to see Ms Belacourt. They have much to discuss."

I rose from my chair and bowed to Lady Dewan. She nodded, but then rose and took a step towards me.

"You displayed no shock upon seeing my face," she said. "And yet you have not lived among the magissa for long, or I'd have heard of you."

I bowed again.

"Please raise your head," said Lady Dewan. Her voice was soft. "Even our kind can find Hydros a little disturbing. Believe me... there are few who would have entered the house of Hydros in order to aid a stranger."

I raised my head, and met her gaze. "My Lady, I don't consider Alison a stranger. I consider her a friend." I felt tears prick at my eyes because of the lie. I was so selfish. The deception was cruel, too cruel. Nevertheless, if it got me out alive...

Lady Dewan took another step forward. She reached out a hand, which I shook. Her grip was firm. This gesture would be a mark of considerable favour among the aristocrats I'd encountered in Selen. In Octavia's quiet, secluded sitting room, it carried crushing weight.

"Susan Fletcher with the cheap business cards considers Alison a friend," she said. She frowned, then strode to a sideboard where vases filled with skeletal flowers flanked a pad of paper, as well as a silver tray containing my business card. She ran her finger around the edge of the tray. "May I keep your card, Susan?"

Why was she... of course she... I gave up. "I would be delighted for you to keep it, Lady Dewan."

She nodded, gravely. "Thank you. I would have liked to have a friend such as you when I was Alison's age. So it goes. Now, to business..."

She scribbled on the pad of paper which lay next to my card. She tore the page free, folded it in half and handed me the slip. I accepted it with a respectful dip of the head.

"Paget is upstairs. Fida here will take you to the library, and then ask Paget to join you there. Give her that note, it asks that she take you on as a protégé. Please examine it if you wish, the contents are not secret. Paget will also be best placed to summon the astynomia, they are more her asset than mine. I have certain wheels I may set in motion if the need arises."

"Thank you, my lady."

She nodded to me. I bowed back and followed Fida as she drifted from the room.

That was my task mostly complete. All I needed to do now was get out of my meeting with Paget Belacourt in one piece, get her to actually summon the damned astynomia, and I'd be out of here faster than winking.

The servant led me down a corridor and up a cavernous set of stairs. Modern photographs adorned the staircase walls, many were clearly of Alison's ancestors. Alison herself featured in two pictures. She stood boldly, one foot slightly in front of the other, chin raised, hands splayed. Her pose stood out amongst the other portraits of stuffy, reserved aristocrats. She looked extremely pleased with herself. I was willing to bet the pose had been her idea.

At the head of the stairs, Fida coughed respectfully. I jumped, and apologised as I scuttled up the remaining stairs to join her. The first floor of the house was less lavish than the ground floor. Simple, warm colours made the place feel homely, and there was a gratifying lack of tiny ornaments on trestle tables.

Fida opened a door for me, revealing a cosy library. I thanked her and stepped through. Even as I did so, a small part of me suspected some sort of trap. I might have given myself away in front of Lady Dewan and she'd given instructions for me to be taken to a torture chamber disguised as a library.

I checked for distortions in the carpet which might hint at secret doorways, and I checked under every table and chair for secret torture implements. The place seemed mundane enough. Bookshelves, armchairs and tiny tables. Each bookshelf had an armchair, and each armchair had a tiny table, and each tiny table was piled high with books. I picked an arm chair whose usual occupant clearly enjoyed novels with shirtless people on the covers, and sat.

Paget would expect me to have some experience with offers of patronage. I was already supposed to have been through one from Lady Callas. I should probably just agree to everything she said until I was able to escape. But – no, it wouldn't do to suck up to her. The magissa evidently respected strength of character. Presenting as a worm, wowed by Paget's presence, would probably lead to... consequences.

So, I should present as being confident in my abilities. I was less sure of what those abilities were since entering the Callas death trap. I should start with my osto.

A jolt of panic crackled up my spine. I had no idea what Charites' osto was. Did I have a memory anchor for it? I was sure Alison had said something about it… I must have anchored what she'd said. Where?

My right hand darted from anchor to anchor. Magissa, things I mustn't do, subgroups, the bracelet of teeth, details of payment, lies about my shared history with Lady Callas…

Footsteps in the corridor outside. I froze. Blinked. Shook my head. I needed to get my game face on and maintain my cover. I could keep checking for anchors as long as I did so subtly.

The door opened, and a nightmare filled the doorway. I breathed. Not a nightmare. Only a magissa – tall, with black hair pulled up in a tight bun. A battered black suit drank in the light, whilst a copper wolf pin scowled from her lapel.

She smiled at me. Her mouth was the size I was used to from humans, but she still managed to show more teeth than either Alison or Lady Dewan had managed. "Paget Belacourt. I'm delighted to meet you."

I stood, bowed and held out Octavia's note. "Lady Dewan wished that I present this to you."

Paget smiled. "Interesting." Her voice had an aristocratic edge to it, even though her clothing and stance didn't suggest one who had come from the highest levels of society.

She peered closer at the note, before stepping to the left and examining it from a new angle. She did the same from the right. Given she was inspecting the note, rather than me generally, I used my free hand to check for lost memory anchors.

Left hip – nothing. Left thigh – nothing. Left waist – the schedule Lady Callas had concocted for my reports into the magissa. Left ear – the people I'd encounter at the mansion. Left temple –

Paget took the note from my hand. How long had she been staring at it? I focussed. She wasn't staring at the note. She was staring at me. I smiled, weakly, and tried to disguise my hand tapping my temple by scratching.

Something was strange. Paget hadn't closed the door behind her. Padding footsteps approached. Paget turned, then stepped aside to reveal the most enormous dog I'd ever seen. It stalked into the room and, as soon as it saw me, it started to growl.

Chapter Eleven

Paget peered at the wolf, reached to her wrist, and slipped a tooth into her mouth. She growled – actually growled, the noise canine. Low and rumbling. The wolf sniffed, then yipped, before padding about the library, sniffing at chair legs.

Paget beamed at me. "You're Charites, yes?"

I still hadn't found my anchor. I should lie. No, Lady Dewan would have said I was Charites. Damn. I nodded. "Yes, Ms Belacourt."

Paget's smile stretched further across her face. "Wonderful! Can you talk to Bloodfang?"

I looked at the wolf. It bared its fangs. They were red. Talk to Bloodfang... Talk to Bloodfang... That was it, I *did* have a memory anchor for Charites osto! I scratched the back of my head. Of course! Alison had said—

"Are you using memory anchors?" Paget asked, her voice saccharine.

I froze. "Sorry? Oh, no, I was just... No, you asked if I could talk to Bloodfang. I can't." I swallowed. "My osto allows me to speak with," I swallowed again. "Fish."

Paget raised an eyebrow. "Fish? How remarkable. Well, no matter. Would you mind taking off your shoes for me?"

"I'm sorry?" I asked.

Paget flew towards me. Before I could even blink, she was looming over me, holding a knife to my throat. I took a step back and collapsed into my chair. The knife followed me down.

"I asked you to take off your shoes," she said, her voice still sickly sweet.

She knew. I'd been found out. I wanted to scream, or cry, or both. I'd been so close...

Paget eased the knife closer to my throat, until the blade brushed against my flesh. "The memory anchors were a hint. Were circumstances different, I'd advise you to work on using subtler recall gestures. However, I suspect you won't get the chance to practice.

"Even if I'd been blindfolded, meaning I'd missed your clumsy use of anchors, Bloodfang would still have spotted you. She says you don't smell like one of us. You smell like a human."

Bloody, bloody dogs. "Oh no," I said, trying to sound at ease with the situation and failing completely. "I'm not human. I'm a magissa."

"What's wrong with your voice?" asked Paget. She squatted in front of me, dropped her knife, and tugged at my shoelaces.

"Nothing. I always sound like this. Please leave my shoes alone."

I tried to rise from my chair, but Bloodfang thundered across the room to stand next to Paget. It reared, placing its front two paws on the arms of my chair. I was treated to an intimate view of the crimson jaws which would devour me if I made one wrong move.

Paget yanked my left shoe off. "What's this?" She gasped, theatrically. "Your feet don't end in claws as every Charites' feet should! My, my, Bloodfang, I fear we've an infiltrator here." She scooped her knife back up and rose to her full height.

"No!" I squeaked "No! I'm not actually an infiltrator! I was invited!"

"Not by Octavia you weren't," said Paget. "Bloodfang, darling, maybe you should rip her throat out."

"No! No! I was invited by Lady Marie Callas! She had a plan and needed my help. She knew I was human."

Bloodfang, blessedly, didn't move. Paget tapped the flat of her knife to her lips. Her gaze wandered across the ceiling. "You wouldn't lie to me, would you?"

"Well, I've already lied to you several times during this conversation—" I said, because apparently when my nerve breaks, it breaks *hard*, "but not about this! I haven't lied to you about this at all, yet!"

Paget chuckled.

"I didn't mean yet!" I cried. "I didn't mean yet! I meant at all. Just... at all. I won't lie to you again. I promise."

"All right," said Paget. "All right. Come with me, we need to talk. Don't say anything until I give you the nod."

She sheathed her knife and strode from the room. I stared longingly at the empty corridor, but Bloodfang hadn't moved from my side. It growled at me.

"I'm going, I'm going," I said, wondering if Paget meant she didn't mean to kill me at all, or she was just taking me somewhere quiet and wipe-dry so she could kill me with minimal fuss.

I felt as if I was watching myself walk... as if someone had taken *me*, the me who lives behind my eyes, and pulled me back away from my vision a little. At arms length from the world.

Bloodfang padded after me as I followed Paget's implacable back down a few corridors until she opened a door and stepped through. I followed, wondering if prisoners on their way to the gallows had felt similarly back in the old days.

Through the door was... a mess. The walls were obscured by a haphazard collage of photographs displaying different breeds of dogs.

Books, folders, and loose papers were scattered all over the floor. A strong, floral-sweet smell I didn't recognise hung in the air.

Paget flopped down into the room's only chair. "Shut the door."

I tried to shut the dog out, but it was too quick for me.

"So," said Paget, "Lady Callas knew you were human."

I nodded. My throat felt tight. I couldn't be sure that I'd be able to get words out if I tried to speak.

"Did she want you to do anything for her?"

I nodded.

"What did she want you to do?"

I opened my mouth. No sound emerged. Was there a way out of this? Bloodfang was faster than me so I couldn't run. Was there a way I could convince Paget I was harmless? Begging wouldn't be enough. I'd no doubt she'd seen people beg before. A show of strength, even if such a thing were possible, would be even more futile.

"Susan." Paget clicked her fingers. "You're kilometres away. Come back."

I'd been staring at the floor without even realising it.

Paget sighed. "Do you have any proof that Lady Callas knew you were human?"

I nodded.

"What is it?"

Lady Callas' briefing documents were under my bed. In my house. *Where my dads were.* I couldn't let her know about them. I forced my lips shut and stared intently at the floor.

"Bloodfang, come here," said Paget. The massive dog padded past me and sat at her mistresses' feet. The door behind me was now unguarded, but even if I ran, I'd never make it out of the house.

Paget scratched the dog behind the ears. With her free hand, she reached into a cupboard, drew out a rolled tobacco paper, and lit up. The floral odour rolled through the room with renewed strength.

"Look," said Paget, "I don't want to kill you."

Well that was good news.

"How old are you?" she asked.

I tried to reply. It should have been really, really simple to answer Paget's question, but I couldn't. I couldn't even form the thought, let alone speak it.

Paget took a drag on her roll-up. "I need to know why you're here. If you've seen Octavia, then you already know too much. If I'm not satisfied with your reasons for being in this house, then I'll have no choice but to kill you. I'm sure you know why, but just in case, let me be clear: I'll not allow you to threaten my friend's life by revealing her existence to your people." She leaned forward in her chair. "I will *not*. So. Let me ask again. How can you prove Lady Callas knows you're human?"

No. Anything else, but not that. I clenched my jaw tight. Resolved. This was it.

Nothing happened. I'd expected threats. Recriminations. Outrage at my refusal to answer. I risked a glance up. Paget was studying me, taking a long drag of her roll-up. She exhaled pungent smoke, tapped ash into a tray and took another drag. "You're protecting someone," she said, eventually. "Who are you protecting? A girlfriend?"

I returned my gaze to the floor.

"A boyfriend? A non-binary partner of some persuasion?"

I closed my eyes.

"Your parents," she blew smoke at my feet. "The proof you have is in your home. You think I'll go there, retrieve the evidence, and kill everyone inside."

My concerns hadn't been quite that specific, but I nodded anyway.

Paget stubbed out her roll-up. "Look. Your parents are part of this now, whether you like it or not. If you have evidence that will permit me to spare your life, then I'll extend the same courtesy to your parents, of course. If your proof is insufficient, then I'm afraid it won't matter. Now, I need you to tell me what the proof is, where it is, and what your address is. I'll send an agent to retrieve it. They won't harm your parents without being instructed to do so."

I opened my mouth but, again, I couldn't speak. I wanted to cry.

"I had things I wanted to do today..." said Paget. She rose, took me by the hand, and half dragged me to a desk, which was only just visible beneath drifts of paperwork. She shoved a stack of reports aside, revealing six partially completed notepads. She grabbed a pen, took my hand, and introduced one to the other. "Write it down."

I wrote my address out for her, along with the location of Lady Callas' briefing notes. I thought about including the quiz sheet I'd made for dad in my screed, but my hands shook too much every time I began. I'd asked them to burn the quiz. If they hadn't... we'd deal with that if we were all still alive tomorrow morning.

I returned the paper and pen to Paget with shaking hands. She glanced at my notes, nodded, and slipped them into her jacket. "Don't go anywhere," she said. She brushed past me and out of the room. The door clicked shut behind her, leaving me alone in the room with Bloodfang.

I cracked, then I broke. I collapsed into a ball on the floor and shook. Tears ran down my face. Sobs tore from my throat. All there was in my head was a terrifying, thunderous silence which rolled from one side of my brain to the other, obliterating everything in its path.

I had no idea how long I lay trembling on the floor. Eventually, the silence became less oppressive and thoughts crept back into my head. My first thought was that I'd probably just got my dads killed. It was such an unbelievably huge, terrible thought that I feared it would take over from the deafening silence I'd just escaped. Then, another thought came: I was probably going to be killed. And another: if my dads weren't already dead, then I'd completely ruined not only my life, but theirs as well. Some second chance this was turning out to be.

Something wet prodded me in the back of my neck, interrupting my cacophony of oppressive thoughts. I yelped, but the same thing prodded me again. It didn't feel as if I was being murdered. I uncurled a little and rolled over to see what was prodding me.

Bloodfang towered over me. I barely had time to wonder what she was doing before her massive jaws opened and her head moved forward with dizzying speed. I had a moment to make peace with what I imagined was my impending non-existence, before her tongue emerged and gave me a massive, slurpy lick on the cheek. Another lick followed on the other cheek, and Bloodfang settled into this activity with gusto.

It's really quite hard to despair about your entire world being ripped away from you when a dog is licking your face. Something about her weird wet, raspy tongue short-circuited my brain, causing a treacherous smile to play across my face.

Paget cackled from the doorway. "Good girl, Bloodfang!"

I jumped, nearly head-butting the enormous dog on the nose.

Paget strolled into the room. "Are you feeling any better?"

"A little," I said, my voice cracked and horse. "Did you harm my dads?"

"Absolutely not, and neither did the agent I sent to infiltrate your house. She affected entry via your bedroom window, which you had not secured, by the way. Your dads never even knew she was there."

This was good news, assuming Paget's word was worth anything.

Paget rolled her eyes at my sceptical expression. "I've no reason to lie to you, and you have no reason to lie to me ever again." She flourished Lady Callas' briefing notes. "Why don't you tell me everything in your own words, and then we'll see what's to be done about this mess."

Paget settled into her chair as I recounted how disastrous my final year of school had been, and how Lady Callas had tested me, alongside others in a similar position. Bloodfang snuggled up next to me as I warmed to my subject. I relayed the full story to my captor, although I needed to stop twice to ask for a drink of water.

"She was going to expose us?" Paget asked, once I was done. "Really?"

I shrugged. Recounting my story had given me time to think, and there were important matters that needed attention. "Look," I said, "we'll have to finish up our business here, I know that. The thing is – Alison Dewan and the others in Lady Callas' house are in danger. Whether I go or not, you need to send help for them as soon as possible."

Paget's expression softened slightly. "As it happens, whilst I was waiting for my agent to report on the contents of your bedroom, I put out the call. The astynomia should be on their way very soon."

I exhaled. "Good." If nothing else, everyone in the house should be safe once help arrived.

Paget frowned at me. "Good? Why is it good? I mean... it *is* good. Put it this way - I know why *I* think it's good, but why do you?"

I sighed. I shrugged. At that point, I didn't even know how to answer her question.

"Curious," she said. She picked up a knife, and flourished it artfully as she spoke. I couldn't tear my eyes from its tip. "We both know I can't just let you go, given what you know. Perhaps you might consider accepting an offer of employment."

"What?" I asked, too shocked to think of a more intelligent reply.

"I need agents in the human community," said Paget. "It's my job to know things of interest to the magissa, so I find it useful to have a network of well-placed informants here and there. I think you'd do well in such a role, given sufficient training."

"You want me to spy on my own people for a group that actively preys on them?"

Paget looked amused. "Well, you don't have to. I mean, I could just kill you and your family. That's the more sensible option, but I'm trying to help you, softie that I am."

"Well, since you put it that way..."

"Good. We'll sort out the full details of your employment later. For now, we need to get you, along with the astynomia, to Lady Callas' mansion. Oh, and I need to introduce you to your minder."

I pinched the bridge of my nose. "My minder?"

"Well, yes. I can't just employ you as a spy without any guarantee that you won't run off and spill the magissa's secrets all over the place. You'll need supervision. One of my hounds will pose as your familiar."

Bloodfang was sitting attentively by Paget's feet.

"Like her?" I asked, pointing.

"Very like her, yes," said Paget. "I'll go and fetch him. One second."

Paget slipped out. I stared at Bloodfang. Would my minder have a name like Bloodfang? Would I be assigned a gigantic grey beast named Razorclaw, or a huge shaggy creature named Swiftshadow?

The door opened. I turned. Paget strolled in, followed by a small, white, fluffy creature. He looked uncannily similar to my aunt's pet lapdog.

"Er..."

"Say hello to your minder," said Paget.

"Hello."

"Say hello, Constable Woofington," said Paget.

Constable Woofington yipped, padded towards me, and nuzzled my leg.

"Constable Woofington?" I asked, incredulously.

"Yes. What? Why are you looking at me like that?"

"But... your dog is called Bloodfang!" I said, outraged. Was this supposed to be an insult? Had I not gone through enough for the magissa to be afforded even a modicum of respect?

"Yes. My mentor named Bloodfang when I joined her service. I raised Constable Woofington from a pup. Do you have a problem with my choice of name?"

I considered my position. "No, no," I said. "It's a lovely name."

Constable Woofington tried to place a paw on my leg, lost his balance, and fell over.

"The thing is," I said, "the Constable is supposed to be my minder, but won't I spend most of my time minding him? He seems pretty harmless."

Paget grinned. "You don't know anything about dogs, do you?" She used a set of tongs to pick up a finger-width crimson rod, and held the far end of the rod in the flame of a gas lamp.

I was utterly fed up with the magissa and their infinite tests of knowledge. "No, I don't know anything about dogs."

Paget, rotated the rod so the flame heated it evenly. "People are impressed by Bloodfang because she's big, and she looks like she could crush your skull in her jaws, and she can, but she won't. Bloodfang is a big softy, aren't you, sweetie?"

Paget leaned down with her free hand and scratched the enormous demi-wolf behind the ears. The dog's tail thumped and she made a contented doggy noise.

"If you want a really vicious, evil creature, you have to go for the small dogs. They're the ones with something to prove. They'll have your hand off if you annoy them, and go for your throat if you disrespect them."

"You're kidding." My hand froze. I'd been playing with Constable Woofington's ears.

"By all means, test the limits of the constable's patience if you don't believe me," said Paget. "Just not whilst you're in the middle of a job. You're to keep him with you at all times. He'll report to my other agents when he sees one. For your part, you're to send me written reports to this address on a bi-weekly basis. Now, do you need to grab anything? The astynomia should be here any minute. You'll head back to the Callas mansion as soon as they arrive."

"Aren't you coming?" I asked.

"I've matters to attend to here. After all, a conspiracy to reveal us to humanity has just been revealed. Lady Callas might not have acted alone. Oh, yes. See that bookshelf over there?"

"Yes?"

"No, not that one. *That* one."

"Oh, yes?"

"There's a tin box on the bottom shelf, grab a booklet from in there, would you?"

I did as I was told. The booklet was around fifty pages long, although it had been printed in an oversized typeface.

"Read that at your leisure. For the love of Eleos, don't lose it."

"What is it?"

"An employee handbook. All my agents get one. It has essential clan information, details on how we'll pay you, our disciplinary and sickness procedures, everything you should need."

"Oh," I said, staring at the incongruous document. "Good. By the way, should I be maintaining my cover? Pretending I'm magissa?"

"No," said Paget, slightly amused. "Well, perhaps you should in the Callas mansion until everything is sorted out. After that, you should let our people know what you are. Many of them will have worked with human agents before. They don't like it, but they know it's for the best."

"Thank you."

"Not at all," said Paget, "but there is one last thing. Take your jacket off and roll up your shirt sleeve."

"Why?" I asked.

"Because I asked you to," said Paget, mildly.

I raised an eyebrow and did as she asked.

"You may find the magissa slow to trust," said Paget, "so it's sensible for our agents to identify themselves using signs known only to them. That way, we know who our friends are. Open that window, would you?" she inclined her head towards a window on her right, my left.

"Are you going to give me a badge or something?" I asked, opening the window and turning back towards Paget.

Paget turned towards me. She carried the rod that she had been heating in the gas lamp with her. The end glowed red hot.

"Something like that," she said. She grabbed my wrist with her left hand, winked at me, and plunged the red hot end of the rod into my forearm.

Chapter Twelve

Sausages sizzling in a pan. That's what being branded smelled and sounded like. I'd squeezed my eyes shut when I'd realised what Paget was doing. I cracked an eye open. The monster was staring at me. I stared back.

"Why doesn't it hurt?" I asked.

Paget grinned, infuriatingly. "Working for magissa. A career filled with surprises."

"I'm serious."

"So am I. I asked Apollo – one of our medics – to build a painkiller into my brand. It leads to fewer complaints in the long run. Now get a move on, the astynomia await."

I found four magissa waiting in a coach outside the house. I had to help Constable Woofington in, after he tried and failed to jump up the steps three times. I sat next to a woman wearing at least three thick winter coats – only her forehead and ice-black braided hair were visible. Constable Woofington fell asleep on my foot as the door shut behind me. I shifted, and then gasped as a trickle of icy water ran down my back.

"Hello," said the bundle of clothes which may or may not have contained a person, "I'm Heledd. Don't worry if you experience chilling supernatural phenomena. Chilblains. Mysterious gusts of cold air.

Ice cubes on the back of your neck. Freezing water down your spine. It's not real. It's just happening because you're sitting next to me. Oh. Oh. I haven't felt this one before. A cold spot on my ankle. It's not even that cold. Oh, wait. No. It's a dog. He's touching my leg with his nose. Hello little fellow. Anyway, yes, don't worry. You'll get used to it."

I didn't get used to it.

The other three astynomia were Dawn – a lithe woman with mottled brown fur covering most of her skin. Elin, who sat hunched forward, with his elbows on his knees, because he had nubs of bone protruding from his back. Finally, Callan, who wore a sharp suit and a bracelet of teeth which wound around her arm in a double helix of muted silver.

Callan introduced the others once the coach was on the way to the Callas Mansion. "So," she said, sitting back. "I've not met you before. You're one of the wolf pack?"

Paget's brand had been of a wolf head. I still didn't know how I felt about being permanently marked. I found my lack of reaction a little worrying. I'd clearly had so many life-changing revelations in twenty-four hours that a little light assault from my new employer didn't really register. Still, respect was respect. "Yes," I said. "I'm one of the wolf pack."

Callan nodded. "Right. You worked with astynomia before?"

I shook my head.

"Spirits preserve us," said Dawn.

"*Those outside ourselves*

Alone are nothing but rage

With us, they're angels," said Elin.

Dawn stared at him. "You what, mate?"

"Can we focus, please?" said Callan. "Okay, wolf, here's the deal. You don't work for us, we don't work for you. Don't try and order us about, that never ends well. We all have the same goals. We meet them with the minimum of fuss, everyone goes home happy."

"I won't be happy," said Heledd.

"I'm going to try and get some sleep," said Dawn.

"Dawn, you're not going to sleep," said Callan. "Look, wolf, you've been in the house, right? What can we expect?"

I nodded. "Right. Two murders in the space of maybe four hours. Alison Dewan and I had an encounter with someone wearing a cloak and hat, who we chased through the house's steam tunnels."

Callan whistled. "They walked away after a tangle with Alison Dewan? Noted."

"*Five weapons, a hand*
Open palm or curled fingers
Or blood drawn by blade?" said Elin.

Dawn folded her arms and closed her eyes. Callan stared at Elin, her lips moving soundlessly. Eventually, she clicked her fingers and turned back to me. "I think Elin was asking if the person who attacked you had any weapons."

"Oh, well done Callan," said Heledd.

"A sword. No firearms. They were careful not to use their osto around us, so we think they were one of the residents. Er... one sec." I tapped my left ear. "Right. So, at the house were Lady Callas – Charites, now deceased. Teleri – Hephaestus, caterer, now deceased. Betsan – Silenus, head of security. Mr Das – Erebus, housekeeper. Charles Varma – Deimos, resident. Praxi Tolis – Hydros, resident."

Callan nodded. "Any details on their ostos?"

I shook my head. "Alison would know Praxi's, but I haven't experienced any others. Oh – there was a… damn. What was it… can a osto be poured into… something like a trap?"

"What do you mean?" asked Callan.

I gave a brief description of the disjointed, unnatural guilt spiral I'd experienced in Teleri's room, moments before her death.

"Sounds like an infusion, right enough," said Callan. They can be used as a trap if you have enough time to prep. And it sounds like Deimos's work. Charles has some questions to answer. Okay, wolf, you got anything else for us?"

I rubbed my hands together, trying to get back into the frame of mind I'd been in before fleeing the Callas house, when I'd been concentrating on solving the murder because it meant my best chance of survival. Concentrating was hard, because an ethereal freezing wind kept stinging my cheeks.

"Okay," I said, after I'd got my thoughts into a line. "Any murder needs means, motive and opportunity."

"Read a lot of detective stories have you, kid?" asked Dawn, her eyes still shut.

"I thought you were going to sleep, Dawn," said Heledd.

"I am. Shut up."

"Opportunity," I said. "That's an easy one. Everyone in the house was incapacitated using poison. Anyone heard of the Flower of Tartarus?"

That got their attention. Callan, Elin and Heledd's gazes all snapped to me. Even Dawn opened her eyes momentarily.

"Were they poisoned with the Flower of Tartarus?" Callan asked.

I shifted, uncomfortable in the heat of their gaze. "Maybe, I'm not sure yet. What is it?"

"A tool of spycraft," said Callan. "A problem with poison generally is it's unpredictable. Give two grams of a certain poison to three people – one may die, one may be knocked unconscious, and the third may merely have a stomach ache.

"I believe, for this reason, the Flower of Tartarus isn't considered a poison, technically. It's closer to anaesthetic. It incapacitates those who consume it, with a low fatality rate. It's extremely difficult to get hold of. If the killer used the flower, they either work in intelligence or know someone who does."

I mentally filed that information. "Right, that's helpful. Returning to our suspects having the opportunity to murder Lady Callas: any one of them, given the right moment, could have poisoned the food and incapacitated the household. That person could have easily faked their symptoms, or else ingested a small amount of the poison after murdering Lady Callas.

"I found uneaten pork under the servant's dining table. If that was the poisoned food, then it was likely that one of the servants was the killer. Of them, Teleri was the most likely – she was a regular at the Pitt club."

"Oh, her," said Dawn, cracking an eye open. "Yeah, I've had previous with her. Definitely seemed to be running from something."

"Right," I said, "and whatever it was caught up with her. Lady Callas insisted on hiring her, specifically, over Betsan's objections. I've no idea why, although there's a connection to Charles. Anyway, the next question is motive. Lady Callas didn't like Betsan, but I don't think that stretched as far as murdering someone. Otherwise... how much do you know about me?"

Callan shrugged. "You work for Paget. You're wolf pack. Human."

I nodded. "Right. So... there's a wider issue involving Lady Callas and a project she was working on – a project she was attempting to use me for. If anyone in the house found out about the project, that would be a strong motive, but we have no idea if anyone knew about me."

Callan shifted in her chair. "Are you going to tell us what the project was?"

I grimaced. "I'm not sure if I'm allowed to."

Callan sighed.

"Means," I said, hoping the question of motive could be left behind. "Means are simple. Someone held Lady Callas' head under the water until she drowned..." Dead eyes staring up at me... Sodden clothing clinging to me as I'd hauled her out of the bath... I closed my eyes, and pressed on. "The killer had to be strong – possibly discounting Charles or Mr Das.

"Then again, Lady Callas had been poisoned, and the killer hadn't. That might account of any difference in strength between her and the killer."

Callan considered this. "So, out of the four possible suspects, you've eliminated none of them."

"That's right," I said. "and it's still technically possible that there's an intruder in the house who isn't one of those four."

Callan nodded. "All right. Thanks, wolf."

Dawn opened her eyes. "Why are you thanking the wolf? You just said she didn't actually tell us anything useful."

Elin grinned at her.

"*She who speaks loudest*

Words travel from ear to ear

Not shedding meaning.

What words may fly, from mouth through mind, from ear to ear,
meaning denied."

Dawn growled. "Are you calling me thick?"

"Let's not fight," said Heledd.

"Susan told us plenty," said Callan. "We know the murders were focussed around stealth and deception. The killer disguised themselves when they targeted Alison and the wolf. First thing we need to do when we get to the house is search it, top to bottom. Make sure there aren't any intruders. Dawn, stick with Heledd. Elin, you're with me. No splitting up – don't give the killer an opportunity."

"What do I do?" I asked.

Callan shrugged. "Whatever you think is right, wolf."

That would have been acceptable advice written on the back of a cereal box. For Susan Fletcher in the year 739, I wasn't a fan. I was starting to think I was a terrible judge of what was right.

Still, I could work with Alison to answer one crucial question: If Marie Callas told someone about her plan to expose the magissa, and that person killed her... who would she have told? Who was she closest to?

Waves crashed against black rocks as the coach crossed the bridge to the Callas mansion. Angry clouds massed out to sea. The astynomia climbed out, and stared, sullenly at the gathering storm. I knocked on the front door, and was pleasantly surprised when Betsan opened the thing almost immediately.

She nodded to me. "Ah, a sight for sore eyes. Good to see you again, Susan. Astynomia, welcome. Can I be of any assistance?"

Callan declined. Betsan stood aside whilst the astynomia strode into the mansion, two by two.

"I was worried something had happened to you, Susan." Betsan said. "Also, why do you have a dog?"

This question took me by surprise until I remembered Constable Woofington. He must have followed me out of the coach. "Paget Belacourt assigned me a familiar."

"You met Paget?"

"Oh, yes. Got to know each other pretty well, as it happens."

"Huh. Remind me not to get on your bad side."

I shrugged. "As long as you're not the person who murdered Lady Callas or Teleri, we'll be fine. Have you seen Alison? I want to catch up with her, share some discoveries, that sort of thing."

Betsan shook her head. "Not for a while. She's been scouring the place for clues. Up in the cottage then down in the residence. She kept coming to talk to me after you left – I think she got lonely. I wasn't the sparkling conversation she was hoping for."

I didn't know what to say to that. I settled for giving an awkward thumbs up. "I'll go find her, then."

Betsan swung the front door shut. "With the murderer still out there?"

"The murderer will have bigger problems than me right now, with four highly trained astynomia on their tail... I assume the astynomia are highly trained?"

Betsan shrugged. "In combat, certainly. Exceptional stamina for chasing down suspects. Not always the best critical thinkers, but that's law enforcement for you."

"Right. Well, I'll be back."

"Good luck."

I searched the cottage for Alisons. Constable Woofington followed, snuffling constantly. Every once in a while, I heard a thump, and would turn around to see that he'd stumbled into a table leg and was in the process of picking himself up.

A thought struck me after the third time this happened, and I was still suffering from an Alison deficit. "Can you understand me?" I asked the Constable.

The Constable yipped.

He must be able to understand me... He wasn't going to be much of a minder if he couldn't tell Paget who I was meeting with and what we talked about.

"Tell you what," I said, "bark once for yes and twice for no. Can you understand me?"

The Constable barked once.

Of course, if he didn't understand me, he might just be barking at random. I pointed to my three-buttoned suit jacket. "Are there two buttons on this jacket?"

The Constable barked twice.

Well, that was more encouraging. "Can you track down Alison for me?"

The Constable barked twice.

"Why not?" He sat down and tilted his head at me. "Is it because you don't know what she smells like?"

The Constable barked once.

"Fair enough. She and I spent a lot of time here over the last day. Are there any scent trails which closely follow mine, but don't belong to the four magissa we were in the carriage with?"

The Constable snuffled around for a little while before barking once.

"You've found her trail?" I asked.

The Constable barked.

"Can you follow it? I want to find her as soon as possible."

The Constable barked twice.

"Why not?"

The Constable tilted his head at me.

"Is the trail too weak?"

The Constable barked twice. He sat down and started opening and closing his mouth.

"Are you thirsty?" I asked.

I swear the dog gave me a patronising glare before he barked twice.

"Do you want me to give you something as a reward if you find Alison?"

The Constable barked.

"Okay, yes, fine. You can have whatever you want, but please find Alison. We'll get you a treat or something once you've found her, okay?"

The dog barked and then sprinted down the ramp to the great hall. I had to run to keep up with the little rocket. I was having such a weird day.

The dog checked that I was following half way down the ramp, and then ran to the stairs down to the lower floors, pausing occasionally to sniff.

He clambered down the stairs to the level housing the bedrooms, ignored the turning which would have taken us to Praxi and Charles' rooms, and instead scampered towards Lady Callas' room.

I was having trouble keeping up. The constable seemed to be built for sprinting, whereas I'd always been a walk fifteen minutes then catch a trolley bus sort of person. Still, when the constable got too far ahead, he'd bark and then spin in circles until I caught up with him.

The door to Lady Callas' room was shut. Constable Woofington or, as I mentally dubbed him, CW, scratched at the no-doubt antique mahogany. I opened the door for him, and he bolted inside before scratching at the closed bathroom door.

I had a bad feeling about that door being shut, especially since what had happened last time. Still, I called Alison's name and opened the door.

Alison was inside. She was hanging by her neck from a rope tied to a light fixture. Her legs twitched. Her gaze found me.

"Alison!"

Her eyes shut.

I dashed forward, grabbed her legs, and lifted as best I could, so the weight was taken off her neck. I needed to cut her down, but I'd lost my blasted sword in the spirits-damned, motherfucking steam tunnels.

Did Alison have her xiphos in her belt? Her coat was blocking my view. I wasted precious seconds manoeuvring myself before catching sight of the hilt of her sword. I reached up and grabbed it.

Great. Now I had a sword. I needed to cut Alison down *right* now, but I couldn't support her weight and cut through the rope at the same time. I'd have to leave her suspended and suffocating, briefly, to cut her free.

I breathed out, and I breathed in just once before gently letting her weight rest. She let out a terrible rasping rattle. I scrabbled out from under her and slammed the toilet seat lid closed. I climbed up onto the lid, and slashed at the rope.

The sword bit a chunk out of the rope. I swung again – cut it half way. My hands were slick on the sword hilt. Alison spun, suspended from her neck. I might be too late already. I slashed again, the rope creaked. Threads snapped free. One more swing – I *missed*. I was so fucking useless. I focussed. I fucking focussed, and struck one more time, and the rope *snapped*.

Alison dropped to the ground limply. Her head cracked sickeningly on the tiles. Blood smeared the pristine porcelain. I dropped Alison's sword, scrambled down and tugged the rope away from Alison's neck. The pressure relieved, I worked at the knot at the back of her neck, teasing it free as best I could with trembling fingers. Eventually it loosed, revealing a ring of ripped, red skin where the rope had bitten into her flesh.

She wasn't breathing. She wasn't breathing. I took a deep breath, opened Alison's mouth, and pinched her nose. I placed my mouth over hers. Too damned wide! I couldn't make a seal where my lips met hers. I repositioned myself and tried again. There. I breathed into her twice before compressing her chest, trying to remember the method my old science tutor had shown me.

Thirty compressions. I was pretty sure I was supposed to do thirty compressions, and then try two more breaths. I lost count after twenty. Constable Woofington had run off while I'd been cutting Alison down, so I wasn't even getting moral support from my dog.

The room stank of death. I was also pretty sure Alison had soiled herself. After completing something close to thirty compressions, I breathed into Alison's mouth twice and, miracle of miracles, Alison drew in a breath.

Her first breath was shallow, but her second was stronger. Only a minute later, she was breathing properly once again. I hauled myself over to a wall, sat with my back against it and stared at my friend. I cried very quietly for a few minutes.

"Susan, hark? This dog doth bark!"

That was the voice of... what was his name? Elin, the medical magissa. He sounded different. Still... "Hi! Yes, I'm in here!"

Constable Woofington thundered into the bathroom, with Elin in tow. His eyes widened when he saw Alison. "Oh, bugger."

I got out of his way. The bathroom wasn't really large enough for three people, one corpse, and an excitable dog. I waited in Lady Callas' bedroom for maybe ten minutes. Constable Woofington waited with me. I didn't move. I barely breathed.

Eventually, Elin emerged, drying his hands. "I've done what I can. She should be okay, but we need to get her to a doctor. You got to her just in time. You found her hanging?"

"Yes," I said. Barely a whisper.

"Your familiar came and found me. Good thing, too. Her blood flow had been disrupted. She might have some brain damage."

"Fuck..." Tears welled up behind my eyes.

"If you hadn't found her, she'd have died. I'm going to fetch one of my colleagues and we'll take her upstairs. Can you find her a change of clothes among Lady Callas' things? I need to change her and perform a little clean-up. This whole experience has been rough on her." He bowed to me and left the room to fetch his friend.

I wanted to check on Alison, but the thought of entering that bathroom yet again made bile bubble up my throat. Instead, I searched the various cavernous cupboards in Lady Callas' room until I found a selection of day clothes which looked as if they'd fit Alison.

Elin returned with Callan in tow. Callan strode into the bathroom, whilst Elin grabbed the clothes I'd laid out.

"Elin," I said. My voice faint.

"What sound from yonder Susan breaks?"

I frowned. "That. You were all... whatsit. Poetic in the coach. I thought it was the curse of your clan, but you spoke normally when you realised Alison was in trouble."

"That's not my curse," said the medic. "The bones in my back are my curse. I just like poetry. Now, please wait for us in the servant's sitting room. I'd like to keep Alison up there. Stay with her. Keep an eye on her and come get me the second anything changes."

"Of course, whatever's best for Alison." I said.

Elin nodded. "She's lucky to have you, wolf."

Chapter Thirteen

I found myself in the servant's sitting room. I presume I walked there myself, but given the state I was in, I wouldn't have noticed if winged fiends had carried me there in their claws.

I waited.

After some time – maybe a few minutes, maybe seventeen years – Elin and Callan carried Alison in and placed her onto a sofa. Callan had changed Alison into Lady Callas' clothes and, whilst the garments didn't fit as well as her own clothes, they were at least clean. I suspected this was an improvement.

"We need to get back to our search," said Callan. "Can you stay with her and send your familiar to come and get me if her condition worsens?"

"She needs a doctor," I said.

Elin nodded. "And she'll get one. We've only got the one coach, and we can't send Alison back to Selen with the murderer still in the house. Soon, Susan. She'll be fine. Keep your fingers crossed."

I nodded. I didn't want to look at Alison, and sought a distraction. "I found a sample of the meal the residents were eating when they were poisoned. Can you test it?"

Elin grinned. *"Pushing through dank mist*
Knowledge cannot hide for long

The mist shall be cleared."

I groaned. "Was that a yes?"

Elin nodded. I retrieved the pork from its hiding place in cold storage, and handed it to Elin, who promptly swallowed a tooth from his bracelet and nibbled on a piece of meat. He waited a few moments and then grimaced.

"Blood flows thickly yet

Sluggish—"

I cradled my head in my hands. "Elin, can you give me a straight fucking answer, please, without the embellishments?"

Callan patted Elin on the shoulder. "Probably not the best time, old chap."

Elin shifted. "Yes, I'm sorry. The sample was definitely poisoned. I can't be certain of the active agent, but the way it was acting on my system before my osto cleared it out makes me suspect the Flower of Tartarus."

"Right. Thank you."

"Will you be okay if we continue our search, wolf?" Callan asked.

I shrugged. They left.

Teleri might have killed Lady Callas. Vials of the Flower of Tartarus... or at least vials *labelled* the Flower of Tartarus had been in her pack. The only problem was, I had no idea why Teleri might have wanted to kill Lady Callas.

I slumped in my chair. Speculation was pointless. It was still possible that the astynomia would find an intruder, and that would be that. I'd be free to go. Back to my dads. Begin my life as a traitor to humanity in earnest.

I stared at Alison's limp body. I had to watch for a long time before I saw her breathing. A lump in my throat grew, and grew, and grew, until I had no choice but to let go.

"I'm sorry, Alison. I should never have left you. I should have got back sooner. If I'd made it back sooner... if Paget hadn't caught me, maybe I could have stopped this. I'm sorry. I'm so sorry... and I *know* that you'd hate me so much if you knew what I was, but – I couldn't let anything happen to you. You've suffered enough at the hands of humanity. You won't suffer any more because of me."

The rest was a little incoherent.

Twenty minutes later, I'd dried my eyes. Another ten minutes later, footsteps approached my sanctuary. Constable Woofington rolled over to look at whoever was coming in, but he didn't yap or growl.

Callan stood stiffly, a model of professionalism. "So, we've searched the mansion from top to bottom. We've been through all the tunnels. No intruders. I took a look at the security system. No-one other than you and Alison entered the mansion before we did."

"The killer is one of the residents in the house, then."

"Just so. We're going to get to work untangling that puzzle – thanks for the briefing. We'd welcome your help, but Elin said Alison really needs someone with her. Up to you, Wolf"

"I'm staying with Alison," I said, my gaze on the floor.

"I think that's the right call. Stay strong, let any of us know if you need anything. Except Dawn, best not to ask Dawn." She waved, and left.

Constable Woofington went back to sleep. Alison continued to breathe terrifyingly slowly. I chewed my lip. The astynomia would finish the investigation. I could just stay here with Alison and make sure nothing bad... Make sure nothing bad happened...

Wanting a distraction, I reached for the employee handbook Paget had given me and flicked through it.

'Welcome,' the first page began, 'to the interesting and exciting world of being a covert agent of the Senate! We hope you'll be very happy working with us. We consider our agents part of the family, which isn't to say we'll have a massive row every Winter Frost celebration and refuse to pay you. Rather, we mean that we really care for each of our agents.'

There were another two pages which continued in a similar manner. I skipped them.

Page three explained the pay which agents were entitled to. As a new agent, I'd be paid a surprisingly large amount of money, which would increase as I completed training and reached professional development milestones.

Page four contained drawings and descriptions of various signs which agents needed to know, including the sign that Paget had branded into my arm – the mark of the wolf pack. Paget's brand was not only designed to identify me as someone who could be trusted, but even permitted me some small authority in certain circumstances. I was to be given access to Senate property and intelligence.

Page five provided information about the various magissa clans. There were twelve of them, although the twelfth didn't exactly count as a clan. The twelfth clan were categorised as Proteus - magissa who didn't display characteristics of the other eleven clans, and while they were rare, they weren't unheard of.

To me, it sounded as if the magissa were cheating. They had categories for eleven clans. They then took everyone who didn't meet these categories and put them in a twelfth clan. Examples they gave included a woman who could turn her blood into acid and a man who could perform magically induced miracles in the bedroom, if you follow me. What had these to do with each other?

Page five proved to be fascinating. I read about the clans of Charites and Hydros. I read about the clans of Silenus and Morpheus... and then I read about Deimos – Charles' clan.

Deimos, the handbook informed me, most commonly manifested the ability to manipulate terror in other people, but other known manifestations included inducing dread, panic, trembling, and guilt.

I read the entire handbook cover to cover, before going back to re-read a few key sections. One of these concerned infusions, as the astynomia had described them. Certain magissa could, indeed, lay traps with their osto. Some of these traps were motion-activated, while others needed a specific trigger, like a certain time of day, or for the intended victim to move from sleep into wakefulness.

Charles. Charles' osto forced Teleri to kill herself. Callan had said Charles had questions to answer. To me, that seemed like a serious understatement.

I closed the employee handbook, and shuddered. The motive made sense - Charles blamed Teleri for Tova's death, although we still didn't know if that was justified or not. Teleri hadn't known her victim's name.

I reached out to stroke CW, but he barked at me, clearly outraged. I stared at him, surprised and a little worried. Then, I remembered I hadn't yet given him anything for finding Alison.

Guilt gnawed at me. I rooted around in the cold storage with CW until we found an appropriate payment for the part he'd played in saving Alison's life. Six sausages later, CW jumped up on the sofa next to Alison, spun in a clockwise circle three times, lay down, and fell asleep.

Alison lay still. Too still. When I'd first met her, she'd been maintaining this stern, dignified facade, which made much more sense since meeting her mum. Since she'd learned of the trouble at the mansion, she'd been vibrant. Alive. Amazing.

Who could have done such a thing to her? Who had the power? Who had the nerve? I'd find them, and I'd punish them.

Five minutes later, Heledd slumped past my door, with Betsan and Mr Das in tow. I asked what she was doing. Getting all the suspects together in one place, apparently. Stop them causing mischief. I was annoyed that I hadn't thought of that.

Alison slept, and I talked to her. She didn't respond to anything I said, but it still helped. I wanted to tell her that I was a human, both because of my growing guilt for lying to her, and because if anything was going to bring her back, I was sure it would be that.

After the end of the first hour when she was still unresponsive, I cracked. I told her I was a human. I said I was sorry for how she had to live her life in fear of my people.

She didn't respond. She didn't open her eyes and ask further questions. She didn't leap from the sofa and try to strangle me. She didn't fulfil any of the optimistic images I'd filled my head with to help pass the time. She just lay there, unresponsive.

Eventually, my miserable guilt gave way to boredom. Elin had dumped Alison's Xiphos next to the sofa, as well as a leather satchel I hadn't seen before. Or... That wasn't quite right. It had been on Alison's body when she had been hanging, hadn't it? I couldn't remember exactly, I'd been preoccupied.

I emptied the bag onto the sofa next to me. A black, hard-backed notebook fell out first, followed by a sheathed dagger, a collection of leather pouches, a metal tin and finally a scrap of paper floated down to settle on top of the pile.

I hadn't been sure what to expect from Alison's satchel, but... maybe the collection was what I should have expected? Had I given any thought to the idea that I was in a nightmare, or hell, or something? Probably. That seemed like the sort of thing I'd do.

The scrap of paper was blank except for one line of exaggeratedly scraggly handwriting. It read: 'I kNoW wHaT yOu DiD'.

"You don't know what I did," I said. "You're just a note." I frowned. Yes, it was just a note, but why had I felt the need to say that? I wasn't having a good day.

I tried to focus, dropped the note and unsheathed the dagger. Blood flecked the blade. I grimaced, and re-sheathed it. The leather pouches were empty, and they set off some bell of recognition deep within me, but that was all. The tin contained rows of amber capsules, a physician's note detailing how they should be taken, as well as the name of the medication: 'Testosterone undecanoate.'

"Alison," I said. "Alison. Hey, Alison. Where did you get all this stuff from?"

No reply. I opened the notebook and worked my way through its contents. It turned out that, whilst Alison had many magnificent qualities, keeping coherent records was not one of them. The first page was occupied in its entirety by the words: Found knife in bathroom!!!!!

"Alison?" I said. "Alison? *Which* bathroom, Alison? When did you find it? Where *in* the bathroom did you find it?"

No response. She probably meant Lady Callas' bathroom? Although surely we'd have found it. We'd searched in there, hadn't we? We must have searched in there. Still, the other possibilities were stranger. Why would Alison be finding knives in other bathrooms?

The next page was thick with handwriting which began in an elegant cursive, but quickly devolved into a scraggly scrawl. I had to read it a few times before concluding Alison had found the knife stashed behind Lady Callas' bathtub.

The next few pages were dedicated to interactions between Alison and Mr Das. She'd noted his mannerisms and attitude in minute detail. Probably. It was hard to tell. I've met doctors with neater handwriting than Alison's.

"Hey!" I said, after re-reading a paragraph for the fifth time. I brandished the notebook in front of Alison's closed eyes. "What does this say, Alison? Was Mr Das behaving shiftily, shitily, or shinily? Was he shirking? Alison? Was Mr Das shirking? Was he? Was he, Alison?"

The comic absurdity of yelling at an unconscious Alison made me feel slightly better, but then I remembered how serious her condition was, and I was right back where I'd started.

The next page was occupied by an idea which Alison had decided to write three lines high: 'CURSE: CAN ONLY SAY ONE WORD AT A TIME! SOLUTION: WRITE THINGS DOWN. IM A GENIUS'

My fingers twitched until I relented and drew in an apostrophe between the 'I' and the 'M'.

The following pages were a conversation between Alison and Mr Das. He was clearly distressed to hear of Lady Callas' death, and wrote that he bore Lady Callas no ill will. Further, he could not think of any reason anyone would have to harm her. Alison had asked a load of questions about the steam tunnels, which Mr Das had answered in exhaustive detail.

Alison noted that she'd also taken the time to search his room during their conversation. I could only hope she had done so subtly. She'd found the leather pouches in a drawer, along with the pill case.

Ah. That made sense, at least. Alison had been baffled by the pills, which was odd considering the first half of their name was simply the word 'testosterone'. They were hormones - for hormone therapy. Mr Das was likely born female or intersex. The hormones assisted him in living his true life. It was the sort of thing that could have been used as blackmail a hundred years ago, but these days there was no shame to it. I discounted the evidence, feeling as if a weight had been lifted.

The next page explained that Alison had found the 'I kNoW wHaT yOu DiD' note on Teleri's body, in one of her pockets. She'd asked the residents of the house about the knife. Praxi hadn't recognised it. Charles had claimed innocence. Betsan said she'd found the knife when searching Teleri when the caterer had first entered the house. She'd been allowed to keep her knife, because when you're a magissa, a knife isn't a significant weapon compared to your osto.

So. Teleri's knife possibly found at the scene. The note on Teleri's body… What if Teleri had killed Lady Callas because she was being blackmailed by somebody else? Then, once Teleri's usefulness was over, the blackmailer had taken her out of the picture? That would explain everything… except the blackmailer's motive for wanting Lady Callas dead. That last piece of the puzzle was still missing. Unless, as I'd speculated, the blackmailer had found out about Lady Callas' schemes.

Who could have been responsible? Only Charles and Praxi were likely suspects. I needed to find out more about their relationships with Lady Callas before I could narrow the search any more. I could interrogate my new suspects directly, or else could ask Betsan for more information. Unfortunately, both of these plans would mean leaving Alison alone and unprotected.

I grumbled, quietly to myself. I thought about waking CW up and asking him to fetch one of the astynomia, but he looked so peaceful… I closed my eyes and thought about the puzzle.

Half an hour later, I was roused by a cold breeze chilling my cheeks. Heledd slipped into the room shortly afterwards. "Hello," she said. "I hope Alison isn't dead."

"She's not," I said. "Stable. Look, I have some questions I want to ask the suspects. Can you watch Alison whilst I'm doing that?"

"Oh," said Heledd. "Well, I suppose. I haven't been much use downstairs, to be honest."

"Okay," I said. I checked Alison's breathing, then touched her shoulder, self-consciously. As I turned to leave, my foot nudged her xiphos, still in its sword belt. Alison wasn't using it currently. I was heading down into a house with a murderer. I swapped my sword belt for my friend's.

Heledd chattered away as I gave CW a stroke to wake him up. "Yes," she said, "You see, they brought me because I can freeze the blood in someone's veins. It's a useful trait when you might be attacked by a shadowy figure. Not so useful when you're conducting a complex investigation. I think I get on their nerves."

CW yipped, scratched, and jumped down from the sofa.

I nodded to Heledd. "Well, thanks. I'll be back quickly – come tell me and Elin if there's any change with Alison!"

"I completely understand," said Heledd as I left, her voice mournful, like a foghorn.

I found the suspects in the library, along with Elin. Mr Das huddled in a corner, Charles stood stiffly inspecting a bookcase, Betsan paced in a small circle, and Praxi...

"Where's Praxi?" I asked.

"*She who crafts water—*" said Elin.

"Damn it, Elin, just tell me."

"Sorry, yes. She's being interrogated. How's Alison?"

"No change," I said. "Heledd is watching her whilst I check on some things. Can I have a quick word with Betsan?"

"I don't see why not."

Betsan yawned, then padded after me.

"I heard about Alison," she said. "Are you doing okay?"

"Fine."

"Do you have any idea why she'd have wanted to take her own life?" Betsan asked.

"What?" I rounded on her. "She didn't try to take her own life. Who told you that?"

"Dawn. She's Silenus. She wouldn't lie to one of her own clan."

I rolled my eyes. "She's not lying, she just hasn't taken the time to learn the facts of the matter. When Alison left you, she said she was going to check on something, yes?"

"That's right."

"A matter of minutes later, I found her hanging from a light fitting in Lady Callas' bathroom. What, exactly, is supposed to have happened in the meantime?"

"Maybe the stress of being hunted got to her."

"Oh, she was having the time of her life during the investigation. Besides, why choose Lady Callas' bathroom, of all places? No, It's far more likely that she went to talk to whoever our killer is, and she said the wrong thing. She made the killer think she was onto them. The killer then took her to Lady Callas' bathroom and hung her."

"I mean... that does sound... more..."

"So, I need you to tell me *exactly* what she said last time you spoke with her. Who was she going to see? Because that person is the one who, in all likelihood, killed Lady Callas."

Betsan leaned towards me. "How do you know it wasn't me?"

"Well, obviously I don't, but I don't think you did. You don't fit the motive I believe to be behind the murder."

Betsan stepped back and shrugged. "Okay, well, Alison said she was going to go and check on something. She didn't say what, she didn't say she was going to talk to anyone."

"Did she say anything else?"

Betsan splayed her arms. "Not about the case! She asked if you were back yet and made sure I knew she'd found evidence that she wanted you to look at."

"I found the evidence at least. Well, thank you. Whilst I have you – I'm after background information on Praxi and Charles. Can you provide an unbiased view of those two?"

Betsan growled, thoughtfully.

"Do either of them hold a grudge against Lady Callas?" I asked.

Betsan made a face.

"What?" I asked.

"Well, it's hard to say. I know Charles didn't. He was a close friend to Lady Callas. Praxi, though..."

"What about Praxi?"

"Look, Lady Callas saved Praxi's life when she was quite young. When Praxi was still a child, her village got attacked. Lady Callas saved her from the attackers. Praxi's parents were dead and she didn't have anywhere else to go, so Lady Callas brought her back to live here with her and Victoria."

"That's exceptionally generous," I said.

"Lady Callas liked to offer people second chances," said Betsan.

I couldn't help it. I burst out laughing. Betsan looked as if I'd just farted. I fought to get myself back under control, but I couldn't manage it. "Sorry, Betsan," I said, as soon as I physically could. "Sorry, I know it's in terrible taste. It's just... you just... never mind. Look, Lady Callas gave Praxi a second chance. Why doesn't Praxi feel indebted to Lady Callas as a result?"

"Oh, she does. But even so, Praxi didn't know anyone over here. She's from Talvik, originally. Big old place to the south – heard of it? Magissa live in the open down there."

"Seriously?"

"Oh yeah. The magissa have only managed to stay hidden in Selen because of centuries of isolationism. Desert to the north, massive treacherous ocean to the south. Wall of chains blocking casual travel. It's helpful."

I ground the heels of my palms into my eyes. "Okay, look. We're wandering off topic. What about Praxi being from Talvik was a problem?"

"Mostly the language thing. She had to learn a whole other language when precious few other than Lady Callas and her fellow diplomats were able to teach her. Plus, Praxi's Hydros, so she couldn't socialise much outside the mansion. When she grew up, Lady Callas offered her an informal job as gardener. Praxi liked the garden."

"So?"

"So, I think Praxi *might* have ended up resenting Lady Callas. There's a fine line between offering someone a sanctuary and offering them a gilded cage. I know Praxi was grateful to Lady Callas for rescuing her but – well, you asked."

"This resentment–" I said, but Betsan jumped in.

"No, I don't think the resentment was a strong enough motive for murder."

"Fine. And how would you describe the relationship between Lady Callas and Praxi? Would they share confidences with each other?"

Betsan probed the interior of her left ear with the tip of a finger, thoughtfully. "Possibly."

"Charles, then?"

"Oh, they definitely shared confidences."

"Charles is Deimos yes? Can he tap into people's guilt in some way?"

"You'd have to ask him. He hasn't used his osto much in my presence."

"He's been reluctant to use it since the death of his protégé?"

"I think so," said Betsan, stretching. This drew my attention to something that should have been obvious.

"Your condition seems much improved, Betsan."

"Yeah, the poison's effects are essentially gone. I was able to check on everyone else when the astynomia gathered us all together. The others are recovering slower than I am, but they're making good progress."

"Good. That's good. Okay, how close were Lady Callas and Mr Das?"

Betsan sighed. "I don't want you to get the wrong idea about Lady Callas, but she didn't mingle with the staff much. Victoria hired Mr Das a few years ago. Lady Callas didn't show much of an interest in him until Victoria went on her first really long business trip of the year."

"Okay... What happened then?"

"Mr Das was summoned to Lady Callas' room after Victoria had been away for about a week."

"Couldn't it just have been to give Mr Das instructions about new housekeeping duties?"

Betsan shook her head. "Lady Callas wouldn't have invited Mr Das into her rooms for that. She'd have given instructions in the great hall, or come up to the cottage. Whatever happened in that room was something Lady Callas didn't want observed."

"Did something similar happen in the last few days?"

Betsan shook her head. "No. It's happened a few times since then, but not for six months or so."

Damn. Maybe it was nothing to do with the case after all.

"You think Charles killed Lady Callas?" she asked. Apparently, she'd given my earlier line of questioning some thought.

Charles was, in my opinion, the most likely suspect, but I'd not expected Betsan to be so quick on the uptake. "I still don't have enough hard evidence to say one way or the other, but it seems possible."

Betsan growled. I reached up to rest a hand on her shoulder. "Betsan. I'm light on actual evidence. I have an idea, and the facts of the case currently fit that idea, but there's probably only one person who actually knows. The astynomia are working hard, as am I. We'll find out who did this, don't worry. Two murders and one attempted. This won't stop until we stop it."

Betsan frowned at me. "Did something happen to you when you went to get help?"

"Sorry?"

"Did you not understand the question?"

"Er..."

"Never mind."

Praxi was still being interrogated when we returned Betsan to the library. Charles was still examining the same bookshelf he'd been staring at fifteen minutes ago. I didn't particularly want to question him, but if he'd been the one to attack Alison...

"Elin," I said, "could I borrow Mr Varma for just a moment? It's about a rather delicate matter."

Charles turned, a little too slowly and a little too smoothly for it to come across as natural. He looked to Elin, who shrugged. He looked at me. I smiled. He shifted – he *definitely* shifted his weight from one foot to the other. He smiled, nodded, and followed me out into the corridor.

I strode ten paces down the corridor, then turned to face Charles. I wanted to be far enough away from the library that we had the illusion of privacy, but close enough that I could shout for help if needed. "I wonder if I may ask you a question or two, Mr Varma?"

"I've spoken extensively with the astynomia..."

I smiled, and nodded. "Of course. The astynomia are pursuing their investigation, however our objectives are not exactly aligned. Do you know Paget Belacourt, Mr Varma?"

Charles' face greyed. "Ah, yes, of course. Paget. Have you known her long?"

I grinned. "Not very long at all, actually! The reason I bring her up is... well, she's Charites, as I'm sure you know, so when she heard about Lady Callas, we had a chat and, long story short, she's asked me if I could look into one or two things. Strictly... well, I won't say confidential, but... I'm acting in a less formal capacity than the astynomia."

Charles nodded. "Less formal, I see."

"Precisely. So, I was wondering if you might tell me a little about Tova Oster."

Charles looked as if I'd just applied scorching bio-fuel to the soles of his feet.

Chapter Fourteen

Charles had insisted on finding somewhere a little more private. I was wary of going anywhere particularly secluded with him but, after some haggling, we wound up in the mansion dining room with the door open.

"Why do you want to know about Tova Oster?" Charles asked, as soon as he was seated to his satisfaction.

On the one hand, I didn't want to have anything to do with this murderer than I had to. On the other hand, if Charles *hadn't* made the attempt on Alison's life, I would dearly like to know as soon as possible. There were games I could play here, potentially fatal games. There was also the truth, or different flavours of the truth. I'd caught myself up thinking about conversations as games of Sako before. Always trying to be three moves ahead. Right now, I couldn't be faffed with that.

"I want to know about Tova Oster, because there have been three crimes committed in this mansion over the last twelve hours. Someone murdered Lady Callas, someone murdered Teleri Parry, and someone tried to murder my friend Alison."

Charles' gaze focussed on me only when I mentioned my friend. He glanced at the door, then back to me. "Is she okay?"

I rested my hand on the hilt of Alison's xiphos. "This is the problem, Mr Varma. There are a very small number of people who might have attacked Alison, and you're one of them. So, I hope you'll understand if I don't freely give out information as to my friend's health."

Charles' gaze flicked to where my hand rested. If his hands moved... if it looked as if his right hand was going to dart to his left wrist, to the bracelet of bones he no-doubt wore there, I'd draw. I'd draw, and when he was distracted by the sword, I'd grab a wine glass and hurl it at his face.

Charles held himself terribly still. "We've all been through a lot over the past day," he said. His voice had lost some of the superciliousness I was used to. "It's understandable that you would be upset by someone making a move on your friend's life. Please be assured that I had nothing to do with it."

My palm was making the brass pommel at the base of Alison's sword slick with sweat. "Nothing to do with it?"

Charles shook his head. "Nothing at all."

I nodded. "Good. That's good. So, Tova..."

"Tova, yes... I don't think you actually... Look here, what do *you* know about Tova?"

This man might have overpowered Alison. I held up a forestalling finger, stood and unbuckled Alison's sword belt. I unsheathed Alison's sword, slowly and with as little hauteur as possible. I placed it on the table, in the space where my chair's place setting should have been, then discarded the belt and sat back down.

Charles's gaze was locked on the sword. His bracelet of teeth sat at his wrist, untouched. I dried my hands, and then drew out my notebook and pen. They were light. Easy to drop. The sword was only centimetres away. I was as safe as I could be. Time for a gamble.

"Mr Varma," I said, my voice sounding distant. "I should say first... I should make it very clear that I'm not particularly concerned about the circumstances of Teleri Parry's death."

Charles held himself still. "I don't understand what you mean, Ms Fletcher."

I sighed. "I mean, I am not concerned that you, Charles, infused your osto into the floorboards under Teleri's bed. I am not concerned that your infusion was designed to activate when Teleri woke, forcing her to relive her guiltiest moments. Or perhaps one guilty moment in particular. I am not concerned that this osto caused her to take steps to end the guilt you forced into her head. I am currently only concerned with the murder of my patron, and the attempted murder of my friend. Do I make myself clear?"

I turned a page in my notebook, the paper rasping away the silence which fell between us. The sword still lay on the table, undisturbed, its tip diamond sharp, its edges gleaming.

Charles sat very still, his gaze on the sword. "You understand I couldn't possibly comment on such... such..."

I waved my pen, airily. "Baseless speculation, undisputable truth. But you see, Mr Varma, that baseless speculation is why I want to know about Tova. You forced Teleri to take her own life because you were convinced she murdered Tova. As far as I can tell, there's nothing which links Teleri's death to that of Lady Callas. Let's leave aside Teleri's death entirely. It's not important. I merely wish to know a little about Tova.

"Help me, Mr Varma. Currently there are too many schemes in this house. If I understand what happened to Tova Oster, I hope that I will be able to separate the facts of Teleri's death from Lady Callas'."

If Charles was going to attack me, he was going to do it in the next few seconds. Only Lady Callas' murderer would know that Teleri's knife had been left in Lady Callas' bathroom. If Charles had murdered Teleri and *only* Teleri, he wouldn't know about her knife. He might not know about the Flower of Tartarus in her pack. But, if he was responsible for everything terrible which had happened over the past twelve hours...

A sheen of sweat glistened on Charles' brow. His evening suit was crumpled and stained. He'd clearly made an effort to pull himself together, appear the ever-dignified, unflappable gentleman. His eyes were cold. His expression was void. At any moment, he may decide that enough was enough.

I felt disconnected from the danger, which was disturbing, yet useful. What I felt dreadfully, painfully connected to, was my half-lie about being unconcerned about Teleri's death. There's an old saying, 'Whoever fights monsters should see to it that in the process she does not become a monster.'

Blaming my callousness on the house, on the magissa would be easy. I reached down and stroked CW's back. I'd been living lies for too long. I wanted Alison to get better. I wanted to get out of here, go home, hug my dads. Find out what my life was going to be from now on. I didn't want to become a monster.

Charles looked as if he might be about to talk. I held up a hand. "My apologies, Mr Varma." I dropped my notebook and pen next to my sword, then ran my hands over my face and back through my hair. "As you said, it's been a long day. Tova is none of my business. I grew overly focussed on... and Teleri was... there's this numbness..."

"Tova..." said Charles. His voice strained. "Tova was my protégé. My first. The only protégé I've taken."

I sat back in my chair, letting the silence stretch.

Charles sagged. "She was, in many ways, unremarkable. She enjoyed art and drama before she was discovered. One of our doctors found her, in the way they find many of us. She was Deimos – do you know of our curse?"

I closed my eyes, trying to remember what I'd read in Paget's handbook. "Deimos waste away if they don't use their osto?"

Charles nodded. "That's right. Only below the neck. Our faces remain much as they always had been whilst, below the shoulders, we turn increasingly skeletal. Our ribs begin to show, our stomachs turn concave. Our bones become brittle, and break. Eventually, every Deimos has one fundamental choice to make: use our powers, or suffer a fate akin to starving to death."

I let out a breath – it hissed between my teeth. "That makes Charites clawed feet seem like a trifle."

Charles nodded. "Thank you for saying so. I agree. Tova Oster, a happy fourteen-year-old girl, didn't want to use her powers. She wanted to stay in her school. Live her life. She had no interest in the magissa or our world of witches and monsters, especially if it meant she had to choose between wasting away and inflicting terror on people."

"Fourteen?" I said. "I thought magissa were initiated at eighteen."

"Initiated yes, but not everyone is found as late as you were, Ms Fletcher. Your friend Alison would have been born magissa. She will have had multiple mentors throughout her life."

"Lucky her."

Charles frowned, possibly wondering if I was stooping to sarcasm. "I was young back then, and Tova came to me after a difficult relationship with her first mentor."

"When you say 'relationship'," I said.

Charles smiled at my insinuation, "Nothing inappropriate. Mentor and protégé. We take such things extremely seriously, Ms Fletcher. Anyway, Tova was assigned to me when she was seventeen and I was approaching forty."

I grimaced. "That doesn't pass the vibe check."

Charles slapped his hand on the table, making the glasses jump. "Exactly, Ms Fletcher! Exactly! I was the youngest Deimos available. Imagine being a young... well. I don't have to, do I?.

"Tova was furious at being required to leave school and abandon her friends in order to maintain strict secrecy. I was mentor to her, yes, but I was also her only remaining companion. We discussed art. We read and enjoyed the same ridiculous books series. I wish that had been enough, but depression slowly sunk its claws into her."

I nodded. "Makes sense. I've certainly had my ups and downs since this whole... thing started."

Charles sighed. "Yes, well... usually, when a magissa abandons their human life, they find a strong community of new friends to help them adjust. They have an exciting world to discover, and a new clan to take care of them. Some take longer than others to adjust to their new life, but few reject it outright. I was dreadfully worried about Tova's future, which is why I was overjoyed when she agreed to start using her powers."

I drummed my fingers on the table. "Too little, too late?"

Charles nodded. "Something like that. Tova's osto caused her victims to suffer panic attacks. She initially used her power on those who could use a little fear in their lives."

"Vigilante justice?"

"Exactly. Industrialists, press barons, and politicians. The sort of targets who are insulated from the consequences of their actions through wealth."

"That's one way to make the best of a bad situation."

He smiled, although his gaze remained vacant. "I wish it had been enough. She couldn't keep up her crusade for long. The guilt grew within her, until she had to insulate herself from her actions. She'd walk into crowded streets and just brush past people, causing panic with every touch. She never looked at who she was touching, she simply used her power and moved forward, then repeated the process until her hunger was gone, and she could stop again for a few months."

"How do you deal with this problem, Mr Varma?"

"Needing to use my powers or starve?"

"That's right."

"I try to follow Tova's example, and only give guilt to the deserving."

"You're still torturing people who haven't hurt you."

Charles nodded. "Yes. Yes, I am. That's a nice coat, Ms Fletcher. Did you buy it?"

"It was a present."

"Ah. Good. Do you know where it came from?"

I shook my head.

"We've left the evils of slavery behind, Ms Fletcher. We're a modern civilisation. However, if you were to trace the cotton your coat was made from, or the dyes used, or the metals required for your buttons..."

I waved this aside, "Yes, yes, but I don't have a choice – I need clothing to survive."

Charles splayed his hands, "And if I don't use my powers, I starve to death. You only see that as morally objectionable because I'm active in the process. The suffering you cause others through merely surviving is at a distance."

I held up a finger. "Maybe don't get too high up on that horse, before I remind you of what you did to Teleri Parry."

Charles winced. "First, of course I have no idea what you're talking about, I didn't do anything to Teleri Parry. Second – fair point. However, I'm still right. If I am to be condemned because people suffer as a result of my existence, then I have extremely bad news about literally everyone in our nation."

I groaned and sat back in my chair. "We've become waylaid by politics, Mr Varma."

"Just so. Well, Tova put on a brave face, even as she spiralled into depression. I thought she was improving at the time. Had she still been in school, someone might have recognised the signs of her failing health. Had she been in contact with more friends, she might have felt that she had more to live for. Had I been more experienced, I might have realised something was wrong in her life."

I nodded, "I think I can see where the story ends. She grew more and more desperate. She wanted the pain to stop. Anything would be better than living the way she was living."

"It's deeply sad that one so young can run ahead of this particular conversation."

I didn't know what to say to that.

Charles smiled, sadly. "Anyway. I only pieced all this together after the fact, but Tova was a question looking for an answer. The answer she found was the Pitt Club."

"Teleri Parry?"

"A brawler with an ego who wouldn't back down when provoked. She set Tova free."

I had the past and I had the present. Where were the links which could join them? Betsan had mentioned being furious at Callas because both she and Teleri were members of the Pitt Club, but Callas had only condemned one of them... "Lady Callas insisted that Teleri should be hired for the initiation."

Charles nodded. "Someone must have had a word with her. Asked her to hire one particular caterer, as a favour."

"I see."

"Tova's death was useful, in a way." Charles said, staring at some distant thing only he could see. "The Senate used her death as a lesson. Sought out mental health problems waiting to manifest before they caused a crisis. Relaxed what rules they could, regarding maintaining contact with humans. They tried to make sure that what happened to Tova would never, ever happen again. Still... too little, too late."

Charles sat, lost in a past hell. I'd expected tears, but he seemed resolute. Resolute about what, though? Was he going to try and kill me when the conversation wrapped up, now his confession was essentially complete or... had a certain someone talked with Lady Callas about revealing the magissa to humanity? Was I in a room with the architect of Lady Callas' plan?

I stood, and nodded to the radical Deimos. "Thank you, Mr Varma. You've been most helpful."

"Find out who killed Marie, Ms Fletcher," said Charles. "Find them. Please."

"I will." I slipped Alison's xiphos back into its sheathe, buckled her sword belt on and strode from the room. Charles remained behind. Every second that passed, I expected him to rise, chase after me, and jam a blade into my spine. He defied my expectations.

I bumped into Callan on the way back – Praxi was with her. It was the first time I'd seen Praxi awake. She looked as if she'd been through hell. A hell I was about to add to. "Ah, Callan," I said. "I wonder if I could have a word with Praxi? I have some questions." Praxi shook her head and kept walking. "Praxi?" I said.

Praxi walked into the library and shut the door behind her.

"Rude," I said.

"I gather she doesn't talk much at the best of times," said Callan. "And I probably didn't help. You can try and persuade her to talk to you, but I wouldn't hold out much hope."

"Great," I pinched the bridge of my nose. "I don't know how actual detectives do this. Oh, I should say – Charles is in the dining room. I left him there in case he tried to kill me on the way out. If you want to keep the suspects together you might want to go get him."

Callan nodded, and strode off. Moments later, she returned, Charles in tow. "So," she said, as Charles disappeared into the library. "How's your investigation going?"

"Frustratingly," I said. "Yours?"

"Same. We can't keep everyone together like this much longer. I was going to get my people together and discuss next steps. Can you attend our little get together?"

I shrugged, helplessly. "Sure, but I need to go and check on Alison. Can we do our meeting up there?"

"I don't see why not. See you in ten."

Nine minutes later, the servant's sitting room up in the cottage was full to bursting with five magissa, a human, and a small fluffy dog.

"Thank you, everyone, for your work so far," said Callan. She looked as if she wanted to strangle someone but was putting a brave face on it. "Dawn, Heledd, Elin, any updates?"

"I found a xiphos and some jewellery in the steam tunnels," said Dawn. "Figured it might be important." She reached into her pack and pulled out a familiar sword.

"Oh hey," I said. "That's mine."

Dawn scowled at me. "What was it doing in the steam tunnels?"

"I lost it fighting the murderer. I must have mentioned that."

Dawn handed it over, sullenly. "Well, the jewels are a good find anyway, right?"

"Yes," said Callan, at the same time I did.

Callan turned to me. "You agree, wolf?"

I slid my xiphos into its sheathe on the third try. "Yeah. Valuable looking things, are they?"

Dawn shrugged. "They glitter. Beyond that, I don't know diamond from those synthetic aug-glass stones the jewellers have." She fished out a pouch from her bag and opened it, revealing five items, the value of which I shuddered to think about.

"Right," I said. "Good. That's good."

"It can't be that good," said Heledd.

"No, it is," I said, "it means the murder must have been hastily improvised."

Dawn glowered at me. "I don't believe this."

"Ah," said Callan. "I see what you mean. These must be the jewels which were missing from Lady Callas' bedroom. So, the fact that they were dumped in the steam tunnel rather than somewhere outside the house means the murderer had no time to prepare. Is that what you're thinking, Susan?"

I preened, slightly. "More or less. The murderer must have been hoping they'd be able to dump the jewels somewhere once the lockdown was lifted. They didn't anticipate anyone getting into the house before that."

Callan nodded. "Right. So, the murder was hasty. Maybe not a crime of passion, spur of the moment sort of thing, but likely the work of only a few hours. That means the murderer will have made mistakes. They'll be stressed, scared, and praying to make it out of here undiscovered. The good news is, we have a stratagem for just this sort of occasion."

"Oh, no..." Dawn said, lolling her head back.

"I'm not being the detective this time," said Heledd.

Elin chuckled. "*Failure is progress*
Moving past our dead past selves

We release you, love."

"Does Elin always do that?" I asked Callan.

"He's a very useful astynomia in many other ways," said Callan. "Anyway, Susan, how would you feel about a little deception?"

Chapter Fifteen

"No," I said, jumping to my feet, "absolutely not."

"What?" Dawn said, giving me a contemptuous look. "It's fine. We do it all the time."

I had to close my eyes and take a breath. "That's worse. You realise that makes it worse?"

Callan held up a hand, "Sorry, Susan, it's my fault. I shouldn't have let Dawn explain the deception. Look, all we propose to do is get all the suspects together, set out the facts of the case, and then we accuse the person we think is responsible for the murders. If they're the murderer, there's good odds that they'll confess, helpfully skipping over our relative lack of evidence."

I held my head in my hands. "You do this a lot?"

"No, no, no. Every once in a while."

"And this has led to innocent people confessing to a crime they didn't commit... how many times, exactly?" The astynomia exchanged looks. I threw up my hands. "Never mind! Look, even if that strategy didn't have serious problems, we can't use it here, we just don't have enough information."

"*The fire burns bright*
Consuming plans, whilst never
Birthing plans herself," said Elin.

I glared at him. "Are you saying 'You come up with an idea, then?'"

Elin scratched his cheek, his eyes wide, a faint smile ghosted on his face.

Callan cleared her throat. "I think that's what he's saying, yes."

I collapsed back onto the sofa. Alison still lay on the sofa opposite. Still breathing. Still asleep. Still unrousable. We needed to get her to an actual doctor. The astynomia were right about one thing: We'd run out of time.

"I don't have a plan," I said. "Can I just... explain why we can't do your bonkers idea?"

Callan smiled, magnanimously. "Please, wolf. Tell us."

I closed my eyes again, trying to slot everything into place in my head. "Okay. Let me just check on something." I flicked through my employee handbook, looking for a section on dealing with classified information. I found what I needed in a yellow box-out on page twenty-nine. The short version was 'agents should use their discretion'. Very well, I'd use my discretion.

"There's an element to this case which you might not be aware of. Lady Marie Callas had a plan to expose the magissa to humanity."

Dawn growled, Elin gasped and Callan flinched. Heledd didn't seem particularly surprised.

"This is a problem," I said, trying to maintain momentum, "because it's a motive which all of our suspects share, and none of them share at the same time. If any of them were aware of the plan, that would give them a motive which trumps all others, but it's exceptionally hard to know if they were aware of the plan. You follow?"

"That tracks with our findings," said Callan. "We followed up on several of the leads you gave us, wolf. Betsan's grudge against Lady Callas does seem particularly weak, but if Betsan had found out about this plan..."

I nodded. "Exactly. That's reason number one why we can't accuse someone and hope for a confession. Unless someone wrote in a diary somewhere that they knew about the plan, or low-key confessed – which I'll get to – we just can't know."

"Right," said Callan. "but this is all too fragmented already. What are the facts of the case?"

"Someone poisoned the meals of everyone in the house with the Flower of Tartarus." I said.

"Oh," said Heledd, "I spent some time with Betsan, speaking of life and the difficulties found therein. The long nights, the longer days, the nights after the longer days which are even longer still... but I did ask about the meals the household ate as well. Betsan said they have a cook who comes from the village nearby. She prepares meals for the household in the cottage kitchen. Anyone would have had access to the meal whilst it was being prepped."

"So it's likely the Flower of Tartarus was added to the meal at its source, rather than plate by plate," I said. "We should talk to the cook when we have more time. So, Person X poisons the food. They pretend to eat the meal with the others. They wait for everyone to fall ill. Then, they go to Lady Callas' room and murder her."

"By drowning her in the bathtub," said Callan.

I exhaled through my teeth. "Maybe."

"You found her in the bathtub, kid," said Dawn. "She was still there when we got here. We took her out. Wolves have no respect for the dead."

"Mm," I said. "But the thing is, just because we found her in the bathtub, that doesn't mean someone drowned her in there. Praxi is Hydros. Does anyone know what her osto is?"

Four blank looks. Three of the astynomia shrugged, whilst Callan appeared thoughtful. "You're saying Praxi could have used her osto to murder Lady Callas, and then disguised her involvement by placing her body in the bathtub."

"Yes, exactly. That's problem number two – we don't even know *where* the murder was committed. Sorry, I'm getting distracted again. Back to the sequence of events. Person X has just murdered Lady Callas.

"They take some jewels from her dresser and... maybe they try to dump them out of a window, but find that Betsan has already locked the house down. They make the best of a bad job and dump the jewels in the steam tunnels instead. Did any of you examine Lady Callas' body?"

Dawn nodded. "There was a cut on her throat."

"Deep?" I asked.

"Non-fatal," said Dawn.

"Right. Alison found a knife in Lady Callas' bathroom. So, maybe she was killed in the bathtub – Person X held the knife to her throat as they held her under the water. Or, maybe Person X drowned her some other way and left the knife to implicate Teleri Parry."

Dawn groaned, and paced around the sitting room, which was already rather cramped without a restless Silenus stomping about the place. CW was sitting on my lap because everywhere else he'd tried to fall asleep had resulted in him nearly getting sat on by an astynomia.

"Whilst all this was going on," I said, "Charles Varma was enacting a plan against Teleri Parry. He all-but confessed to me earlier. He blamed Teleri for his protégé's death, and infused his osto into the floor under Teleri's bed so, when she woke, she was hit by amped up guilt about Tova, which led to her taking her own life.

"The real question is – did Charles blackmail Teleri into murdering Lady Callas, and then murder Teleri? Or were the vials of the Flower of Tartarus planted in Teleri's pack by Person X, who also planted her knife at the scene of the crime."

Callan held up a finger, dropped it, and then held it up again. "If there was blackmail," she said, "it was likely to be remote. Teleri was extremely imposing, whilst Charles isn't. I doubt he'd have tried to blackmail her to her face."

This flicked on a light in my head. "Right! Alison found a note in Teleri's pack. 'I know what you did'."

Callan frowned. "Nothing else?"

Dawn sniffed. "Short note. Too short for blackmail."

Callan smiled, "So, Charles *didn't* blackmail Teleri."

I shook my head. "Hold on. 'I know what you did' might have been supposed to spark guilt in Teleri's brain, which could then be focussed by Charles' osto. Remember, if Charles is Person X, then he was running two schemes simultaneously. Just because we've found one note, that doesn't mean that one note was all there was to find."

Dawn turned to the nearest wall and started bashing her head against it.

"I'm sorry!" I said. "But this just proves my point! We don't have enough information. Merely speaking from my investigation, I've had a decent chat with Betsan and Charles, but I've only got one word out of Mr Das, and I didn't even get that out of Praxi.

"Put it this way. Working through the suspects: Mr Das. There's something going on with him and pouches of teeth being passed to him by the Callas family. Maybe blackmail, I don't know. Seems thin. He's also pretty slender, not the sort of person I can see overpowering Marie Callas, or hauling her body to the bathroom.

"Betsan – definitely has the strength, but we lack a convincing motive. If she found out about Lady Callas' plan, she'd probably just rip her throat out rather than come up with an elaborate poisoning scheme. Charles seems like he'd be philosophically aligned with Lady Callas about exposing the magissa to humanity, so had an anti-motive there. He almost certainly killed Teleri, however.

"Finally, Praxi. Maybe Praxi resented Lady Callas, maybe she didn't. She's Hydros so has the most to lose from the magissa being exposed to humanity. She has water powers. That's two flags, but we have nothing concrete to go on."

"Someone attacked Alison," said Callan. "It'd have to be someone who could overcome Hydros in the prime of her youth. Alison was armed, and actively expecting trouble. Someone must have taken her by surprise. Mr Das could have done that, or Praxi."

My gaze slipped back to Alison, a weight dragged at my chest. "Right. So, supposition is pointing us to Praxi. Did she say anything to you which would rule her out, Callan?"

Callan shook her head. "Single word answers, only. Didn't want to talk to me at all."

"Nor me," I said. "So, that's why we can't just make a show of accusing Praxi. All anyone has to do is ask what actual evidence we have to suspect her, and we'd be stumped. 'It makes sense when you think about it' isn't the best reason to accuse someone of murder.

Light glinted in Elin's eyes. "*A flower of night,*
Poison from murder's mother
The source is the key."

Callan thumped the arm of her sofa, "Of course! The Flower of Tartarus. It's not easy to get hold of, and we've established that Lady Callas' murder wasn't planned. All we need to do is find out who acquired the flower!"

I grinned. "Great. How do we do that?"

Heledd slumped in her chair. "We'd have to talk to the spy-mistresses. Paget and the others. They might know. Otherwise we'd need to interrogate back-alley alchemists, merchants and importers. We might get an answer right away or we could spend six months searching."

Alison's chest lay terribly still. I watched, waiting for a breath. Finally, she drew in air, her chest only rising slightly.

"We're running out of time," I said. "Alison needs a doctor, and the longer we leave the suspects, the more obvious it is that we've got nothing."

"We can't just let them go," said Callan. "This is why we proposed the accusing gambit."

I sighed. "Right. I see why you'd be tempted, but I really don't think it's right for this situation. It would require us to set out the facts of the case as we saw them, and that would essentially tell the murderer we were guessing, unless we got lucky. It's too specific. What about..."

I scratched CW behind the ears, his silken soft fur helped me think. "Okay, how's this for an idea. It's similar to your gambit but it's more general. It focusses the suspects on what's already eating away at them. Assuming our murderer feels any guilt at all, it might just work..."

Twenty minutes later, Callan, Elin and I had finished setting up in the cottage's dining room, whilst Heledd and Dawn had left to get the suspects.

"Who do we see first?" I asked. "Praxi? Or Charles? They're the most likely suspects from my point of view."

"*Shadows live and die*," said Elin, gathering up spilled food from under the table,

"*Never may a shadow lie*

Shadows purify."

Callan and I exchanged a glance.

"Mr Das?" I said.

"Obviously," said Elin.

"Do you want to take Mr Das, Wolf?" Callan asked.

I paused in the act of moving crockery to a sideboard. "Er... yes, I think so. I think he's likely to be wrong-footed if it's me. He might just clam up if you do it. Not that he'll have much of a choice. Speaking of, we need pen and paper."

"*Like the wings of spring,*" said Elin, on his way out of the door.

"I hope he's gone to get paper and he's not hibernating or something," said Callan.

"I'm guessing you wouldn't recommend the astynomia as a career choice?" I said, trying to suppress a smile.

"Are you asking to swap jobs, wolf? Because yes, I'd dearly like to swap."

"Thanks, but I'm not actually sure what my job is, yet."

"No-one ever says yes," said Callan, giving the dining table a spiteful polish.

We stacked all but two of the chairs against a wall, and then hauled the dining table into the middle of the room. We placed the remaining chairs on opposite sides of the table – one between the table and the wall, one between the table and the door. I sat in the chair which faced the door, and waited.

Elin returned, with Mr Das in tow. He led Mr Das to the empty chair and placed paper and a pen on the table in front of him, before strolling around to join Callan, who was propping up the wall behind me.

"Mr Das," I said. "We know it was you."

His eyes widened. He drew in a breath. His hands wrung together in his lap. I reached forwards and pushed the pen and paper towards him. He snatched them up. His hands shook as he wrote two sentences. Once he was done, I took the paper from him, doing my best to maintain an expression of stern authority.

Mr Das had written: 'It was all my idea. Please don't punish Mrs Callas.'

Presumably Victoria Callas. I nodded, gravely, and passed the paper back to Callan. "Tell us, in your own words, Mr Das. Obviously, we don't want to involve Mrs Callas in this, but…"

Mr Das had been rolling the fountain pen between his fingers, until I trailed off. He looked up at me, and nodded. He set to writing.

Ten minutes later, he handed over two pages of densely packed prose. I read them over, nodded, and handed them to Callan. "Thank you, Mr Das," I said. "That will be all."

He stood, nodded, and slipped from the room, looking a little baffled.

"Right," said Callan. "So… Mr Das has a human brother… and he's deathly ill. The Callas' were paying their housekeeper at least partly in teeth so he could hire Apollo to minister to his brother."

I sat back in my chair. "Is white-market witchcraft a thing?"

"This wouldn't exactly be white-market," said Callan. "Disapproved of, certainly, but not illegal. Grey-market at worst."

"Right," I said. "Good. All right. Who's next?"

"Betsan," said Callan.

I stood, "You'd better deal with her then, she knows I don't really know what I'm doing."

"If you don't know what you're doing, then why are we going with your plan?" asked Callan, sitting.

I tapped Mr Das' confession, then went to stand by Elin. CW pawed at my leg and wouldn't stop until I picked him up. He fell asleep in the crook of my arm.

Dawn led Betsan in. She sat, the chair creaking under her weight.

Callan steepled her fingers. "Betsan. We know it was you."

Betsan's gaze darted from Callan, to me, to Elin. Was that a hint of a snarl at the corner of her mouth? Had she tensed up? "Hm," she said. She stared at Callan. Callan stared back. I waited... but she didn't crack.

Eventually, Callan gave up. "Thank you for your time, Betsan."

"Ah, a bluff," said Betsan. "Thought so."

She stood to go. Dawn was waiting on the other side of the door.

"No-where near the others, please, Dawn," called Callan, before turning to me and raising an eyebrow.

I held up my hands. "Fifty-fifty result so far. Better than we'd have done with your get everyone together plan. You can only do that once."

Callan shrugged. "Let's take Charles next then, you sure you don't want to take him?"

I shook my head. "Last time we chatted, I presented myself as a cold heartless bastard who didn't care that he murdered Teleri. If I'm stood in the corner looking all stony, he'll think I told you all sorts of stuff, but he won't know what *you* know. Better coming from you."

"Charles," said Callan, once Deimos was seated at the table. "We know it was you."

Charles glanced at me. I nodded. He sighed, and sat back in his chair. "Ah, it's like that is it? Well, this was always a possibility."

"We're not just talking about Teleri Parry," said Callan, a rasp of anger in her voice.

Charles froze, his self-assurance fled. "Oh. Well, look... I... There's a very good... If you think about it, really it's in everyone's best interests that—" He shut his mouth in one quick, tight motion. He drew himself up. "As I was saying. I have no idea what you're talking about. Unless, of course, you'd like to discuss something specific?"

My mind raced. Pieces fell into place. I placed Constable Woofington carefully on the floor, where he snuffled and rolled over.

Callan nodded. "I think you know what we're talking about."

Charles nodded, smiling to himself. "Oh, I do, I absolutely do. If you could just remind me? You wouldn't be trying to bluff me, would you?"

Callan sighed. "Thank you, Charles—"

"No!" I bellowed. Ripping the bracelet of teeth from my wrist, I stalked to the table. "Charles, you murdered my patron. I know you did. Well, these fools may be willing to let you leave, but I won't. I'm going to summon every spider, beetle and snake in the Obsidian Coast, and they're going to tear you to *shreds*."

I plucked the remaining four teeth from my bracelet and slammed them into my mouth. I clambered onto the table and cackled for a moment, before looking down at Charles. His expression was *perfect*. Halfway between self-consciously neutral and amused at a joke only he knew the punch-line to.

I jumped down from the table and faced Callan. "See? Absolutely no reaction to Charites summoning a whole load of animals to gank him. He knows my threat didn't have any weight behind it. He knows I'm human. He and Callas must have planned the whole 'expose the magissa' thing together."

Charles scoffed. "I've never heard of anything so ridiculous."

I waved a hand at him. "Give it up, Charles, you've already confessed."

Charles flinched. "Sorry?"

"You didn't react when I said I was human, only when I mentioned your plot with Callas. A magissa would be shocked to learn a human was wriggling around in one of their sanctuaries... unless, of course, you already knew one was coming."

"Do you have anything to say, Mr Varma?" said Callan.

"I'd like a lawyer, please," said Charles.

"Absolutely," said Callan. "Dawn!"

Dawn opened the door. Callan asked her to secure Charles, and I was privileged to see the murderer of Teleri Parry, and the man who had indirectly led to Marie Callas' death, along with the assault on Alison, being led away by the astynomia.

"Well," said Callan, once Charles was safely secured. "We might have found a replacement for our 'get everyone together and bluff' gambit."

I shrugged. "It helped that he'd come damned close to telling me anyway. I didn't think he'd murdered Lady Callas – he asked me to find the killer. Pretty sure he meant it too."

Callan patted me on the shoulder. "Either way, that's the plot to expose us dealt with."

I frowned. "Mm. Maybe. You're going to want to see if you can account for Charles' movements over the last few... I don't know. Days, weeks... maybe even months? We don't know if this was the only part of his plan."

"That sounds paranoid," said Callan. I opened my mouth to object, but she steamed on regardless, "but it definitely makes sense to check."

"That's fair," I said. I cracked my neck. "This whole nightmare has really thrown my..." I found I'd raised my hands – my fingers pointing at invisible dancing stars, "My whole... my sense of what's likely and unlikely. Right, one more to go. Let's get it done so we can get Alison to a damned doctor."

"Right," said Callan. "Let's get Praxi in here."

Alison's mentor looked as if she'd not slept for a week. She shuffled to the chair and sat, her gaze looking everywhere but at the chair I sat in.

"Praxi," I said. "We know it was you."

She leapt to her feet and kicked the table. It slammed into my chest, knocking me to the floor.

Chapter Sixteen

"Astynomia!" cried Callan as the chair fell on top of me.

I rolled – a rippling spear cracked through the chair. The door burst open – running feet. I crawled under the table. Legs danced incomprehensibly. Alison. I had to get to Alison. If Praxi was the one who'd attacked her...

Dawn roared, and one set of legs morphed, swelling in size. Fur engulfed them. Heledd wailed. An icy wind crashed into the table, knocking me to the ground at the same time as it picked up the table and hurled it against the wall. Glass shattered.

I picked myself up, saw a gap between the tangle of fighting magissa, and made a break for the door. CW barked and skittered past me. I reached the doorway. Passed through. More glass shattered. Another blast of icy wind sent me stumbling. CW dodged around me, then jumped – he threw himself at me, hitting me in the side. I staggered, and a shimmering spear hurtled through the air where I'd been only a moment before, biting deep into a wall.

I ran to the sounds of bestial wails and icy gales. The stairs were steep. I took them three at a time. We'd stashed Alison in the servants' kitchen. She lay on the table, unharmed. I dashed into the room, waited for the constable to follow, then slammed the door shut and shoved a chair under the handle. I drew my xiphos and held it in a duelling stance. Then, I thought better of it. I grabbed Alison's sword as well. I gave the blades an experimental twirl as I checked the windows.

An almighty crash echoed from upstairs. An athletic blur landed on the lawn, then dodged out of sight. A furry maelstrom followed – claws, teeth and ochre fur. Dawn in her war form. She picked herself up, and glanced around her.

"Hey!" I yelled. Dawn's head snapped around. I pointed after the fleeing figure with my xiphos. "That way!"

Dawn howled, and thundered off in pursuit.

Stepping away from the windows, I let myself relax a little. I couldn't put the swords down just yet, although they were mostly for my benefit rather than Alison's. I could barely fight with one of the things, let alone two, and Praxi knew that perfectly well, assuming it had been her I'd fought in the steam tunnels. Still, I felt more capable of defending Alison with both blades at the ready.

I paced the kitchen, listening for tell-tale sounds of movement behind the walls. There weren't steam tunnels in the cottage, but I wouldn't have put it past this nightmare house to have doubly-secret secret passages up here as well.

Ten minutes past, then twenty. The door handle rattled after forty minutes. "Speak 'friend' and enter!" I shouted, trying to sound intimidating. I mostly sounded exhausted.

"It's me," said Callan. "Praxi's fled. Dawn's in pursuit. Heledd's taking Charles to Selen. He's going to be handed over to our criminal justice people there, but they left the coach for us. Elin's going to take you home, and Alison to a doctor. You okay to come out?"

I nudged the chair away from the door with my foot, and hefted my swords. "Come in!"

Callan opened the door, with Betsan standing behind her. Betsan nodded, whilst Callan grinned at me. "Good job. I can take Alison if you want to carry on guarding her?"

Had they come to take care of me? The final loose end? "Er..." I slumped. I gave in. I had to trust someone. "Yes, please. It's been a long day."

Callan and Betsan picked Alison up, more gently than I'd have given them credit for. I strode with them to the coach, CW watching my back. They loaded Alison into the coach we'd used to travel here from Selen. We waited for CW to have a bit of a sniff about, and a pee. Then, finally, Alison and I were on our way back to Selen.

The coach rocked. I closed my eyes. "What's the time?"

"Coming up to seventeenth hour," said Elin. *"And whilst the sun sets*

Duty still travels with us
Our burden and friend."

I groaned, forced my eyes open, and stared at the scenery. Crashing waves, throwing surf onto dark rocks, tinged crimson by the setting sun. Scrubland, then farmland, then Selen.

The coach stopped outside a grey two-story house in Holly, Selen's only boring district. Elin jumped out of the coach, and knocked on the grey house's off-white front door. The door opened, revealing a tall woman in smoke-coloured overalls. She exchanged a few words with Elin, before disappearing inside, and emerging again carrying a stretcher.

"You're a doctor?" I asked, as they approached. The grey woman nodded.

The three of us loaded Alison onto the stretcher, before Elin and the doctor carried her inside.

"Take good care of her," I called.

Ten minutes later, the coach was rattling through Selen's streets once again, this time to the Dewan residence. I'd wanted to go home, but couldn't have left without letting Alison's mum know what had happened.

The coach parked up outside the mansion, and I was just trying to wake CW up, when someone knocked on the coach door.

I jumped. "yes?"

"It's your employer," said Paget.

"Ah. Come in!"

Paget looked frazzled, but stepped up into the coach with little fanfare. She settled down opposite me. "Well. I think we're going to be quite busy for the next few weeks. Why don't you tell me what's happened since we last saw each other?"

I filled her in, trying to be thorough, but also lacking the energy for actual conversation. Twice, Paget interrupted to ask a question, and twice I snapped at her for interrupting. She seemed to understand.

"Good work today," she said, once I'd caught her up. "Don't worry about Octavia, I'll tell her about Alison. I wouldn't want her to find out about your humanity, and the news regarding her daughter at the same time. She might become... irked. You said Alison was at the grey house?"

"Yeah."

"Right. I've a friend who works there. She'll keep me informed. Anything to add, Constable Woofington?"

My minder barked. Paget smiled.

"What did he say?" I asked.

"He said you were an S-tier bitch," said Paget. "It's a compliment from a dog."

I didn't know what to say to that.

We'd past evening rush hour by the time Paget left the coach, so the streets were relatively clear for my journey home. The city felt different to me now that I knew what lurked in some of its shadowy corners.

My house looked ridiculous compared to the mansions I'd spent most of the day in, but I wouldn't trade. Not unless someone else was going to take care of cleaning the damn thing. I let myself in, and CW set to excitingly sniffing about his new home.

The grandmother clock in the hall told me it was nineteen-half. I'd been gone for just over thirteen hours. It felt like a lot longer. I stumbled through to the living room. Papa met me in the doorway, and I enveloped him in my arms. Dad was there too. Hovering, as he does. After I let Papa go, he nipped in to hug me as well.

Constable Woofington approached and tried to join in with the hugging, yipping happily and hopping on his back legs. Papa yelped in surprise.

"Please," I said, "don't ask. I promise I'll explain tomorrow. Very long day."

Dad looked from me to the Constable and back to me again.

"Okay," he said.

Dad fussed about me whilst Papa found two bowls for the Constable. He filled one with water, and the other with leftover pork which was only slightly off. CW didn't appear to mind.

For my part, the dads filled me with fish cakes and the remains of the dried dates we'd been saving. Dad even offered me a beer. Papa scowled at him, but I turned it down anyway – now was not the time.

"My assignment," I said, staring at the table, "had some issues. Some danger. Investigation. I was offered a job because of my actions, and Constable Woofington is part of that. He used to live with my employer. He's sticking with me for the foreseeable future."

"You know," said Dad, "when you're deliberately vague like that, it just makes me more curious."

That, thankfully, broke through the fog of fatigue which was smothering me. I laughed, but my mirth quickly faded. I excused myself, let CW out to relieve himself, and then retired for the night.

I removed my jacket and checked on my wolf brand. The skin looked perfectly normal around the mark, no blisters, not even any reddening. For all that I could say about the magissa, their medicinal skills were wonderful.

I hung up my jacket and xiphos. I changed into my night clothes, and crawled into bed. I was absolutely done with everything about today. CW leapt onto the bed with me and burrowed under the covers. The bed was much warmer with him snuggling up next to me.

I'd been worried that the stresses of the day would prevent me from drifting off to sleep. I needn't have worried – I dropped off almost immediately. Still, I didn't sleep well. My dreams were intense and difficult to follow. Being chased. Under attack. Falling.

A noise woke me in the small hours. Convinced it was one of Paget's agents breaking into my room, I lit the candle by my bed. The room was empty. I lay awake whilst the candle burned low, listening for the noise again. I'd never liked the dark but now I apparently needed a night light.

***

Sun glared through a crack in the curtains. CW snuffled next to me. I checked my pocket watch - just gone nine. I lay in bed staring at the ceiling. My mind was locked. I didn't know what to do with myself. I was trapped.

CW whined. I tried to ignore him, but he jumped down from the bed and fussed about the place until I worked out that he needed to go to the toilet.

I hauled myself out of bed and changed into clothing suitable for winter in Selen. CW scampered off in the direction of the kitchen, rather than the front door. I followed him, realising he must have heard voices. We had visitors, it seemed. A woman was speaking with Dad.

I stumbled through to the kitchen. Constable Woofington sat in the doorway, Papa leant against a wall. Dad sat at the kitchen table, and Paget Belacourt sat in the chair opposite him.

Chapter Seventeen

"Good morning, Susan," said Paget.

"Morning!" said Papa.

I felt as if I was drowning. She was having, what was that, tea? She was having tea with Papa. Had she threatened him? Was this a power play? Was she reminding me that she could have any of us killed at any time?

"Merion, Encarl, I'm so sorry to ask this, but could I borrow two minutes alone with your daughter? We've a matter I must clarify with her urgently."

Dad and Papa exchanged looks.

"Yes?" said Dad.

"Take as long as you like, the sitting room's just through there," said Papa.

Paget stood, her chair barely making a sound where mine had always scraped against the kitchen floor. She breezed past me, and I followed like the dolt I am.

She assessed our sitting room – a comfortable enough room as long as no more than three people tried to use it. There were three arm chairs, which she inspected in turn – one black and stern, one battered and comfortable, one patched with technicolour cloth. She pointed at the stern one. "This one is yours?"

I folded my arms. "No."

She gave me an appropriately sceptical look. "Well, never mind, I can't be right about everything. So, I wanted to drop in on you for a couple of reasons. The first – have you decided what to tell your fathers about your employment?"

"What do you mean?"

"You have to decide whether you're telling your fathers about the m-word or not."

"Oh... yes." There had been a section about family in the employee handbook but I couldn't remember what it had said. "I expected to have to keep it a secret from everyone."

"No, no, no. We tried running things that way for a few centuries, but it didn't really work. Loved ones get suspicious and start conducting investigations of their own, or tailing our agents. It's far easier to just let them know. Immediate family and long-term partners are fine."

Would the dads be better off knowing? Or should I save them from the nightmare world I'd stumbled into? "How long will I be working for you?"

"That depends on how happy we both are with your services. If either of us want to terminate your employment, then we can work out a mutually beneficial arrangement that doesn't involve us killing you and everyone you love. No-one wants that. In theory, you can work for us until the day you die."

"Ah," I said. "Tuesday."

Paget winced. "I promise the work isn't always as dangerous as your first day might have led you to believe."

"Promises, promises."

Paget drummed her fingers on the back of my arm chair. "I can't decide if I should be impressed that you've gone from being terrified of me to rather cheeky in record time, or if this is a sign that you're suffered some pretty significant trauma. Best to schedule an appointment with one of our doctors, just in case."

I narrowed my eyes. I was sure Paget was working some kind of angle, trying to manipulate me. But, the question of why stuck in my head. She was the head of a spy organisation, and she had dozens of agents like me. She didn't have to manipulate me. She almost certainly had better things to do with her time. It was just possible she was being genuine. "That'd be most kind," I said, just in case. "And yes, I'd like to tell them."

Paget nodded, as if I were one of her hounds who'd just learned to roll over. "Very good. That's why I came – it's best to be able to demonstrate magic to the sceptical, otherwise disbelief is inevitable."

Paget explained to the dads. The dads didn't believe her. She demonstrated her powers by communicating with CW, then getting CW to listen to something and then going to tell Paget... it took a while. The objections took even longer.

The dads' were most put out by the initial set of threats to my wellbeing if I revealed the magissa to humanity. I understood their concern. I'd resented her threats at the time as well. Still, I defended the magissa's right to live a life free of human mobs trying to murder them for being different. After all, the magissa hardly sought their transformations of their own volition. The dads seemed to think that my defences of the magissa were unreasonable. I explained that they were being reactionary and bigoted. Dad pointed out that Paget had threatened my life.

Not long after this little exchange, the dads started making unhappy noises, and asked to speak to me in private. This request caused Paget to hold up a hand. "I'd usually never stand in the way of parents speaking with their child, but I wonder if I could bring Susan's attention to another matter first."

"What is it?" asked Dad, grumpily.

"Alison is awake," said Paget, "and she's been asking for Susan."

I leapt to my feet. "Why didn't you say so earlier? Let's go!"

Both dads leapt to their feet as well, expressing serious objections to me running off again without having the opportunity to give me a fatherly lecture first. Paget then took the wind out of their sails a little by inviting them along as well.

"It would be good, I think," she said, "for you to see a little of our world."

The ride to Alison's home was tense. The dads tried out a new line of argument: That I was unsuited to espionage and skulduggery in general. They were, and I'm loathe to speak like this of my parents, a little patronising.

We arrived at the Dewan residence after going through the same arguments about my personal safety a mere thirty or forty times. Fida, the servant who'd escorted me through the house on my last visit, greeted us at the door. She ushered us all in, taking my dads' hats and cloaks. Paget had a quick word with Fida once the visitors' accessories were stored. The servant nodded, and withdrew two small silver badges from a sideboard.

"I requested for the security system parameters to be changed for today," said Paget. "I anticipated we might have human visitors."

The dads glanced at each other.

I grinned at them. "It's nothing to worry about, you get used to it very quickly."

Paget grinned at me. "That's the spirit. This way."

She led the three of us through winding corridors, through strangely shaped halls, and even crossed an exterior courtyard, where I caught glimpses of movement out of the corner of my eyes, no matter where I looked.

"Susan," Paget said, as we were passing a painting of sailors drowning in the Jade Sea, "I told Octavia about your species."

I winced. "Noted."

"Stay strong, wolf cub. She had to know. Better now than later."

I took in a breath, then another. My chest felt too tight. Paget strode ahead, leaving me with my thoughts.

Finally, we stopped in front of a door, decorated with carved whirlpools. Paget turned to face my dads. "I must warn you... you're about to meet someone with a very unusual appearance. Please don't be alarmed."

Paget led us into a sitting room – low ceilinged and cosy. A fire crackled contentedly. Octavia Dewan stood by a drinks trolley, a large jug of water stood out amongst the slender bottles of spirits. My dads stopped dead in their tracks when they saw Lady Dewan. I bowed to her.

"Ms Fletcher," Octavia said, nodding to me. Her expression had none of the warmth it had when last we'd met.

"Lady Dewan," I said. "It's an honour to be invited back into your home. I unreservedly apologise for my deception during our last meeting. I was under significant stress due to circumstances you already know about, but that's no excuse. I hope to earn your forgiveness, but I will completely understand if you have no intention of granting it. Given my dealings with the magissa so far, I'm deeply sceptical about second chances myself."

Lady Dewan nodded. "Thank you, Ms Fletcher. I will consider what you have said. You should also know that I've told Alison of your deception."

My face fell. "She must be furious. May I visit her? I'd love to apologise to her as well. If she'll see me, of course."

She turned away from me to pick up a tumbler from the trolley. I'm sure she meant to hide the fingers of her left hand tightening into a fist. "You saved my daughter's life, Ms Fletcher. You may see her to apologise."

"It was Ms Belacourt's hound who found Alison." CW heard this and attempted to stand to attention. He failed.

Lady Dewan turned back to me. The corners of her eyes sparkled. "You came to warn me about the danger to Alison's life." She advanced upon me. Fury fought with fear in her eyes, but there was something else... She stopped a mere pace from me. She stared down at me, a tidal wave crashed in her gaze. "Tell me the truth. Why did you do this?"

I couldn't hold her gaze. "Lady Callas offered me a commission, my lady. I'd hoped to lift myself and my family from... but that's not important. I—"

"Not the deception," said Lady Dewan, her voice softening. "Paget has told me of the deception. I meant: why did you come to warn me? I had words with the driver who brought you here yesterday. You initially asked her to take you to an address in Kipejo, but you changed your mind and asked to be dropped off here. You could have fled. You intended to flee. And yet... you didn't. You came here to warn me. Why?"

My shoes were scuffed and stained. I must have pulled them on before heading out without really looking at them. How could I have come here without cleaning my damned shoes? Lady Dewan must think she was sharing a room with a sloven. I was piling disrespect on top of disrespect. "I..." my breath caught in my throat. "I'm sorry. This is going to sound self-serving, as if I'm fishing for an answer I'd think you wanted to hear. But I've lied to you enough for one lifetime."

My mouth was too dry. The edges of my two chipped incisors felt sharp against my tongue. "I'd..." Why couldn't I say it? I closed my eyes as the tears came. "I wanted to help Alison. She was in danger and... I wanted to help her. I needed to help her. She's suffered so much because of people like me, but she never harmed me. Neither have you. No Hydros has. Well, Praxi Tolis hit me with a table, but there were extenuating circumstances behind that. I couldn't leave Alison in danger without at least warning you. I fully planned to flee afterwards."

Lady Dewan let out an amused huff at that last bit. "Very well. I cannot deny you a visit to Alison."

"She's also asking to see Susan," said Paget.

"Yes," said Lady Dewan. "That too. Fida will take you."

She turned to face the dads, who were trying not to huddle together for protection.

"You must be Merion and Encarl," she said. "I'm glad to meet some fellow parents who share the pain of raising a talented, yet chronically unpredictable daughter."

Fida led me to an ornate bedroom door, before drifting off. The door's otherwise imposing effect was rather thrown off by a print depicting a group of scowling musicians which had been stuck to it using adhesive tape.

I stared at the print, trying to fit it into the image of Alison I had in my head. I was still staring when the door opened. I jumped back in alarm – a small, fussy woman was on the other side. She wasn't Alison, of that I was about fifty percent sure. I remembered Alison being taller. Younger. More deamon-y.

"Mm?" said the woman, tugging spectacles from her pocket and examining me. "No, no, this won't do at all. One moment." She rummaged around in her hip pocket, then the waist pocket of her battered suit and then the other waist pocket, before pulling out an orange bottle of pills. "Take two of these daily, for two weeks, at two o'clock in the afternoon," she said.

I squinted at her. "Why?"

"For the trauma, young spud, it's practically leaking out of your ears. Now, I must converse with Lady Dewan. Call my secretary and tell him how you get on with the pills. And he'll then tell me, I don't intend for you to strike up an everlasting friendship with Markoth, he's hopeless. Misplaced his house keys four times in one day once. Still, he's Pyros, we must make allowances for Pyros, mustn't we?"

I nodded, wide eyed. "Mhm."

"Dr Grout!" bellowed Alison from her bedroom. "Are you harassing our staff again?"

"What?" the small doctor asked. "No, no. Not staff, no. Human, I think? You can tell by the unfocussed eyes. And the wolf brand, of course. Clearly in some distress. Currently backing away from me and staring at your door. Fascinating."

"Susan?"

My mouth opened and closed all by itself.

"Susan, is that you?"

Dr Grout poked my ribs with a reflex hammer. "I believe she's talking to you, young shaver."

I swallowed. "Yes? Yes, it's me."

"Do you want to come in?" Alison asked.

I shuffled towards the door. I could only see a sliver of Alison's bedroom – vermillion and coal decor was only occasionally visible under the mess. I couldn't see her, but if I kept walking, I would. The thing was... the thing was that I very much wanted to continue living in a world where I was friends with Alison. At the moment, that was still the case. If I stepped through the door, Alison might explain that she never wanted to see me again.

I shook myself, and stepped in.

Alison's room looked surprisingly normal, excepting her obvious affinity with the colour black. Her curtains and furnishings were mostly black, as were her bedclothes, and the strata of garments littering the floor. Her wardrobe was covered with collectable cards of various sorts that had been pinned to the ancient wood. More prints of furious musicians adorned her walls.

Alison herself was sitting up on her bed – a thin sheen of sweat shone on her forehead. Rumpled pyjamas enveloped her. There was no hint of the elegant aristocrat I'd met at the Callas mansion – except she'd kept her silver ear cuff on.

She was glaring daggers at me, much like the musicians she was surrounded by. She stood from her bed and wobbled towards me. She reached me after four unsteady steps and punched me, very hard, in the shoulder.

I yelped. "Ow! What was that for?"

"You're human. And you didn't tell me."

"Ah, yes. That."

Alison glared at me. "You must have thought I was stupid. Naïve Alison, doesn't get out much for fairly obvious reasons, I can glom onto her and get her to fill the massive gaps in my knowledge. She'll never even notice."

"No—"

"I thought we were friends, spirits damn you. And there you were, laughing at me the whole time."

"N—"

Alison closed the gap between us, tides surged in her gaze. "Well?"

This was it. I'd known this was coming. There were probably words – the right words. Convincing Alison wasn't impossible. She hadn't actually attacked me that much, considering. And yet... that face. Her expression – agony at the corners of her eyes. Her lips stretched into a defensive sneer. I'd made her strap armour on for this conversation. I'd lost before I even entered the room.

I wanted to apologise. Stammer out something – anything. But I drowned under her gaze. It was too much. It was all too much. An entire year's worth of events had happened yesterday, and now this. I let go.

The floor hit my knees. A dresser cracked the back of my head as I slumped back. Kneeling? I must be kneeling. Everything was tinged with red and white, blurred by tears. My breath only came in shudders.

Part of me, the part who was always watching, was hoping that Alison would see my unclothed grief and see my sincerity. She'd understand that I hadn't wanted any of this. The next thing I'd feel would be her arms around me, drawing me into a hug. I'd say I was sorry. She'd forgive me. And then...

My misery stretched. My brain awash with overwhelming dread. 'Alison was seeing a doctor', part of me said. 'you saw her walking strangely. You didn't get to her in time. This is because you were too slow.'

That, at last, broke through. "I'm sorry," I said, the words barely understandable. Choked.

"And you think that's enough?"

"I'm sorry, I was too slow. I didn't make it in time. I'm so sorry. If I'd been quicker... if I hadn't been caught. If I'd been smarter... you got hurt and it's all my fault."

"What the f.. what the *fuck* are you talking about?"

"The... when I got back... and you weren't... but CW tried and... I shouldn't have needed to ask... you were... your neck..."

Tears streamed from my eyes, snot leaked from my nose down to the corner of my mouth. My chest crushed my lungs at every sob.

A breath of air. A sigh. A swallow.

My tears stopped streaming down my cheeks. They paused, holding their position... and then they were gone. The shimmering which had blotted out my vision cleared as the tears were whisked from my eyes.

Alison knelt in front of me, her hand hovering by my cheek. Steam rose from my eyes, my cheeks, my mouth. Rapid evaporation. Evaporation without heat. Alison, the miracle.

"I'm sorry," I said.

"Why don't you tell me about it?"

So, I did. She stumbled back to her bed and flopped down next to an unheeded walking stick as I talked. Her expression shifted between a concentrated scowl and deep scepticism, but she didn't interrupt. She didn't even say anything after I finished.

I couldn't look at her. Everything I said was insufficient, but I couldn't bear the silence. "I'm really, really sorry."

"Yeah, well, what you said roughly correlates with what Paget said. And mum said. And Elin said when I woke up in his bloody doctor's surgery. Besides, Praxi's on the run, and everyone thinks she murdered Lady Callas, which means she probably attacked me..."

She stared at me. Her expression reminded me of the conversation we'd had in the steam tunnels. Alison had explained, in some detail, why humans couldn't be trusted. She'd have killed me there and then, if she'd known what she knew now. I knew that. She knew that.

Alison picked up a book from her bedside table. She hefted it in her hand whilst staring at me, then shook her head and put it down. She picked up a smaller book and threw that at me instead.

It bounced off my chest. "Ow."

"That hurt?"

"Yeah."

Alison nodded. "Good. Okay, here's the way I see it: we can try to trust each other and see how it goes. If it doesn't work..." She gave me the sort of look a shark gives a careless diver. "Well, never mind that. Still, we've been through a lot together. It would be nice to..." she trailed off. Her attention snagged on something at ground level.

"Why is Constable Woofington with you?" she asked.

"He's my minder. Paget assigned him to me."

"Oh. Good. You'll like him. He's a good boy."

She was holding her right arm stiffly. Her right leg seemed to be causing her trouble as well. She flopped back onto the bed and pain flashed across her face.

"How are you feeling?" I asked.

Alison groaned, rolling her head back and glaring at the ceiling. "I'm *fine*. Everyone keeps asking how I'm doing and they don't listen when I tell them I'm fine."

"Because your leg—"

"My leg. Is. Fine. The hanging was a little bit hard on my system. Dr Grout said this would happen. Something to do with lack of oxygen to my brain. Translation: It's fine. I'll get better. Stop worrying. I just need to shake this off." She gestured with her right arm. It seemed... uncontrolled. "So. You think Praxi murdered Lady Callas?"

"Yes, but you could confirm that for me – what did you go to check on immediately before you were... erm."

"Hanged? I can't remember."

I raised my eyebrows.

"Don't look at me like that," snapped Alison. "All my memories from soon after you left are just a bit foggy. Apparently, that's *normal*."

There was another silence.

My eyes darted about the room, fluttering from a book I didn't recognise, to a cleaning kit for a pistol, to a small jewelled egg, to a gramophone, to the interminable prints of musicians. I pointed at one of them.

"I don't recognise this group."

Alison was slow to react. "Mm?"

"The group in that print behind you. I don't recognise them. Tell me about them."

Alison looked over her shoulder. "Oh. Oh yes. *Cannibal Stars at the Gates of the Morning*. Have you not heard of them? They're very good."

"Have you been to see them perform?" I asked, before mentally kicking myself.

She grinned. "I have actually. These bands, they all cultivate a certain aesthetic. I don't know if you've noticed."

"I think I might have."

"It's all about darkness, death, decay, all of those fun aspects of mortality."

"Yes, I think I've noticed, now that you mention it."

"Oh, good. So, the sorts of people that go to these things tend to be a little bit ghoulish. I fit right in. I can wear my veil and no-one bats an eye."

"Huh. It's good to know you're not completely trapped."

Alison waved her hand. "Well, it's not completely terrible to be trapped in this house. There are books. I've a fascinating collection of board games I play with the servants. There's also an abundance of marijuana begging to be stolen from Paget's room."

"Oh, so *that's* what that smell was."

"Notice it, did you?"

"It was quite hard to miss."

There was a knock at the door.

"No!" called Alison.

"I'm afraid it's urgent," said Paget from the other side. Constable Woofington's ears perked up.

Alison glanced at me, raising her eyebrows. I shrugged.

"Come in, then," she said.

Paget opened the door, brandishing a newspaper. "We have a problem."

Chapter Eighteen

The Dewan family residence appeared to either have a war room, or a dining room which had sufficiently imposing decor to function as one. Newspapers and maps were spread across the needlessly huge dining table. Paget, Lady Dewan, Alison and I were pouring over an article in the *Heraldic Express*. My dads, thankfully, had been ferried home, protesting at the curtailing of what had turned out to be quite a pleasant chat over tea and crumpets.

The *Express* is one of those newspapers which isn't so much written as it is gradually distilled from the contents of Selen's sewers, and is generally read by people who don't like to think too much about what they are reading. Such readers like to be told what they already believe, but in a way that will make them just a little bit angrier about their own imagined persecution. In Selen, few people pay attention to this joke of a newspaper. Nevertheless, Paget, Lady Dewan, Alison and I were all paying very serious attention to one congealed article.

'Monsters Among Us!' screamed the headline.

The body of the article began: 'Every year, thousands of foreigners swarm into Selen, but we can now exclusively reveal that amongst these scroungers dwells a deeper menace: witches.'

The article then went onto describe the osto of Silenus, Hydros and Deimos in vivid detail. It then darkly hinted that such 'creatures' had

infiltrated even the highest levels of Selen society. The really dangerous part was on page two – it described the curses of various clans,
including Hydros. A spotter's guide to magissa.

It was the sort of article I was supposed to have written for Lady
Callas the day after the initiation ceremony. Well, I'd have written
something less sensational. Still, whoever the source had been for this
article had intimate knowledge of the magissa.

"I feel the need to point out," I said, "that this wasn't written by
me."

"Yes, thank you, Susan, we'd managed to deduce that on our own,"
said Paget.

"I trust you to be able to spell 'machinations' for a start," Alison
said.

"So," said Lady Dewan, "If this wasn't Susan–"

"And it wasn't," I said, just for the sake of absolute clarity.

"–then who the blazes was it?" Lady Dewan said, frowning.

"Charles Varma." I said at the same time as Paget.

Alison rolled her eyes. "Oh, that guy."

"Yes, that guy," said Paget. "Susan suggested that I, along with the
astynomia, should check into who Charles had been meeting with,
along with any other suspicious behaviour, to see if he had any con-
tingency plans in motion. Thankfully, I had already been moving in
that direction, but I should probably have words with my latest cub
for telling me how to do my job."

"Ha," said Alison, "you're a cub."

"A *wolf* cub," I said. CW barked from his spot under the table. I
helped him up onto a chair so he could be involved with the planning.

"My agents and I found that Charles had sent a number of letters
to influential figures around the city. These had been held in trust,
to be delivered this morning. We managed to stop them. Apparently,

we missed some similar letters that Charles sent to Selen's blasted newspapers."

"Right," said Alison. "We can't let this spread any further – information on our curses in the public domain is a nightmare scenario. So, we burn this place... the building the *Heraldic Express* is in to the ground, torching any evidence they had in the process."

Paget waved a weary hand at me.

I turned to Alison, "Right now, precious few people will probably believe an article such as this, because it's utterly preposterous. I certainly wouldn't have believed it seventy-two hours ago. If you attack the newspaper, though, people start asking questions. What was the motivation behind the attack? And then people might start looking at this article and wonder if actually the *Express* was onto something after all..."

Paget nodded to me. "Exactly."

Alison groaned. "Fine, so what do we do?"

Paget dragged a map of Selen into the space between us. "Selen has newspapers here—" she circled a building on the map, "—here, here, here, here, here, and here."

"And there," I said, pointing.

Paget frowned. "There's no newspaper there. That's... isn't that building one massive squat which the landlords have been trying to tear down and redevelop for the last decade?"

"Yeah, and one of the things they print from their squat is a weekly newspaper. *Solidarity in Selen*. Fairly standard socialist material. The police confiscate their printing presses around every six months, but they have friends in high places, so they always get a new one donated to them."

"I doubt Charles would know about a small-scale periodical such as that..." said Lady Dewan.

"He seemed aligned with the periodical, in certain non-murder based ways, when I interviewed him at the Callas Mansion," I said.

Paget shrugged, and circled the building I'd pointed out. "Right, well that makes things just a little bit harder. Most of my agents are busy with urgent work right now. I can spare a few people but all of these places need to be paid a visit, and whatever Charles sent them has to be found and removed with all due haste."

"Okay," I said. I stared at the map. "I can probably take care of that at *Solidarity in Selen*, and once that's done… yeah, the offices for the *Express* are pretty close by. If I take care of those two, can your agents deal with the rest?" Everyone was staring at me, except CW, who'd fallen asleep with his chin on the table. "What? What's the problem?"

Paget shook her head. "No problem. I'm just glad I've got a good eye for potential assets."

"We'll see," said Lady Dewan.

"Urgh, mum, you're so embarrassing," said Alison.

It was my turn to stare at Alison.

"What?" she said. "What did I say?" She frowned. "What *did* I say? There was something and then…"

"Dr Grout said you need to rest, my dear," said Octavia.

Alison rolled her eyes. "Yes, well, when a mob of angry humans shows up to drown us all, the servants can tell them I'm resting and to come back later."

I brushed my shoulder against hers. "It won't come to that."

Alison nodded. "Damn right. We'll make sure it won't. That's why I'm coming with you, Susan."

Tears formed behind my eyes, my stomach flipped, and I couldn't stop smiling. I nodded to Alison, trying to hide whatever emotional reaction I was having. "Glad to hear you say that. I need you along to make sure the job's done right."

"Supervisor Alison to the rescue."

"No," said Lady Dewan. "Absolutely not. You're injured, Alison."

Alison groaned. "Stop embarrassing me!"

Lady Dewan folded her arms. "Dr Grout said—"

"Dr Grout told *me* that I should keep living my life. You won't let me train, you won't let me leave the house. Let me live my life, *mum*."

I turned to Paget. "Is Dr Grout still here?"

Alison and Octavia immediately asked Fida to see if Dr Grout had left. Five minutes later, Alison had forced Dr Grout to admit that there weren't any specific medical reasons for her to not accompany me. Five minutes after that, Alison had changed into street clothes, including her veil and had joined me on the steps outside her house. Normally I'd have waited inside, but Lady Dewan kept glaring at me. I felt like a disreputable paramour.

Seeing Alison under her veil was a little distressing. I'd grown to like her features, and it was sad to be reminded of the isolation she was forced to live in because of my people. Once we were out on the street, people looked at her with some curiosity, but not as much as I was expecting.

We eschewed the Dewan family coach in case we needed to make a quick getaway through Selen's perpetually clogged streets. We walked, instead. I kept striding ahead, and then realising that Alison was struggling to keep up. She'd left without her cane, and her right leg was obviously hurting her. I did my best to not ask if she was okay.

The *Solidarity* building was a fairly typical squat. The ground floor windows had been boarded up after some of Selen's angrier citizens smashed them. The walls were pristine brickwork, because the inhabitants had to regularly clean hateful graffiti from the walls.

I knocked on the front door. It opened, to reveal a short, harried-looking woman. "Yes?" she said. She glanced from me to Alison, who was getting her breath back. "Can I help you?"

"I've done some work with Jasjot," I said, letting a bit of street twang into my voice. "Are they in? It's important."

"Extremely important," said Alison, straightening.

"Names?"

"Susan Fletcher."

"Ethyl Duff-Coopin," said Alison.

"Wait here." She said, then closed the door.

"Don't have any painkillers do you?" asked Alison.

I shook my head.

"Damn."

Silence stretched.

"Why didn't your mum want you to come with me?" I asked.

Alison sighed. "Her little prodigy acquiring a brain injury has made her paranoid."

I winced. "I'm really—"

"If you say you're sorry one more time, I'm going to thump you."

"Righto."

"Oh, don't look like that. Did I ever thank you for saving my life, by the way?"

I shook my head. The door to the squat opened, revealing Jasjot, the androgynous dish I'd done work experience with last year. "Hello Susan. Who's your friend?"

"A mysterious figure who lurks in the darkness, sees all and understands even more," said Alison.

Jasjot nodded. "Okay then..."

I took a step forwards, "Jasjot, did you receive a letter recently talking about witches, powers, curses... that sort of thing?"

Jasjot stared up at the sky for a moment, then their gaze snapped back to me. "Huh," they said. "One moment." They closed the door.

"Problem?" asked Alison.

"Not sure yet. So, we were talking about you thanking me for saving your life?"

"Oh, yes, we were. Well, I mentioned it. I only mentioned it because I wondered if I had, you see?"

"Right..."

"And if I hadn't thanked you, I thought I probably should, if you see what I mean? Because, you know, it would be just... I don't like being in debt to people, and I know that's not exactly... I mean... the information I fed you about the magissa probably stopped the residents of the Callas mansion murdering you a couple of times, so from that point of view, you owe me."

I nodded. "You're right. Thank you, Alison. Genuinely. I couldn't have got through this were it not for you."

Alison kicked a pebble into a drain. I slipped my arms around her and drew her into a hug. She stiffened, but relaxed after a moment.

"Thank you," I said.

"You're welcome."

The door opened again. Alison didn't pull back immediately – she held the hug for one, perfect moment, before dropping her arms.

Jasjot stood in the doorway, a hefty document folder in their hands. "Sorry to interrupt... Got the letter here, along with the manifesto sort of thing they included."

Relief washed over me. I held out my hand for the folder.

Jasjot gave me an appraising look. "Susan... does your Papa know you're here?"

I shook my head.

"Would he approve of you being here?"

I nodded.

"Hm. So I can ask him about this later?"

"Sure. He probably won't know what I'm up to but it's not a problem for you to tell him."

"Right. Okay, put it this way. These documents... they're important, aren't they?"

"That's right."

"Will people get hurt if we publish them?"

"Yes."

"More people than if we hand them to you?"

The magissa fed on peoples bones. Still, they paid for them. Some of them. My teeth had paid for our winter fuel, and Dad's finger...

"Yes," I said.

Jasjot glanced at Alison. "Can you tell me what's going on?"

"No," said Alison. "Sorry."

"Not yet," I said.

Jasjot glanced at the document folder, then shrugged and handed it over. "Implausible rubbish anyway." With a wink and a twirl, they slipped back into the squat.

"You have weird friends," said Alison.

"*I* have weird friends?" I said. "You, Alison Dewan, are telling me, Susan Fletcher that *I'm* the one with weird friends?"

CW barked in outraged solidarity.

"I have no idea what you're getting all bent out of shape about," said Alison. "Right. The *Heraldic Express* next?"

"Right. And its not going to be as easy. It's more of a formal institution. You might need to wait outside."

"Hey, don't be a twat, Susan. You've got a genius with the combat expertise of a fully trained assassin, the social manoeuvring acumen of a budding politician, and the infiltration skills of a spy at the top of their game. I came along for a reason. Let me help."

"You're right. Okay. I did a work placement at the *Express*. It's not a tight ship, but they still might get antsy about random people wandering in off the street. I was planning to see if I could just breeze in, claiming my work placement never ended. Not a fool-proof plan, given I haven't been there for a few months, but it was the best idea I had."

"Hm. That won't get me in. Is there a service entrance or something? Anything where we could get in unobserved? We could get in and find the records room ourselves. Might lead to fewer questions?"

"Can you open locked doors?"

Alison's expression hovered between amused and annoyed. "Can I open locked doors? Can Alison Dewan, Hydros prodigy, most talented magissa initiate in two hundred years, open a locked door?"

I resisted the urge to say 'Is that a yes or a no?' because we were in public. I responded with a shallow bow instead. "Ms Dewan's prowess is, of course, legendary. Her skill with her osto is merely one rose in the bouquet of her talents. Her investigative skills, her sharp mind and razor wit are, of course, remarkable, and that is before we discuss her aptitude with blades and firearms. Her talent for skulduggery is similarly beyond reproach. I merely wondered if she would stoop so low as to open a mere physical lock. Where is the challenge? Where is the opportunity to demonstrate her true skill?"

Alison stepped forward, her movement light and fluid. She placed her hands on my waist and drew me towards her. I could feel her heart pounding in her chest. This close, I could see her eyes flashing behind her veil. "Susan," she said. "If we were somewhere more private, would you enjoy it if I kissed you?"

"Er..." I said, suddenly very confused. My heartbeat had fallen in sync with Alison's. "Yes, I think so."

"Right." She let me go and nodded. "Right. Let's get that manifesto and then have a chat. How close are we to the *Express* offices?"

"Er..." I said, "Two streets away. I'll lead. Look, what just happened?"

Alison kept pace with me, but her right leg was still causing her grief. She strode with her left leg and had to drag her right to keep up. "What just happened? You mean me making a move on you?"

"That was a move? You've done that before?"

"Well, no, but someone did it in this book I read once. It sounded like fun. Was it?"

I was definitely blushing. "Yes. Yes it was. So..."

We turned a corner onto Wye Street – where five of Selen's major newspapers were set up, as well as the *Express*. Lunchtime was fast approaching, so the street was packed with tired journalists scavenging for sustenance, delivery girls rushing about the place with sustenance for tired journalists, and delivery coaches doing their best to avoid running anyone over.

"So... what?" asked Alison. Tension hummed in her voice.

"Er, down here, I think..." I said, pointing to an alley. "How long have you wanted to kiss me?"

"Oh, you know that's actually a pretty good question," said Alison, clasping her hands behind her neck. "I'm not sure. I kept wondering if that's what I wanted, but I haven't had many close friendships, so I didn't know if I wanted to make a move on you, or if I was just enjoying being close with someone. That was before I found out you were human, of course. But you know. No-one's perfect. Well, most people aren't perfect."

"Right, right. Cool." This wasn't what I'd expected from today, so my mental gears were grinding against each other.

"How about you?" asked Alison. "How long have you wanted to kiss me?"

"Well, I'm demisexual so I tend to find out if I want to kiss someone when they kiss me."

"Ah. So we should try it and see if we like it."

"On, like, a date?" I'd only dated one person before. It had been very confusing.

"Sure. Is this it?"

Alison was pointing to a sheet metal door halfway down the alley, sandwiched between an industrial refuse bin, and a closed set of roller shutters which presumably guarded a loading dock.

We'd past three doors like the one Alison had picked already... I checked back way we'd come, counting under my breath. "Next one along, I think."

A padlock squatted under the door handle, daring me to pretend I knew anything about picking locks.

I pointed. "So, Alison, Prodigy of Hydros, wooer of Susans, the lock is here. Please, cast it aside and let us be done with this duty, so that we may dine together somewhere pleasant to us both."

Alison poked at the lock. It was secured to the steel door by a D ring on a metal plate. Alison checked both ends of our alley, lifted her veil, and spat onto the plate.

"Mm," I said. "I'm rethinking our date."

Alison waved a hand. "Not for long, you're about the be in awe of my power."

Her right hand moved to her left wrist, where her bracelet of teeth clung. Her right hand gripped the bracelet, but not any one particular tooth. Alison scowled. Her fingers shifted – sliding to a different point on the bracelet. Again, she missed a tooth.

"Come on, come on..." said Alison.

I hovered, unsure if I should be offering to help or not.

Alison held up her right hand – her fingers were shaking. "I've got this. Give me a minute. We're still clear?"

I checked for observers again. "Crystal."

"Right." She released her breath, the veil twitching. "Let's give this another try, shall we?" She reached to her wrist, her fingers gripped a tooth and tugged it free. Her fingers clenched. The tooth dropped into the stink of waste water on the pavement with a miserable plop.

Alison punched the wall. "Fuck! Fuck, fuck, fuck, fuck, fuck, fuck!" She kicked the nearest bin, staggered and crashed into me. "Get off me!" Alison roared.

CW whined. He was staring down the alley.

"Hey!" called a serious-sounding voice. "What are you two up to?" A sturdy woman wearing overalls and a flat cap was striding into the alley.

I took one, precious moment to panic, before getting my game face on. "Stay here, Ali, I've got this."

"Ali?" hissed Ali.

"Shut up. Come on, CW." I walked to meet the intruder, options flicking through my head. *We'd had bad news. Ali had dropped something – accurate, but didn't explain the strength of Ali's reaction. We'd been trying to do... something... something which would explain our presence in the alley? No. Bad news, best go with bad news.*

"I'm really sorry," I said, as I reached the intruder. "My friend's just had some pretty bad news."

She looked deeply sceptical. "Bad news which you heard in an alley?"

"I didn't want to break the news in public," I said. "And you saw why. It's her dog, you see…" I nodded at CW. "He's not well at all. The vet thinks he's not got long left."

CW looked up at us, his tail thumped, and then he coughed. A tiny, pathetic cough which visibly melted the intruder's heart.

"Oh no!" she squatted down in front of CW, who coughed again. "Poor boy! You're such a good boy…" She fussed over my minder for a good two minutes. CW nuzzled her hand, and thumped his back leg when she scratched him behind the ears. "Sorry about that," said the intruder, once she'd reached cuteness overload. "Thought you were up to no good. Should have known, really. Thieves aren't exactly going to bring a doggy along on a job, are they?"

I laughed, "Right?"

"Can you imagine!"

"No, not at all."

She straightened her cap. "Right. You take care of yourselves, okay?" She strode off.

I stared down at CW. "I didn't know you could act."

CW barked.

"Hey, I didn't say I thought you'd be bad at it. I just didn't know. Anyway, thanks boy. You did a great job."

CW Barked.

"Yes, yes. Bacon when we get back."

Ali, when I returned to her side, was gently bashing her head against a wall. She thrust out her left arm. "Susan, can you grab a tooth for me, please?"

I bit back the first three things I wanted to say in reply. "What sort of quality?"

Ali paused her headbanging for a moment. "Mid-high."

I selected a tooth which looked intact, and held it out for her. She took it with her left hand and slipped it into her mouth. "Thanks." She pointed at the door. The metal plate securing the D-ring *cracked* free, letting the padlock swing limply. "Got there in the end."

"Everyone has bad days," I said, swinging the door open.

Chapter Nineteen

We climbed a set of stairs which seemed to be mostly used as a dumping ground. Drifts of paper, metal trays, and discarded printing-press parts all did their best to trip us as we climbed.

"I did some sorting work in the records room when I did my placement here," I said. "If this stairwell takes us to the first floor, it should be a straight shot to get there."

"Goody," said Ali, her voice flat.

If I'd spent a good five minutes struggling to perform a simple task, I'd not be in the best spirits either. I didn't know how to ask her without being patronising. I settled for: "You want to talk about it?"

"No," Alison snapped. Then, she sighed. "Not yet. Sorry, Susan. Not your fault."

"And not yours either."

We reached a landing, and a door marked 'fire exit', which was almost entirely blocked by cardboard boxes. I shoved the boxes aside, and pulled the door open. Perfect – the *Express* offices hadn't changed much. A corridor lined with battered brown and beige furnishings. Doors in the wall opposite led to journalists' offices, whilst to our left was the enormous, soundproofed door which led to the printing press workshop. That meant the records room...

"This way," I said to Ali. I walked with a measured pace – not too fast. As if I had every right to be where I was, but I didn't actually want to stride about the place because that would have meant working at a dangerously enthusiastic rate. "The door is just ahead on the right."

There weren't too many other people about. A few journalists brushed past me on their way to lunch, whilst a fatigued administrator was lurking at a closed office door, possibly working up the courage to knock.

"Spirits preserve me," said a voice thick with silver from behind me, "Susan Fletcher?"

"Crap." I muttered. "Get to the records room, Ali, I'll deal with this?"

"Girlfriend?" Ali hissed.

"No!"

"Fine."

I turned and smiled at my old supervisor, Ms Kilpatrick.

She hadn't changed much – hair pulled back and held in place with some sort of sour-smelling gel. Her red suit looked expensive, and was at least two sizes too large. She gave a lazy half-wave as she approached. "I didn't know you were coming back in. Another placement?"

"Oh, no, I was just coming in to pick up something I left here. I cleared it with..." crap. What was the administrator's name? "Datan."

"Right, right. Well, it's good to have you back. How did your placement with the pinkos go?"

"Good. Less professional. Nice people, though."

"I told you! Why do you have a dog?"

CW was giving Kilpatrick a sceptical look.

I shrugged. "He needs to go for a walk every day."

"This is an office, Susan."

"I won't let him do his business on the carpet."

"Right. Good."

Someone screamed in the distance. Kilpatrick ignored it. "Anyway, must get on. Lovely seeing you again, etcetera. Actually... if you're not doing anything, we do need some help with the administration, if you wanted to pick up where you left off?"

I might have jumped at the chance a week ago. Working for the *Express* might have been morally repugnant but work was work. "Thanks, Ms Kilpatrick, but I've secured another position."

She smiled, thinly. "Oh. Good. Anyone I know?"

"I don't think so."

Another shout, this one closer. Kilpatrick scowled. "I'd better go see what that's about. Don't be a stranger!"

She gave another half-wave, and strode away. She picked up her pace when more shouts broke through, followed by the crash of breaking glass. I ducked into the records room, where Ali was staring at a shelving rack stuffed to bursting with paper files. The familiar musk of mouldy carpet and pest-repelling pellets, all fermented over many poorly ventilated years made me sway for a moment, nostalgia burrowing deep into my brain, before I was able to focus. "Ali!"

She jumped, and spun to face me, before relaxing a little. "Oh, Susan. Good. Look, these files aren't in any order. How do we find Charles' screed?"

"Yes, right. We might need to hurry because there's a very angry-sounding something going on outside."

"Great. I was going to... never mind. How do we find the thing?"

"Right. Right." I clapped my hands to my cheeks to try and change mental gears. "They use a variant on the Lyladecimal system. The files should be sorted by..." I traced my finger from shelf to shelf. "Yes – year, then category, then full date. The thing is... Charles' letter might not have been filed. See that cart in the corner?"

"No?"

I pointed to an enormous mound of envelopes and loose paper. "There's a cart under that pile. Can you look through there for anything which looks like it might be from Charles?"

"This is a shit first date," said Ali, stomping over to the pile and picking up her first envelope.

I scanned the shelves for the current year. "I thought we were going to try a date later?"

Ali picked up an envelope, tore it open, checked the contents and tossed them aside. "Yeah, but then I realised we were on a mission behind enemy lines, there's some sort of riot starting outside, and you've seen me at possibly my lowest moment since I learned how to use the toilet correctly."

"There you go again, bragging about your skills..." I'd found the correct year and was trying to work out what category Charles' letter might have been filed under.

"Ha. Anyway, if that's not a date, I don't know what is."

"I thought people were supposed to go to the theatre or something."

"Urg. Sitting in stony silence whilst watching actors soliloquise some Gower or Beynon for three hours doesn't sound like my idea of fun."

"I was more talking about independent theatre. You know, the sorts of shows they put on in disused warehouses or under the railway arches."

Ali tore open another envelope, "Nope. Don't know those. Never been. Would my veil stand out?"

"No more than at the fancy theatres, I imagine."

"Mum gets us a box so sight lines to us are restricted as much as possible."

"Ah. Not the theatre then. Have you dated much before?"

"Nope. Don't know many other Hydros I'm not directly related to, and I'm always suspicious of other magissa who claim to find me attractive. Went out with one once. Extremely creepy about my appearance. Not a good time. You?"

"Nope. I don't really notice if people are flirting with me. I only find out when someone mentions it afterwards, and by that time I have no idea if I'd be interested or not."

"Huh."

CW scratched at the filing room door, then growled.

"What's up, pup?" said Ali.

CW barked, twice, then scratched at the door again.

"I'll check it out," I said. "You okay to keep looking?"

"Yeah, yeah." she said, waving a hand.

"If it's any help," I said, "I'm having a good time."

She flashed me a grin, before turning back to her task. I opened the door and followed CW back into the corridor. The smell hit me first – it was sour and clung to the back of my throat. The faint clanging of a fire bell explained the empty corridor. That smell... it was burning rubber and burning paper and... I ran to the nearest window – it looked out over the street. People were streaming out of the *Express* offices. Everyone else was keeping well clear, except for a chain of people passing buckets of water to each other, into the *Express* offices. Something nearby was on fire, and it might well be the building I was standing in.

Chapter Twenty

Ali emerged from the records room, brandishing a wad of paper. "I've found Charles' pain in the arse. What's going on? Fire alarm?"

"Think so. Come on, we've got to get out of here." I strode towards the main stairs, where a haze of smoke blurred all detail. Figures stood in the smoke, moving rhythmically. The bucket chain – they were hauling buckets up the stairs. Good. I'd defaulted to leaving via that main stairs because that's how I'd always left the offices, but we could get out that way easily enough, although we'd need something to cover our faces. Except... CW couldn't do that. I could make him some sort of facemask...

"Susan! Where are you going?"

Ali hadn't moved. I slapped my forehead. We shouldn't head out the front entrance – Ali's veil would invite questions.

Cries of alarm – clangs of metal hitting the floor. Buckets? The smoke was thickening, and a flickering core of orange was spreading down from the upper floors. The people on the stairs had dropped their buckets and were fleeing the flames. No, not the flames. The figure stalking out of the flames.

I stood, transfixed. The figure held a fuel can in one hand, and a shimmering blade in the other. The blade sparked and hissed in the heat of the blaze. A human straggler, slower to flee than the others, turned and charged at the figure. A kick to the chest sent the human reeling backwards, over the railings and down the stairwell. The figure reached our floor and flicked the cap from their fuel can. They strode towards me, dousing the walls and floor.

The figure's form had been hazy whilst it stalked through the smoke. As it emerged, it took on a terribly familiar shape. A battered suit was barely visible under a cloak. Grey cloth was wrapped around their face, leaving only a slit for their eyes, and a smouldering top had sat atop their head. I'd last seen this figure in the Callas' mansion steam tunnels.

"Susan," hissed Ali, "We have to go."

I took a step back. "Ali... it's Praxi Tolis."

Praxi couldn't have heard me over the fire bell, the crackling blaze and her own fuel can sloshing flammable liquid at her feet... maybe it was my movement which finally drew her attention my way. She paused, and dropped the fuel can. She slipped a tooth from her wrist and yanked aside the strip of cloth covering her mouth. The moment she swallowed the tooth, her shimmering blade morphed. It grew thinner and longer – a wicked sharp javelin.

CW nipped my ankle. I shook myself. I took a step back, then Ali grabbed my wrist and yanked me around. "Come on!"

"But it's Praxi! She's... we can stop this, we just need to talk to her."

"Damn it, Susan!" Ali broke into a shuffling run.

Praxi was closing the gap. Raising her spear. I gave up on any attempts at diplomacy, and ran after Ali. She'd reached the fire exit.

"Praxi!" I yelled, once I'd caught up with Ali. "We can talk about this!"

Praxi raised her javelin. I ducked through the fire exit. The javelin buried itself in the doorframe where my head had been.

Ali was hobbling down the stairs. I caught her up just as she stumbled – I grabbed her hand, steadied her. Praxi burst through the fire exit above, javelin in hand. She drew back her arm, trying to aim down the stairwell at us. Ali tugged my hand. I nodded to her – we dodged the final trip hazards and staggered back into our alley.

Smoke and flames billowed from the windows on the upper floors. I kept hold of Ali's hand as we ran, steadying her when she had to put weight on her right leg. It was awkward at first, but we found a rhythm. Her hand in mine felt as if I was home. CW trotted next to us, clearly having the time of his life.

We joined the flow of the crowd at the end of our alley. I checked behind us, but didn't see Praxi. She might not have followed us, or she might have taken shelter behind one of the refuse bins. We followed the flow of the crowd – the press of people moving slowly despite the crackling panic in the air.

CW yipped at me from ground level. He was squeezing up next to my legs. Maybe worried about being stepped on. I scooped him up with my free hand, and he burrowed into my jacket.

The crowd thinned after a few streets. We slipped down a side street, and kept moving until Ali spotted a cab. We gave the driver an address a few streets away from Ali's house. The driver gave Ali's veil a suspicious look, but relented when I offered to double her fare. We settled down inside on the same bench. I finally felt able to relax as we set off. CW clearly felt the same way, because he slipped out of my coat and dropped to the floor, before curling up on Ali's foot.

Ali tugged off her veil – her face was drenched with sweat, her gaze unfocussed. She sighed, and rested her head on my shoulder.

"How you doing?" I asked.

"Been better," she said, closing her eyes.

"Good first date?"

"Memorable."

She fell asleep as our cab rattled through Nine Dials. I stared out of the window. Had the world always changed this quickly? I'd been worried that Ali wouldn't want to ever see me again only hours before. Now... had she only made her move on me because of her injury? Had it messed with her system somehow? Maybe it had lowered her inhibitions. Or maybe she'd had a near death experience and decided to be more impulsive.

Did I actually want to date Ali? Or had I just been swept up in the moment? She shifted next to me, moving her head to a slightly more comfortable part of my shoulder. Her hand moved – I took it. Our fingers interlaced. She sighed, contentedly.

Being demisexual meant my heart didn't flutter if an attractive person... winked at me, or whatever it was that attractive people did. I only really got the feelings I'd encountered in certain types of novel when things had... progressed to a certain point. At that point, my body seemed to suddenly wake up and go 'Mm? What's happening? I like it, keep doing whatever it is.'

With Ali's head on my shoulder, her hand in mine... 'I like this,' my body said 'keep doing whatever it is you're doing'. I closed my eyes.

***

I only woke up when the coach stopped. I roused Ali as gently as possible, and jumped down from the cab to pay the driver, whilst Ali got her veil back in place. We reached the Dewan residence without further incident. Fida opened the front door, took one look at us and ushered us inside, before disappearing.

"She seemed keen to rush off," I said.

"Mhm," said Ali. "Be prepared for an approaching Octavia typhoon."

"A what?"

"Alison!" snapped Lady Dewan, who appeared to have strode out through a solid wall, "What on earth have you been doing? You were supposed to acquire two documents from two newspaper offices."

"Yes," said Ali, testily, "and that's what we did."

"My, you're remarkably dishevelled for two young women who have merely been acquiring documents! And that smell... is that smoke? What happened, Alison?"

"There..." Ali said, before faltering.

"What happened Alison Imalia Mitnick Dewan?"

CW leapt up into my arms and tried to burrow back inside my coat.

"Nothing!" Ali yelled, "You can't control every part of my life, Mum!"

Lady Dewan drew herself up to her full impressive height, while I tried to vanish into a corner.

"I'm trying to protect you, Alison. You were nearly *killed* at the Callas mansion."

"Let me live my life, mum! I hate you!"

That was the least Alison-ish thing I'd ever heard. Lady Dewan was winding up for a retort but Ali turned and stomped up the stairs.

"Don't you walk away from me, young woman!" Lady Dewan said, her tone brooked no disobedience. Nevertheless, Ali disobeyed, finishing her laborious ascent, and disappearing in the direction of her room.

"Er..." I said.

Lady Dewan rounded on me. I explained what we'd witnessed at the *Express* offices, although I left out the part about the change in my relationship with her daughter. "So, I should really be getting these documents to Paget," I said, preferring the leader of the wolf pack over a furious Octavia any day of the week.

Lady Dewan's glare intensified. "Susan. Have you observed any... issues with Alison's health?"

"Er..." it felt like a betrayal to give Octavia ammunition she might use to restrict Ali's movements. Then again, Octavia was concerned about her daughter's health. So was I. "Maybe one or two?" I said, eventually.

Octavia narrowed her eyes and seemed to be building up to giving me an earful before something inside her snapped. She sighed, slumped, and seemed to age fifteen years in front of me. "Forgive me, Ms Fletcher, it's been a trying day."

"That it has. I should probably give these documents to Paget, and then I should probably leave. Check with my dads, make sure they're okay."

"Ah yes. Susan, if I know Paget, she'll have more work for you. I'll send someone to pick Merion and Encarl up. Invite them to dine with us. Do you think they'd be amenable to that?"

"Er..." I thought back to the last time I'd seen dad dine at a fancy house – Papa's old place. Papa's family had... not been welcoming. Still, dining with the Dewans would be less socially complex. "Probably?"

"Good. Fida, take Ms Fletcher's documents to Ms Belacourt. Susan, follow me, we need to talk."

Fida took the documents from me and drifted off upstairs, with CW following close behind.

Lady Dewan stalked away, and I followed. She led me to the sitting room in which I'd first met her. She slumped into an armchair, and waved at the chair opposite her. "Sit down, Susan."

I sat on the edge of the seat, unsure of where this was going. "I'm at your disposal, your Ladyship."

Lady Dewan smiled thinly. "You didn't save my daughter in time "

There wasn't enough air in my lungs. She knew. She knew I'd been too slow.

Octavia's expression softened. "Oh, please don't look like that. What I mean is…. Alison had been hanging for some time before you found her. She'd lost oxygen to her brain, as well as several muscles on her right side. Brain and muscle damage. She'll likely suffer from memory problems for the rest of her life, and her personality may well change as a result. The muscular damage might recover, but it also might not. It's possible she will never fully recover the use of her arm and leg."

I wanted to cry.

"Alison knows all this," said Lady Dewan, "or rather, she has been told this information several times. She refuses to accept it. She won't use the walking stick Dr Grout provided. She won't stay in the house. She's determined to carry on as if her life is exactly the same as it was."

I nodded. I had a horrible feeling I knew where this was going. "You want me to leave her alone so she can recover in peace?"

Lady Dewan laughed, hollowly. "That's what *I* want. Dr Grout has informed me that my desires are ill advised. My daughter is headstrong, Ms Fletcher. She never enjoyed being cooped up. She needs distractions, but she also needs a friend. She had few friends up to this point, but those magissa who knew her will likely not wish to associate with her now. They will see her as weak."

I flinched. "Weak? She's the strongest person I know. I'm pretty sure she saved my life today."

Lady Dewan nodded, gravely. "Well, then, I wonder if you could continue to bring her along on your little misadventures. Dr Grout is of the opinion that she needs the exercise, both mental and physical. It might also help her to adjust to her new life if she's reminded of her new limitations. Will you be a friend to Alison?"

I did my best to keep my face neutral, despite the memory of Ali's hand in mine on the taxi ride home. "I don't think that'll be a problem."

Lady Dewan nodded, curtly. "Good. I'll provide some small remuneration for you time, of course."

I felt as if I'd been slapped. "I don't need to be *paid* to spend time with your daughter." The words 'we're dating, you patronising aristotwat' died, unsaid, at the back of my throat. I definitely shouldn't tell Lady Dewan about that without clearing it with Ali first.

"Well, then, we've nothing more to discuss," said Lady Dewan. She rose from her chair and stalked from the room.

I slumped back in my chair, and closed my eyes. "What is today, even? Today? What is it? Why is it?"

The universe refused to do the decent thing and answer any of my questions, so I hauled myself out of my chair and set out in search of the stairs which would lead me to the first floor.

I made three wrong turns. The first took me to a wine cellar where the walls dripped with either condensation or blood, I wasn't quite sure and didn't want to check. The second wound up with me staring out of an attic window, which was confusing as I was sure I hadn't climbed any stairs. The last opened into the kennels – twelve dogs of various sizes bounded up and sniffed at me. I had to say hello to each of them before I could leave with a clear conscience.

When I finally found the stairs, I was feeling dead on my feet. Once I was at the top, I had a simple choice. I decided to visit Paget first. CW would already have informed her what had occurred, but I had a plan to pitch to her. Then, I could visit Ali and see how she was doing.

"Come in, Susan!" Paget called, when I knocked on her door.

I did as I was instructed. Bloodfang was curled up around CW. Both appeared to be asleep. Paget was flicking through a folder. She didn't look up when I entered.

"So," she said. "You recovered both of Charles' letters, but weren't in time to prevent Praxi Tolis from burning the headquarters of the *Heraldic Express* to the ground."

"Technically speaking, we don't know it was Praxi. There's... I don't know... a five percent chance it wasn't her?"

Paget nodded, but still didn't look up. "Quite. Octavia has had a few curt messages from her clan mothers, talking about due process, how Praxi's actions aren't an admission of guilt, and so on, and et cetera."

I shrugged. "They're right."

Paget turned a page. "Yes, they are. That doesn't make our situation any less fucked. Did you have a reason for coming to see me, Susan? I'd have thought your first port of call after seeing Octavia would have been Alison's sanctum..."

CW opened one eye, saw I was looking at him, and went back to pretending to be asleep, the little snitch.

I rolled my shoulders, and accepted my blush as one tiny humiliation in a worthwhile cause. "If you're happy with CW's report, I have two questions..."

"CW?" Paget asked, raising her eyebrows but still not looking up.

"Constable Woofington is a really long name."

"Ah, yes, and you humans are so short lived, I was forgetting. Your questions?"

"The information about the magissa is out. Even if the humans don't think the *Express* fire is suspicious, it won't take many people pointing out that witches are rumoured to live openly in countries beyond the wall of chains for rumours to become reality. Have you considered that... this might be the right time to reveal yourselves to humanity? If you do it in the right way, it could be a win-win."

"We eat your bones, Susan," said Paget, weariness creeping into her tone.

"Yes, you do. Multiple magissa have – or had - my baby teeth. Same with my dad's finger. You know the most important thing about that? We made it through multiple killer winters because we sold those bones. You have the opportunity to get out in front of this. It's not as if the secrecy you live under is universally loved. Your commitment to secrecy has claimed the lives of three magissa that I know about, and I've only known you exist for forty-eight hours: Tova Oster, Teleri Parry and, of course, Marie Callas."

Paget turned another page. "We don't know for certain that Marie was murdered because of the secrecy."

I shrugged. "Paget, I don't want to argue with you about this. Ali... Alison has a lot to lose if the magissa reveal themselves. I care about the outcome of this. A lot. I just... want you to have considered the question, properly, rather than fall victim to status-quo bias."

Paget sighed, and turned another page. "Fair. What was your second question?"

"Can Ali and I go back to the Callas mansion?"

Paget looked up from her paperwork. "Why on earth would you want to go back there?"

"A couple of reasons. First, I think there might be evidence that we missed the first time around. Second... well. If it *is* Praxi going around burning down buildings, she's adding fuel to a fire because she's terrified of humanity. There's an opportunity to take care of our Praxi problem, and establish who, exactly, murdered Lady Callas at the same time. I want to lay a Praxi trap."

"Alison will want to be involved."

"You're damn right she will, I'm counting on it."

"All right, cub, all right. Run through your proposal for me. In detail, please. I shall be displeased if you're wasting my time."

I explained my plan.

Paget pantomimed having a heart attack. "Well, it's your skin. I won't say I wouldn't be glad to have Praxi out of Selen. It would hopefully give me time to settle the political situation down a little, and give some thought to your first question. Yes, all right. Leave Constable... sorry, CW with me for a little while. He needs to recover and be on top form tomorrow. Say hello to Alison for me..."

Five minutes later, I knocked on Ali's door. No response.

"Ali?" I said. "It's Susan."

"Mmcomn..."

I opened the door, hoping she'd said, 'come in'. The room was dark, the curtains drawn. Ali was in bed. Her boots lay discarded on the floor. She cracked an eyelid, and flicked up the corner of her duvet, revealing she was still wearing most of her clothes. "Come sleep, is sleep time."

"I've got to tell you about a plan..."

"Yes, plan good but later, sleep time now."

I smiled down at her, shrugged, kicked off my shoes and climbed into bed. She shuffled over to make room. I wrestled a pillow out of her control. She scowled at me, but only for a moment. She lay on her side, facing me, her eyelids drifting closed.

"Hey," I said, feeling slightly bold.

She opened her eyes. "Mm?"

"You asked how I'd feel if you kissed me."

Ali smiled. "I did. I remember your answer."

She reached out, drew me too her, and kissed me. Her lips were soft, her touch gentle. When she drew back, she dropped her hand to my waist, where it belonged.

"Thank you," I said.

"Mm, yes, I'm very generous. Sleep now."

I shifted to be a little closer to her, and closed my eyes.

Chapter Twenty-One

Ali stared out of the window as we left the outskirts of Selen behind. I sat next to her in the coach, much as I had during our first trip out of Selen. CW was curled up on my foot, snoring quietly.

"You have to promise me that you won't let me get hanged again. That's all I'm saying," said Ali.

"I won't let anyone hang you."

"Not even Praxi?"

"Especially not Praxi."

"Oh, good. Thank you."

A servant had woken us up for dinner last night, which had only been mortifying for seventeen or eighteen hours. We'd scrambled to make ourselves presentable and then had a full Dewan, Belacourt, and Fletcher family meal. The dads had been lovely to Ali. I was pretty sure they'd already worked out what we were to each other, which was irritating as I didn't know myself.

"So..." I said, trying to sound casual and failing completely. "Are you my girlfriend?"

Ali frowned. "Not now, Susan. I'm contemplating my mortality."

I nudged her. "Well, stop it. I promise you'll be safe. I've got everything worked out."

"Oh, well, as long as you've got everything worked out..." Her left leg jiggled, whilst her right was terribly still.

"Ali..." I said. I touched her shoulder, applied the gentlest of pressure – turning her away from the window.

She sat stiffly, staring at the bench opposite us, left leg still jiggling. "I don't remember being hanged last time, but I'm pretty sure I didn't enjoy it."

"Do you trust me?"

She shrugged – her left shoulder moving noticeably more than her right. I reached across her and ran a finger down her cheek, turning her face to mine. I leaned forward, resting my forehead against hers.

Her gaze settled on mine. "What if she has a gun?"

"She would have used it at the *Express* offices."

"What if she has a knife?"

"She can make blades from water. Why would she have a knife?"

She breathed, stars glittering in her eyes. "Right. Right."

"Ali... Do you trust me?"

Tears glistened at the corners of her eyes. "Yes. Yes, I do."

"We've got CW, we've negotiated for access to Marie Callas' bones, and we're together. This is going to work."

Ali closed her eyes and pressed her forehead against mine. "I'm your girlfriend, Susan. Am I yours?"

"Yes, you are."

"Good, but I'm still not sure about this 'Ali' thing."

"I can go back to Alison if you'd like."

"No-one else calls me Ali. I like that. We'll see how the name grows on me."

The coach drove over a bump in the road, the movement separating our foreheads momentarily, before jolting them together again. We both yelped in pain, and pulled back. I sat with my back against the seat rest.

Ali swivelled and rested her back against the wall of the coach. She lifted her legs onto the bench seat, resting her ankles on my legs. "So, you're being pretty ambitious, Susan. Let's say your plan doesn't go as you expect. Let's say you can't achieve all three of your objectives. Which is the most important?"

I squinted at the ceiling. "Good question. I think getting Praxi to stop doing whatever it is she thinks she's doing by burning down newspaper offices and drawing just... the most attention to the magissa in the process... that's top. It would be good to know if I'm wrong about her and Lady Callas but... my old patron isn't getting any less dead. I think the third objective should take priority over establishing the truth of the Callas case."

"So, if I think Praxi is going to use lethal force, I'll take her out."

I grimaced. "Ali..."

"I know! Dr Grout said I'd have some... problems with impulsivity, but this is someone's life we're talking about. I'm not going to get bored and evaporate the blood in her veins so we can all go home."

"But you will if you think Praxi poses me serious danger?"

Ali shot me a look. "Well, yes. Why, what did you think I'd do?"

I drummed my fingers on a windowsill. "I can't work out if that's sweet or not."

"Oh, trust me, it's extremely sweet. I'm being unbelievably romantic right now, you have no idea. If you were Hydros, you'd be a hair's breadth from proposing marriage."

"Mm," I said, deeply unsure if Ali was joking. "Noted."

"Okay," said Ali, closing her eyes. "Let's talk murder. We think Praxi is guilty because of your 'we know it was you' gambit. She attacked you, then ran away. Is that it?"

"She's our top viable suspect. She had means and opportunity. She had the most to lose from Lady Callas' scheme. Her osto means… what did you say it was?"

"Form shape. She can make water take on particular shapes, like her blades and javelin at the *Express* offices."

"Right. She could have used that power to murder Lady Callas somehow and dumped the body in the bathtub to disguise the obvious water connection. There's also the fact that… someone hanged you. You had an idea and went to talk to someone. I don't think you'd have let your guard down around any of the others. You felt safe around Praxi. When you said the wrong thing…"

"Did you investigate many murders before you infiltrated the magissa, Susan?"

"You know what, I actually didn't."

"Huh. Well, you might have a future in that profession if journalisting doesn't work out."

"All cops are bastards, Ali. In human society at least."

"Ah yes. Still, the case against Praxi is far from watertight. Not a confession, is it?"

"I see what you did there. No. No it isn't. A confession is what we're hoping for this time around."

"With us as bait."

"You, and me, and the doggy makes three."

Ali grinned. "Hear that, CW?"

CW continued snoring.

"So," I said. "The one thing I'd really like to get done before the ambush is find out where on earth someone had been keeping the Flower of Tartarus. The astynomia searched everyone and everywhere."

Ali tutted. "Everywhere in the house."

"Mm?"

"In between mentoring geniuses, Praxi enjoyed spending time in that big old slab of garden. She might have a hiding place somewhere in the grounds."

"Good point. That's the first place to look."

Twenty minutes later, we crossed the bridge to the Callas mansion. Waves crashed against the obsidian rocks on the starboard side of the causeway. Flecks of foam pattered against the coach windows. Ali lowered her window and stuck her head out into the spray, sighing contentedly.

Our driver dropped us off, then rattled off to Irina as arranged. I knocked on the door to the cottage, whilst CW relieved himself, and Ali stared about the place, her expression unfocussed. A pile of folded bedlinen opened the door. I peered around it and caught the gaze of a diminutive maid.

"Good morning!" I said. "Susan Fletcher and Alison Dewan. Betsan should be expecting us."

"Betsan!" shouted the maid. "The spies are here!"

"Yes, well, if you could be just a little quieter..." I said. The maid scowled at me, shifting his grip on the laundry. Mercy got the better of me. "We'll go and find Betsan. you get on with your day."

"Much obliged, I'm sure," said the maid. He gave a momentary bob, which made the laundry stack wobble alarmingly, before staggering off.

"Who were you talking to?" asked Ali, whilst glaring at a herbaceous border.

"You know, I forgot to ask his name. Three days mingling with the aristocracy and I'm already forgetting my manners."

"Right, but why weren't you talking to Betsan?"

"Because I don't know where she is."

CW barked. Ali pointed. Betsan was standing in the cottage doorway. She must have heard the one-act-play the maid and I had performed. It was, apparently, going to be one of those days. "Betsan! Good to see you."

Betsan frowned. "Is it? Why?"

I gave up. "Never mind. Look, we're on an operation. Do you need details?"

Betsan folded her arms. "Obviously."

I told her the details.

She stared at me, before nodding. "Victoria Callas sent me a message this morning. She said Paget was sending some people, and they were to be gifted certain items. You're who she was sending?"

"That's right. Now, can we see Lady Callas' bathroom briefly? We'll be in and out."

Betsan nodded, and ushered us inside. I fed CW the two and a half sausages we'd agreed on, and he scuttled off on his part of our mission.

Betsan escorted us to the murder scene. Ali spent a good twenty minutes making certain selections, whilst Betsan and I made careful notes. Once we were done, Betsan settled into a chair, whilst I stood with Ali at the door to the bathroom.

I held out a hand. "Ready?"

Ali took my hand. "As ready as I'm likely to be."

I eased the door open, and we stepped inside. Ali's grip tightened on my hand. Pain danced in her eyes.

"Any memories being jogged?" I asked, hating how clinical I sounded.

"Desperation," she said. "My feet kicking. Clawing at the rope round my neck. Pain."

"I'm sorry, Ali."

"Nothing really useful so far."

"Come on, let's go back to the bedroom."

Ali let go of my hand and strode from the room. I followed, closing the door behind me. She was staring at a book on the night stand, her breathing quick. I touched her shoulder. She spun to face me, agony and fear fighting for control of her gaze.

I reached for her shoulder, but froze. What if she didn't want anyone touching her? I hated my inaction, I hated not knowing how to take this pain away from her. "Ali..."

She darted forward, arms wrapping around me, her face burrowing into my collar. She sobbed, and I held her. I still didn't know what to say.

Ali came back to herself only gradually. When she was ready to pull away, she dried her eyes and shot a look at Betsan. "Sorry," she said. "That was a little embarrassing."

Betsan gave her a blank look. "Feel better, don't you?"

Ali shrugged.

"Nothing to feel embarrassed about then, is there? I know what happened, Ms Dewan. These things take a toll."

"I..." Ali glanced at me, then back to Betsan. "Thank you. You might be wondering... Susan was just..."

"None of my business," Betsan said.

Ali nodded and straightened her lapels. "Right. Right." She turned to face me. "So, Susan. No memories about who..." She frowned, "Hang on..."

She dragged me back into the bathroom, where she stood, staring at the bathtub. "I found the knife behind there. You'd been surprised by the murderer in the bathroom, and that made me think... why was the murderer in there?

"So, I looked, and there was the knife, wedged between the bathtub and the wall. I was overjoyed... but the more I thought about it, the less my discovery made sense. It was too convenient. You probably would have seen the knife when you found Lady Callas. So... I thought about that, and I thought about how the knife could have got there, and then..." She frowned. "I can't remember exactly... but I'm not sure it was my idea to look for the knife."

"Praxi might have dropped a hint to you after I left?"

Ali nodded. "Maybe. I remember searching for the knife and feeling happy when I found it, and then feeling suspicious about it later... Nothing clear."

"That suspicion... do you think you would have confronted Praxi? Demanded an explanation?"

"Oh, yes. My first mistake."

I nudged her. "Second. You forgot about trusting me."

She glared at me. "I don't think that's especially amusing, Susan."

"Sorry."

"Stop saying you're sorry, damn it. It's repetitive."

"I *am* sorry, Alison. If I'd been here—"

"You cut me down, Susan. Maybe if you'd been here, things would have been different. But, maybe they wouldn't have been. Maybe you'd have been hanged alongside me, our feet dancing with death together. Now, *that's* a bad first date."

I wasn't sure if I was supposed to laugh or not, and by the time I realised I probably should have, it was too late. Ali sighed and returned to the bedroom, where Betsan handed us the bones Paget had negotiated for. Ali took them reverently. then we returned first to the cottage, and then the garden at its rear.

The pristine lawn stretched away to the tree line at the far end of the garden, bordered by artfully crafted flowerbeds and only broken by the garden sheds.

"Right," I said. "Ready?"

"One second," Ali said. She pulled a thigh bone from her pack, opened her mouth, opened her mouth still further, and slid the bone down her throat.

My guts twisted at the sight, but another part of me was in awe of her strength. She licked her fingers once she was done, which spoiled the moment a little.

We took a turn around the garden in companionable silence. The first thing which struck me was the number of birds hanging about the place. I couldn't understand how I'd missed them on my first visit, although maybe it'd been too early for them.

A couple of peacocks were strutting about in one of the flower beds, wild parakeets perched in the trees, and mourning doves *coo*ed from invisible hiding places. Constable Woofington emerged from behind a bush, saw me, barked, and then disappeared again. Hopefully he was sticking to the plan and not getting distracted. I had no idea how much a peacock cost, or how angry Victoria would be if I were called upon to replace one.

"How long do you think we have?" asked Ali.

I checked my pocket watch. "Hard to say. Maybe hang around by the sheds so you're not immediately visible, just in case?"

Ali grumbled as she stomped over to the sheds. She stared at them. "Why are there two?"

"Two sheds?"

"Yeah, two sheds. The Callas' are loaded. Why two sheds? Why not one big shed?"

I shrugged. "Who knows why rich people do... these... The secret entrance to the mansion was a tunnel through concrete which emerged by one of the sheds wasn't it?"

"It was, it was. You check that one, I'll check this one."

I poked my head through the nearest door, and was struck by the smell of mouldering grass cuttings and rusting steel. Long handled sheers, trowels, gloves, and various other instruments that I didn't recognise lay haphazardly on a stone table seemingly built into the far wall.

So far, so normal. It was the opposite of the shed I'd have expected from the magissa. I stood in the middle of the shed and inspected the shelves, the walls, the ceiling, and finally the floor.

Fragments of glass lay in a corner. There was nothing made of glass in the shed. What was I missing? The stone table was curious... The shed's exterior wall was attached to the back legs of the table with a couple of brackets. The floor under the table looked strange – slightly raised compared to the floor in the rest of the shed.

Closer inspection revealed paper thin cracks in the solid concrete. I traced them with my fingertips and found, hidden behind one of the table legs, a hole in the floor. I felt inside, and found a button. I pressed it.

Steam billowed from the cracks under the table. I jerked back. CW barked and dashed to my side, growling at the steam. I ducked out of the shed, the constable following moments later.

"What did you do?" Ali asked, emerging from the other shed.

"I found a hidden button and wanted to see what it did."

"You wanted to see what it did?"

"Yes! I was investigating!"

Ali grabbed the hair at the back of her head and tugged at it. "Look. I understand what's happened to me. Well, what everyone says has happened to me." She paused, looking off into space, before shaking her head. "What was my point? Yes, yes. That was it. Look, this investigation isn't going to work if we *both* have poor impulse control. You can't just go around pressing buttons because you're a bit frustrated at letting a murderer run around, hanging your girlfriend every chance they get."

"Fair point, I'm sorry."

"Was it fair? I couldn't work out if I was being reasonable or not."

"Ali... you're doing fine. I'm not... I don't really understand what's going... when we were at the *Express* offices you had a bit of a moment when you dropped a tooth, but you've seemed fine since then – as fine as I'd expect anyway. Besides... wait. Would you have made that move on me outside the *Solidarity* offices if you weren't having some impulse control issues?"

Ali glared at me. "Maybe? I don't know. Everything's a bit confused up in here at the moment." She tapped at her temple. "I have times where I'm... not myself, but other times I'm perfectly fine. Maybe it's just that I'm forgetting how I was before, but it's possible that I'm also getting better. Right?"

"Right," I said. "Should I be helping with this... this problem?"

"You can help by not patronising me, which seems to be a rare talent at the moment, from what I've seen."

I did a quick scan of the garden. CW was patrolling the alley by the house. We hopefully still had time. I took Ali's hands in mine. "You're a force of nature, Ali. You're devastatingly sharp, supremely powerful, and damned beautiful. I promise—"

Ali snatched her hands out of mine and stepped back. She staggered and had to steady herself on the shed wall. "What?"

"Hey..." I said, staring down at my empty hands. I'd been building to what felt like quite a romantic moment.

"What the fuck did you just say?" Alison said.

"Er..." My brain finally caught up and started going over everything I'd been saying to double check to see if I'd accidentally called her a c-word or something. "I was telling you how awesome you are. You usually like when I do that. It's one of our things. I tell you how awesome you are, you continue being awesome... it's fun."

"Fun?"

Crap. Wrong word. "Al..." I couldn't say Ali. She was angry. I couldn't call her Ali, it would be wrong. Why would it be wrong? *This* was wrong. We were supposed to be setting a trap but I'd fucked that up. "Alison..." the word felt faded and impersonal. "I don't understand what's going on. I did something – I'm sorry. I..."

Alison folded her arms. "You called me beautiful, Susan."

I nodded, unsure of when we'd get to the bad bit. "Yes, I did."

"What about me, very specifically, is beautiful?"

My brain finally caught up with the situation, but I didn't give it a chance to grind to a shame saturated halt. I shook my head, and returned Ali's glare. "Your eyes. They glitter. Did you know that? When you're excited, or working something out, or pleased with yourself. So they glitter pretty much all the time. Your smile. You could light up a decent chunk of Selen with that smile. Your lips make me feel a little wobbly when I look at them. You have..." I glanced down, "a figure I'd kill for." I returned my gaze to her face, and took a step forward. "Your horns..."

Ali stepped back, shaking her head. "Don't..."

"They're part of you, Ali. They're beautiful, because you're beautiful."

"You're making yourself say that! Your expression when you first saw me without the veil was pretty fucking clear. You were *repulsed*."

I ground my palm into my forehead. "Ali... I'm demisexual. I don't understand what makes someone attractive. When people at school would point at someone and make a lewd comment or whatever, I'd nod and smile and not have the faintest idea what they were talking about. I know the theory from books and things, but I never really felt it before. Ali... I know you're beautiful. I know it. I see it. I feel it. You. Are. Beautiful." I folded my arms. "You don't get a say in the matter. Sorry."

Ali's eyes narrowed. "Great. So someone finds me attractive for the first time in... since the creepy fucker, and they only find me attractive because they don't understand what makes someone beautiful. That's great. That's just fucking great."

Lava bubbled in my stomach, welled up within me, and rushed to my head. The tears which had been forming at the corners of my eyes were snatched away in slips of steam. This wasn't the painless evaporation of Alison the Miracle, this was all me. "Alison, would you care to repeat that? I'm not sure I heard you correctly."

Her chin jerked up, her gaze acidic. "I'm pretty sure you heard me just fine."

I closed my eyes. I breathed. We definitely didn't have time for this, but if I let that go, it'd devour me. "Alison... Ali... I don't know if the allos would find you beautiful—"

"Allos?"

"Fucking Allosexuals, Alison! The people who get soaking wet when they meet someone with nice... arms, or whatever. Allos. Now let me finish, okay?"

Alison held up her hands, a bemused expression cracking her defensive sneer.

"Right," I said. "I don't know if the allos would find you beautiful, and, frankly, I don't much fucking care. If others don't see you as beautiful that sounds a lot like they're the fucked up ones, and it's not your place to tell me that I only find you beautiful because I'm damaged in some way. I'm a woman too. Are you going to tell me that I'm broken because I'm not one of the heteros?"

Alison frowned. "No! Of course not!"

"Of course not! Right!"

We glared at each other.

"It appears," said Alison after a long moment, "that I may have made something of a blunder."

I had to clamp my lips together to stop them curling into a snarl. Making myself do this also stopped me from saying 'Oh, you fucking think?', which I was glad of. It wasn't entirely fair. I counted to five, then took a breath. "Ali… I'm sorry for losing my shit. I have no idea what it must have been like to live with people treating you so fucking terribly. I'm sorry. But please… please don't… it hurts to see you assume that this thing we have is lesser than a relationship some vanilla couple would have. You're amazing. You're beautiful. This thing between us is thermite. Don't call it a damp squib."

Ali nodded terribly slowly. "Fine. But I'm still pissed off at you."

I shrugged. "Well, I'm still pissed off at you."

"Good."

"Are you still my girlfriend?"

Alison narrowed her eyes. "For now. Are you still *my* girlfriend?"

"Yes."

"Good."

"Fine."

"Fine."

"Fine?"

"Fine."

Back in the shed, the steam had cleared. Two massive pistons had lifted a section of the shed floor up, revealing a set of stone steps which led down into darkness. Pipes jutted from the walls of the stairwell at odd angles, some descending into the dark, others cutting across the gap to the far side, or to the underside of the shed floor.

Ali whistled. "This is pretty serious."

"It is. Any magissa clans who can... I don't know... build structures like this with their osto?"

"None that I know of. Come on, your weird flirting has cost us time."

She descended into darkness, her steps still uneven and laboured. I followed, and was relieved when pale green light bloomed in Ali's hand – she'd found a stash of glow globes hanging from a pipe.

I held my hand over the nearest pipe – scalding hot. "They must have hooked this place up to the steam tunnels, but not the bio-fuel system..."

Ali held the glow globe up, casting light ahead and behind as she continued her descent. "Makes sense. You need access to the steam feed if you're going to use hydraulics to conceal your lair's entrance. Light was apparently considered more of a luxury. No-one lived down here. At least... not comfortably."

She stepped down into the space beyond the steps, and moved aside so I could join her. A room had been roughly cut into the obsidian rock. Shelves had been bolted to the far wall – empty apart from scraps of wood and drifts of broken glass. Shattered mechanisms, splintered wood, and battered gas canisters lay scattered on the floor.

My foot bumped against a cyrecet bat, lying discarded amongst the scrap. I picked it up– fragments of broken glass were lodged in the business end. "What do you think this place is?"

Ali prodded at two threaded iron bolts set into the wall, then reached down, shoved a coil of frayed rope out of the way and picked up a set of shackles. She examined them, her expression grim. "A torture chamber."

Chapter Twenty-Two

"Torture..." I said. "As in... the bad thing which—"

Ali held up a finger. "Just to... what was... yes. Just to get out in front of the Susan thought train before it really gets rolling, I have a question. Do Selen's police or expeditionary forces ever have to get information from people who'd rather not give it to them?"

Water dripped from the ceiling. The shackles in Ali's hands were stained – black and russet. Oil and blood. There was no process here, no oversight. Someone had made the choice to do this. "That," I said, before I had to swallow – get the taste of death out of my mouth. "That..."

I swallowed again. There was a lump in my throat I couldn't clear. My heart was pounding, my thoughts racing. I could have been bound up in here if I'd been caught. Alison might have dragged me here herself. That fear, that *fear* whilst Ali stared at me... it made something break inside me.

I leaned against a wall, slick brickwork against my palm made me shudder. I closed my eyes. "Ali... can you..."

"Su, what do you need? What's up?"

"I'm panicking and we don't... we don't have time. Damn."

"Su..." A finger lifted my chin. I opened my eyes. A hazel wave washed over me. One good thing... her eyes were one good thing in the room. "Su. I'm beautiful, remember? Tell me what else about me is beautiful."

"The way you frown when you're concentrating... The way you do..." I laughed. "The way you do this. The way you care. You cared about me long before we got to know each other. You've always cared."

"Good. That's good. Come on, let's get you upstairs. I've got what I needed from here."

Ali led me up the stairs, keeping me focussed. The world changed as we emerged from the stairwell – sunlight streamed through the windows. We staggered outside, and collapsed onto the lawn.

"Damn," I said, after a moment. "Sorry, Ali. That was... intense."

"You claustrophobic, Su?"

I rubbed my palm against my temple. "Didn't used to be."

"No panic attacks?"

"Not before the Callas mansion."

"Ah..." Ali was staring up at the clouds. "Good."

"Mm?"

"Oh, sorry, Su. I was being selfish. It felt good for a moment, knowing I'm not the only one who left part of themselves behind in that damned house."

I breathed, rubbing stray blades of grass between my fingers.

"Was it my saying I wanted to stop the Su thought train?" asked Ali.

"Sorry?"

"You got really... upset after I said that."

"Oh, no. I was just... I started thinking that human police and that cellar were completely different, and then I got thinking about how just because human police wear a uniform that doesn't excuse them acting in basically the same way. Then I thought about how I might have ended up in that room if I'd been caught, yesterday. And then... I thought that you might have taken me there if you'd caught me. And then I got thinking about us, and then I tried to think about what mattered to me now, and then I thought about what comes *next* and then my brain broke. Too much... everything."

"Eesh, sorry. Will a clue take your mind off it?"

"Only if it's a signed confession."

"Well, it's not signed..."

Her smile glittered in the sunlight. She flourished a piece of glass at me. Ordinary glass? No. An engraving. 'Tarta—'

"Is that what I think it is?" I asked.

"Found nearly a full set on the floor of that torture chamber before I realised how bad you were getting. Flower of Tartarus. We found where Praxi was storing it. Looks like she either had some seriously messed up hobbies or was some sort of senate agent – not like us, one of the... hardcore ones."

"Right." I covered my face with my hands, trying to block everything out except my thoughts and Ali's voice. "So... Praxi is an agent of the senate – a random serial killer wouldn't have built a secret room under a shed, not without anyone in the house being aware of it. She must have had it put in when they made the tunnel? We'd have to check when the tunnel was built... never mind. Praxi is an agent and she holds captives here sometimes. She has the flower – she keeps some in her room maybe. She kills Lady Callas, and escapes after we do the 'we know it was you' gambit. She slips free of Dawn, returns to her torture chamber, grabs any teeth she kept there and smashes everything else to try and conceal any clues she might have left behind. How does that sound?"

"Plausible. Plausible. There are holes, but we've run out of time to look for them. CW's coming this way."

I cracked an eye open. A small, white blur was shooting towards us across the grass. He bumped his nose against my face and growled, softly.

"What's up, boy?"

He nudged me with his nose again.

"Crap. She's here, isn't she."

He yapped, softly.

"What direction?"

He spun around in a circle twice, before facing the tree line – the furthest end of the garden from the house.

"She's going to climb over the wall?"

He barked.

"Right. Thanks, boy. You hide, okay? Don't want you caught up in this."

He seemed to think about this, before getting distracted by a peacock. He bolted off after the bird, who squawked and fled, flapping up into a tree after a short run up.

"Right," I said, hauling myself to my feet. "Okay. Okay. Game face. Enacting plans. Facing down murderers. You ready to go?"

"Sure."

Ali held up a hand. I grabbed it and, together, we got her stood up.

She cast a critical eye over the garden. "If she's coming from the tree line, where do you want me?"

My legs felt heavy. "Er. Behind that sort of willow thing?"

"That thicket of bushes over there?"

"Sure, that works too. Come on." I stood up straight, rolled my shoulders, and walked towards the tree line, my feet scuffing the grass. "I've just realised... if this plan works then I'm not going to get a proper rest for weeks. Maybe months. Might be easier to just let Praxi kill me."

"That probably sounded funnier in your head."

"Yeah, sorry. Too soon."

"Too soon. You still sure you've got this?"

I cracked my knuckles. "One last task. One last... whatever I was going to say next."

"Hey," said Ali. Her face was serious. "Girlfriend, right? You're sure?"

"I am if you are."

"This plan... it's not *not* dangerous. So..." She unclipped her ear cuff and held it out to me. "A gift of silver for you, Susan Fletcher, on this, our second date."

I stared, open mouthed, at the gift. A gift of silver was a curse, wrapped up in a lie. Maybe not always. I took the cuff. Then, an idea sparking, I slipped the silver bracelet from my wrist. "Silver for silver. You'd make better use of it anyway..."

Ali took the bracelet, her fingers lingering in my hand... CW yipped at us.

"Yes," I said, "I know. Praxi's coming. Thank you for reminding us."

"You've got this, Su," said Ali. With a wink and a wave, she was gone – slipping through the flowerbeds and into the thicker greenery beyond.

I felt terribly vulnerable. Good for the plan, bad for me. I strode to the tree line, fumbling the silver cuff onto my ear as I walked. Dense foliage shaded me from the sun, and birds sung overhead. I found a tree with a trunk I could easily hide behind, and checked if I could see Ali from her hiding place... no. I had to trust she was there. I repositioned the cuff on my ear, taking my time.

Grunting. Cloth scraping against rock. A scramble, then something solid landed in the undergrowth a little way away. I sidled around the tree so that it was in between me and the cracking twigs which marked Praxi's passage.

She had a couple of approaches she might take. She could try and approach the house directly, openly. If a servant saw her, they'd assume she was meant to be there. Alternately she might try and sneak as close as possible through the flowerbeds. There wasn't much cover – she'd probably be better off with the direct approach... and that was the one she took.

Praxi strode from the tree line, bold as blisters. She'd disposed of her hat and veil – or maybe she'd lost them on the journey here. Her trousers were torn, and her jacket was coated with debris.

I rolled my shoulders, and strode from the tree line, matching her pace, matching her heading. We walked in parallel with me a little behind her. She hadn't spotted me. I opened my mouth to begin the gambit, but my throat closed up. There was a good chance Praxi would try to kill me during the gambit, but there was a much higher chance if I didn't speak first – set the tone. I swallowed, walked a little faster and closed the distance, so we were walking side by side.

"Praxi," I said. "Good to see you again. We should have a chat."

She froze, and darted away from me. Her hands hovered over her coat pockets, like one of those duellists from Selen's age of expansion – the ones who were obsessed with drawing pistols faster than their opponents.

"I'm not here to kill you," I said, my voice sounding much calmer than I expected. "I've come to offer you peace. Come with me, explain your actions to the senate. We have more important things to worry about than a petty murder investigation."

I shouldn't have used the word 'petty'. 'Petty' was definitely a mistake. Praxi frowned at me, shook her head, and reached into her jacket.

I forced myself to stay still. If she was reaching for a gun, I'd only invite her to shoot me if I ran.

Praxi drew a flask from an inner pocket, flicked the cap off, and poured out two hefty glugs of water from within. She reached out to the water, which twisted in the air, forming a blade – a dagger. She caught the dagger's hilt as she returned the flask to her pocket.

For my part, I did my best to keep my gaze on Praxi's eyes – but she wasn't looking at my face. She wouldn't meet my gaze. She twirled her dagger, but didn't charge at me.

I smiled. "I wouldn't recommend trying to use that blade on me. You won't want to waste the power it takes to make another one."

Her lip curled into a snarl. She dashed towards me, raising the knife – which burst into steam. Praxi yelped. Her charge faltered. "Alison… where is she?"

I shook my head. "That's not important. Late yesterday you will have learned that Alison Dewan planned to return to the Callas mansion in order to locate one crucial piece of evidence. That was a lie – Paget Belacourt spread the rumour around in the hope of getting your attention. I suspected you'd be keen to stop your former protégé uncovering vital evidence. Maybe you planned to complete your previous attempted murder. You've walked into a trap, Praxi, baited with Alison. I apologise for the deception, but it was necessary. We need to talk."

Her hand flashed back into her pocket and withdrew her flask. "Talk?" She flicked the lid from her flask. "We have nothing to talk about."

"Please don't…" I said.

Praxi leapt towards me, forming a needle from water as she moved. The needle bore down on my chest, but hissed into vapour before it reached me.

I sighed. "I'm not a threat to you, Praxi."

Her lip curled. "Your existence is a threat."

I frowned. Did she mean I was a threat because I knew she'd murdered Lady Callas? Or did she know I was human... How would she have known? Lady Callas might have told her... Still, I had a counter. "I'm one of the wolf pack." I tugged up my sleeve, displaying Paget's brand. "We're on the same side."

Praxi took a step back, then another to the side. She circled me, her gaze darting from me to the sheds, then the trees, then the bushes where Ali was hiding. "How did an infiltrator wind up working for Belacourt?"

"Long story. Look, Praxi. You knew about Lady Callas' plan? You learned about it and put a stop to it."

"Yes," she said.

I clapped my hands in relief. "Good! That's good. I don't know the Senate's laws that well, but surely they'd consider you stopping Lady Callas from revealing the magissa to humanity in a sympathetic light. Honestly, you're Hydros. You could probably argue self-defence well enough."

She spun to face me, eyes wide. For the first time, her gaze met mine. "What are you talking about?"

I had maybe a sentence or two with which to convince her. If I didn't manage it, I'd have to run. I really didn't want to run. "You're acting like a fugitive, and I think that's because part of you feels guilty... but you wanted to keep the magissa from being revealed. The only genuinely criminal thing you've done is trying to murder Alison. And burning down the Heraldic Express offices. My point is, you committed a desperate act. Since then, you've been scrambling, trying to make the best of an awful situation. You've done some terrible things, Praxi, but you have a choice. You can choose to stop. Take a breath."

She turned away from me, taking in the garden. The cottage. The garden walls. The tree line. Searching for Ali… or planning a quick exit.

"Marie Callas was a fucking idiot," I said, my voice cracking. "She wanted to just reveal the magissa in one go. She hired a human infiltrator, for the love of the spirits. Who does that? She saw herself as a saviour. She probably thought she was helping you. In fact, I bet that's what she told you. Her plan was terrible, and I'm glad you stopped it. I wish you hadn't had to kill her, but I bet you do too.

"The thing is, terrible though her plan was, she wasn't wrong. Ever since I've learned about the magissa, it's been clear that the secrecy under which you live is only hurting you. Alison can't leave her home without a veil. Charles lost a protégé, and Teleri Parry lost her life as a result. You live trapped on the obsidian coast because if a human spots you, it risks everything.

"I was brought here to expose the magissa, but Lady Callas couldn't have anticipated Alison Dewan. She showed me how grey my life had been before learning of the magissa. She showed me how strong we could be together."

Praxi glared around the garden again, but her breathing had slowed. She slipped the cap back onto her water flask. She turned to face me. "What do you want, human?"

"I want you to come back to Selen with me and Alison. Fill in a few details for us. We've stopped the plot to expose the magissa, but your attack on the *Express* offices will have made things harder. We'll be able to keep things off the boil as long as you're not charging around burning down newspaper buildings. Then… the house of Hydros has an important question to answer."

"How much do we value the magissa's secrecy?"

How much is the secrecy hurting you?"

Praxi slipped her flask back into her pocket. She rolled her shoulders. "Good effort," she said. "You nearly had me."

She wrapped her fingers around my throat. Her thumbs collapsed my windpipe. Black spots flared in my vision. My throat convulsed – wanting to cough. Crushing emptiness. A ripping, sickening emptiness.

I pulled away. Tried to break her grip. Couldn't. I couldn't break free because I had to hold up a hand – a forestalling palm to where Ali was hiding. She couldn't take that final step. This was my own fault. She wouldn't become a murderer for me.

"Please..." the word limped from my mouth. "Don't..."

"It'll be over soon," said Praxi, in the cold voice of someone who thought she'd heard it all before.

The world was going black. I focussed on holding my palm up. Ali had to trust me.

"Ali will kill you... Please..."

I wanted to say more. Words sparked in my head before fleeing. Damn. I'd failed. Except... Praxi's grip softened. I coughed. My entire body convulsed. I kept my hand still. Nothing else mattered right now.

"What did you say?" Praxi asked, her voice hoarse.

I tried to reply, but only ended up coughing. Praxi sighed and released me.

I dropped to my knees, hand still outstretched. A mistake. Praxi saw my hand – saw what I was doing. Turned to the bushes where I'd last seen Ali.

"Ah," she said. "Hiding in there, is she?"

Fuck. I grabbed at her – found a hand. Grabbed it. Couldn't stop coughing.

She slapped my grip away. "You said something, human. What was it?"

"Ali will..." More coughing. Wrenching. Wracking. "She'll kill you if I can't..."

"Ali?"

Damn. "Alison Dewan."

Praxi frowned. "Who, exactly, is Alison Dewan to you, human?"

"Dating," I said, before my throat convulsed again. Spit spattered down my chin. I drew in a breath, and managed to say: "Girlfriend." Before I was lost to coughing again.

"But... how long have you known her?"

I couldn't reply. I also didn't especially want to.

"How many months?" Praxi asked.

I shook my head.

"Weeks?"

I used my hand which wasn't currently holding back the tidal wave of Ali's rage to make an obscene gesture at Praxi.

"Days?"

I held up three fingers on my obscene-gesture-making hand.

"Three days? A human seduced the prodigy of house Hydros after three days?"

I had to spit to clear mucous from my mouth. "Yeah."

Praxi took a step back. She turned to Ali's hiding place and spread her arms in a 'What's going on?' gesture. She then turned back to me, and examined me with the cautious curiosity most people used when prodding at unexploded fireworks. "She can do better."

I wiped a string of saliva from my chin. "I know. Look, Praxi. if I bring the maelstrom out, will you actually talk to us or are you determined to stick with your plan of murdering one or both of us?"

"I could kill both of you easily. Your faith in... Alison is misplaced. Rapid evaporation is a powerful expression of the Hydros osto, but unless she's gained a gargantuan amount of power from somewhere, it won't be enough."

I wanted to laugh or fall asleep for a week. "When we arranged this meeting, we negotiated for Ali to have access to Lady Callas' bone collection. She recently consumed a femur, two carpals and an ulna. I don't even know what an ulna is. Ali's never had quite this much power buzzing about within her, but she told me she'd have to be quite restrained to only explode *your* blood, and avoid mine."

Praxi's impassive expression wavered. She glanced over at where Ali was hiding. "Ah."

"Right. So will you please relax for two damned minutes? We didn't come here to kill you. Ali is currently being very restrained in not killing you. You have no idea the sort of promises I had to make in order to get her to agree to this plan. Can you, pretty please, promise to not murder anyone whilst we have an actual damned conversation?"

Praxi snarled, but her heart wasn't in it. She threw up her hands. "Fine."

Relief kissed me. I turned my open palm, Ali-forestalling gesture into a beckoning finger. Nothing happened. I had a moment of bone-knotting panic before Ali emerged from the tree line, around where I'd waited for Praxi. Very much not where she was supposed to have been waiting.

"What were you doing over there?" I asked.

Ali glared, splitting her time evenly between me and Praxi. "Well, when you did your 'I don't trust Ali to not immediately murder a murderer, so I'll give away her position' bit, I decided to move."

"Ah." I stood, feeling as if I'd aged twenty years in the past few hours. "Good idea."

"Praxi," said Ali.

"Ms Dewan. Ms Fletcher here said you two were… an item. Is this true?"

Ali rolled her eyes. Her lips twitched for a few moments, occasionally revealing ravenous teeth. Probably biting back a number of bitterly sarcastic replies. Eventually, she set her expression in stony stoicism. "Yes."

"Why?" asked Praxi.

Ali turned her glare on me. "She's hot, smart, adventurous, and she cares about me. Why do you ask?"

Praxi shook her head, but didn't seem to want to say anything. For my part, I was busy blushing.

"So," said Ali, cracking her knuckles. "Let's negotiate."

After half an hour of torturous diplomacy, Praxi agreed to return to Selen with us. We snuck her past Betsan, although Praxi refused to let Ali cover her head with a jacket as if she were an artist trying to dodge a crowd of press outside a night club.

Ali had to burn off some power on the way across the bridge back to the mainland. She'd consumed too many bones from Lady Callas' collection to hold in her tank long term, and she was at risk of having her power leak if she didn't do something about it. She exploded flecks of surf until she returned to a safe level. Praxi tried her best to not look impressed.

Ten minutes later, we'd located the spot where we'd asked our coach to wait.

"Right," I said, once we were settled inside and rolling back to Selen. "Let's get the admin out of the way. You killed Lady Callas, right?"

"I couldn't possibly comment," said Praxi, flicking a piece of lint from her lapel.

Ali bashed her head against the coach's window frame. "Come on, there's just the two of us here. You already tried to murder me once, don't use boredom to finish me off."

Praxi looked as if she'd been slapped with a duelling glove. "You will not speak to me in that—"

"Su, can I explode her blood now, please?" Ali asked.

"Ali, you promised you wouldn't unless Praxi did something which deserved it."

Ali fixed her gaze on mine and nodded, very deliberately.

"No, please don't kill her," I said. "I'll make it up to you later."

"Promises, promises."

Praxi looked aghast. "What.... what happened to you?"

"Okay," I said. "Now you can kill her."

"Wait, seriously?" Ali asked.

Praxi grimaced. "My apologies. I... certain events might have slipped my mind."

Ali leaned forward. "You... you *forgot* that you hanged me?"

"No, no... it's just been a lot and I've had a lot on my mind and I might have not... joined up certain facts... and..."

Ali bared her teeth. "Praxi, just answer Su's questions so I don't have to evaporate your blood. Please?" She sat back, her shoulder brushing mine. She started at the contact, then grinned and took my hand.

"Praxi," I said. "You killed Lady Callas. She told you about her plan to expose the magissa. You had a vial filled with the flower of Tartarus, because you work as an agent for the senate. You poisoned the evening meal, avoided eating it yourself and waited for the flower to take effect.

"You visited Lady Callas, formed a spear or something from water, and forced it down her throat, returning it to water as it went. You drowned her in her own bed, then let the spear return to water, staining the bedclothes.

"You dragged her to the bathroom, hauled her into the tub and filled it with water. You planted the poison vials into Teleri Parry's pack, then returned to your room. Maybe you took a little of the poison but, as an agent myself, I know deception is a key skill of ours."

Praxi looked as if she were swallowing bile at the thought of her skills being compared to mine. I fought the urge to giggle. Ali didn't bother fighting.

"So," I said. "Did I get anything wrong?"

Praxi shrugged. "I actually did take a little of the flower. Best cover story is a real cover story."

I nodded. "Right."

"I still have trouble believing she told me about her plan, and she thought I'd be happy about it."

I nodded. "A little naive."

"Oh, you have no idea."

Ali winced. "I can't imagine how it felt to have the person who rescued you be the one to try and expose us."

Words, sentences, arguments, and counterarguments churned in my head. "Praxi... the magissa are in a vulnerable position right now, and if you agree to stop making things worse, I'm sure we can minimise any consequences you'd see from your actions."

Praxi folded her arms, unfolded them, and then clasped her hands in her lap. "And why would you want to help with that?"

I had to close my eyes to think about that question, because it shouldn't need to be asked. The answer was so obvious that Praxi must already know it. I tried to play conversational Sako in my head, but gave up after only a few moves. "Suffering," I said. "Is bad."

"I murdered someone."

"Yes, you did. Are you going to do any more murders?"

Praxi shrugged, without looking at me.

I sighed. "Right. Okay. Here's the point, the main point. All magissa, but particularly Hydros are living with this burden of secrecy because you all assume that if humans find out about you it'll be catastrophic. And that's not an unreasonable assumption, honestly. I just want to check that you're not sticking with the secrecy because you're long-lived and it's the way you've always done things. Status-quo bias."

Praxi gathered herself together, raised her head and made eye contact with me. "Humans are monsters."

I shook my head. "That's trauma speaking for you. I've spent most of today trying to keep you, Ali, and most other magissa safe. I'm a wolf cub. Am I a monster, Praxi?"

Praxi's gaze slipped back to the window. She shrugged.

Given she wasn't looking at me, I let myself slump, rest my head on Ali's shoulder and closed my eyes. "Praxi. Do you believe that this is as good as life can be? This secrecy is the best possible option for the magissa? Or is there the merest shadow of hope that things could be better? If we all work really hard, could we lift the burden of secrecy a little? Just a tiny bit? Is there any hope at all that things could get better?"

"Hope…" said Praxi, turning the word over and examining it from all angles. "Yes. There's always hope."

I suppressed a groan and reached for Ali's arm. She drew me closer. Held me tight.

"What's wrong?" asked Praxi.

"You gave Su the answer she wanted," said Ali.

"She doesn't look very pleased."

"I'm not," I said.

"Hey," said Ali. She brushed a stray lock of hair from my cheek. "Su?" I opened my eyes. She was smiling down at me. "Are you really not pleased, Su?"

That smile... "I'm overjoyed," I said. "I just need to rest."

Praxi sat back, letting her hands unclasp. "Are either of you going to tell me what's going on?"

Ali kissed me, then straightened and fixed Praxi with an austere glare. "We're going to get back to Selen. You'll be under the care of house Hydros provisionally, for everyone's protection. You can negotiate your own damned parole with the Senate because Su and I are going to take a week off. Then, once that week's over, Su and I are going to take a trip beyond the wall of chains. We're going to visit Talvik, to see how the magissa live alongside humans there. Was what happened to you unusual? Have things improved since then? We need to see if magissa *can* live alongside humanity. We'd like you to come too."

Praxi scratched her cheek. "And if we come away from that expedition satisfied that we don't need to maintain our secrecy?"

"Ah," I said, closing my eyes again. "That's when the real work begins."

Chapter Twenty-Three

The Cracked Dials Workers' Club was generally used for union meetings, bawdy comedy nights, and microbreweries. I'd set up at a table in the quietest corner I could find. What my corner lacked in noise, it made up for with the odours of spilled beer and historic tobacco smoke. I was trying to focus on the bustling hall, the beating heart of Selen, rather than the downsides of my corner.

"Why should we trust bone-eating daemons?" Dad asked. He was sitting next to me, a sheet of questions in his hand.

I tapped the first finger of my right hand against the tip of my right thumb twice. I'd been practicing with Paget on keeping my memory anchors subtle – indistinguishable from merely fidgeting. "First – not daemons. Something we learned during the course of our research is that daemons are a whole other species. and they very much don't enjoy being mistaken for witches.

"But, to your point... We should trust the magissa because we have more in common with them than we do with factory owners, newspaper barons and the neo-nobility. Selen's problems stem from profiteering and exploitation. The magissa have done some of the later, but ultimately they were forced to live in secrecy through fear of how privately owned newspapers would cast them as a scapegoat to distract from how all of us were being exploited."

A weight lifted from my foot. Something must have woken CW up. He padded out from under the table and stared into the crowd which was gathering at the foot of the stage. Two small dogs were scampering in and out of the throng of workers, husbands, and kids. CW ran to the back of the crowd and made little whining noises until one of the kids played chase with him.

"Awwww," said several dozen people in the crowd in unison.

"Spirits preserve us," said Dad.

The crowd parted. One of the smaller kids was riding on Blood-fang's back. Paget was watching from the side-lines. She caught my gaze, and winked.

Papa emerged from the crowd, looking bedraggled. He was carrying three mismatched glasses with the self-conscious care of someone who was determined to not spill a drop, and would inevitably tip half a litre of gut-rot over himself within thirty seconds of sitting down. Jasjot, the dish from *Solidarity in Selen*, strode next to him, taking everything in.

"How can we trust people who need our bones to survive?" asked Dad.

I ran a fingernail across one particular spot on my thumb. "The magissa's senate has agreed to a standardised pricing structure for bones. The magissa won't take your bones, but they'll buy them from you at a price I'm sure you'd find fair.

"That's only how we'd start, of course. It's a system which ex-ploits those who need the money the most, much like many systems we currently have in Selen. The magissa expect that, as part of this transition period, certain power structures in Selen will shift. We have the opportunity to strive for less exploitative systems in Selen. We'd love for the unions to be key stakeholders in the post-transition world. Shape new structures. Create a foundation of trust with the magissa."

"I still think that one sounds a bit corporate," said Papa.

I nodded. "Hopefully Ali can take that question if anyone asks it. She's better at capturing the spirit of the answer than I am."

"She backstage?"

I nodded. "Still not used to the crowds."

Dad studied the list of questions. "Do you know how proud I am of you?"

I frowned, searching for an anchor, then I clicked. I swatted at my dad's arm. "Shut up, dad."

"I mean it."

I gave him a hug. "I know."

"All right!" bellowed a swarthy woman from the stage. "Good evening, good evening, one and all. We've got some proper, old fashioned entertainment for you this evening, but first, we've got a bit of a presentation. I only know a few of the details but believe me, it's going to be a lively one. You here, Susan?"

I hugged my dads again before standing, waving, and making my way to the stage.

"Here she is, workers and wonderers," said the union rep. "Child of one of our members, recently returned from beyond the wall of chains, please welcome Susan Fletcher!"

I climbed onto the stage to the familiar sound of polite, not especially enthusiastic, applause. Ali slipped through the curtain at the back of the stage and joined me at the footlights. Hatted and veiled, she held the crowd's attention.

"Good evening, everyone," I said, trying to sound as if I hadn't given this exact speech twice already this week. "As you heard, my name is Susan Fletcher and this is my girlfriend Alison Dewan. The veil will make sense in a moment."

"She a looker?" yelled someone from the back of the crowd.

"One of the most beautiful people I've ever seen," I said. This prompted a chorus of 'Awww's, as well as a few good-natured heckles.

"Step by step," Ali said.

I reached for her hand. It was right where I knew it'd be. I focussed on the crowd. "I had a stress-induced panic attack during my final school exams. This cratered any chance I had of studying journalism at Selen's universities. Then, a miracle happened. I was hired to infiltrate a secret society by a woman named Marie Callas..."

Ali's hand in mine anchored me. I told the crowd how terrified I'd been when infiltrating the Callas mansion. How Ali would have murdered me if I'd said the wrong thing. Sceptical expressions dominated, until Ali revealed herself, and continued the story from there.

She held the crowd spellbound as she spoke. At one point, the same woman who'd yelled about Ali being a looker staggered closer to the stage, an overly ripe piece of fruit clutched in her hand. Her gaze was locked on Ali, her mouth contorted into a sneer. Paget slipped through the crowd, intercepted her, and lured her back to the bar for a convivial drink.

Papa and Dad watched from our corner, their eyes glimmering. I scanned the crowd for potential trouble spots. Anyone who looked as if they were about to heckle, and break Ali's flow. When I spotted a heckler, I signalled for CW to distract them. I only needed to do this twice. The crowd were warmer than the last two we'd addressed. Besides, no group of humans we'd spoken to had been anywhere near as frosty as the mothers of house Hydros.

Ali wrapped our story up in a bow, and presented it to the crowd. They couldn't help but love her. I knew how they felt. I'd stood no chance whatsoever. I let the silence hang for only a moment after Ali finished talking. Then, I grinned at our audience. "So. any questions?"